If the Fates Allow

An LGBTQ Holiday Anthology
Edited by Annie Harper

interlude press • new york

ISBN 13: 978-1-945053-47-4 (trade)
ISBN 13: 978-1-945053-48-1 (ebook)

Published by Interlude Press
www.interludepress.com
BOOK AND COVER DESIGN BY CB Messer
PHOTOGRAPHY & VECTORS FOR COVER ©Depositphotos.com/
Rawpixel/sellingpix/Mariannette/ kontur-vid/ lazar
10 9 8 7 6 5 4 3 2 1

interlude 🧩 press • new york

For Lex

Contents

Foreword

AT THE VERY FIRST OFFICIAL Interlude Press meeting, we made a list of the stories we wanted to tell and the authors we wanted to work with. One of our founding partners, Lex Huffman, added "holiday collection" to that list. Lex loved everything about the winter holidays. He loved Hallmark Christmas movies, baking cookies and seasonal breads, and listening to carols. And every year, he put up and decorated twenty-seven Christmas trees. (No, that's not a typo.)

It's been nearly two years since Lex passed away in his sleep one August night, and it's been nearly four years since he first added "holiday collection" to our "to publish" list. Since we began in 2014, we at Interlude Press and our young adult imprint, Duet, have published many books on that list—more than fifty novels featuring diverse casts of main characters whose sexual orientation and gender identity are not often represented in literature, characters who, as Lex once said, "deserve happy endings." We have also had the privilege of working with most of the authors on that list—including all five of the novelists who wrote stories for this collection.

If the Fates Allow is a collection of five short stories set during the winter holidays. In "Gracious Living Says It Must Be a Live Tree," author Killian B. Brewer takes us back to the charming town and characters he shared with us in his novel, *Lunch with the Do-Nothings at the Tammy Dinette* (2017). Still happily working at the Dinette, Marcus is determined to have a magazine-perfect Christmas with his boyfriend, local mechanic Hank—no matter what it takes.

In "True North," Lambda Literary Award winner (*Into the Blue*, 2016) Pene Henson tells the story of pro basketball player Shay Allen's reluctant return to her Montana hometown and the resurfacing of her old feelings for her high school crush, Milla. "Last Call at the Casa Blanca Bar & Grille" by INDIE award-winner Erin Finnegan is a story about loss and moving on, in which Jake Volarde visits an once-favorite bar and reminisces with the mysterious new bartender about the man he loved.

In Lilah Suzanne's romantic comedy, "Halfway Home," Avery Puckett's bad luck begins to change when she rescues a stray dog and meets Grace, a beautiful and sweet employee at the local animal shelter. And in "Shelved" by INDIE award-winner Lynn Charles, library clerk Karina Ness, using the magic of books, plays matchmaker for her uncle and a library regular.

We hope you'll enjoy this collection of holiday stories from five beloved Interlude Press authors. And, if you're inspired to do so, please check out other works by Killian B. Brewer, Pene Henson, Erin Finnegan, Lilah Suzanne, and Lynn Charles at www.InterludePress.com.

We still miss you, Lex. This one is for you.

—*Annie Harper*

Gracious Living Magazine Says It Must Be a Live Tree

Killian B. Brewer

Chapter One

MARCUS SUMTER DROPPED ONTO THE turquoise pleather seat of the diner chair and let out a long, slow breath of absolute exhaustion. He propped his elbows on the speckled, blue formica tabletop and rested his head in his right hand. With his left hand, he yanked the hairnet from his head and ran his fingers through his coppery red hair in a feeble attempt to fluff it out of the smashed shape a day of toiling over the diner grill had created. The collar of his apron stuck to his neck, and a bead of sweat rolled between his shoulder blades toward regions below. He closed his eyes and lost himself in the honky-tonk piano sounds that drifted from the jukebox in the corner, letting Patsy Cline soothe his weary mind. As he took another deep breath, his exhaustion surprised him.

In the six months since he had moved to Marathon, Georgia and begun working at the Tammy Dinette, his body had quickly become accustomed to the ragged pace of life in the busy little joint. He had mastered the meticulous square dance that he and the waitresses do-si-doed around each other in the cramped space of its kitchen. Having grown up moving from diner to diner with his transient mother and then working in diners for years as an adult, Marcus found nothing new in the short-order life. In fact, he preferred it to anything else he had tried. Hard work pleased him, and a day in the Tammy usually left him invigorated.

Even after a particularly busy Saturday brunch, the joy of cooking and the comforting presence of his newfound friends would have him floating out of the kitchen. He would settle in the corner booth to catch up on the town gossip with his new neighbors, the Do-Nothings, Marathon's preeminent busybodies. After listening to the henhouse cackling of the women's chatter, he would waltz out of the diner whistling one of the twangy country love songs from the jukebox. He would float down the small-town streets as he ambled the three blocks to Murphy's Garage, all the way hoping his boyfriend, Hank Hudson, would be found bent over the engine of a car with his perfect backside on display. With the comfortable weariness of a good day's work in his bones, he would place his arms around Hank's shoulders, lay his head on his shoulder, and sigh in contentment. "Hey, Baby," he would drawl, "it's been a good day."

But today had been like nothing he had ever experienced. Today he was tired—bone tired—the kind of tired that makes feet burn as if racing across hot coals and limbs drag with the weight of steel girders. His eyes and temples throbbed with the beginning of a headache, and his stomach raised a loud, rumbling protest at not having been fed all day. Since Frankie Jones, the youngest of the owner's daughters, had flipped the lock on the front door and welcomed the first guests of the day, he had not stopped running for six straight hours. His head swam in the constant barrage of requests for more plates of turkey and dressing. Pot after pot of corn and yams and string beans and okra and black-eyed peas and collard greens blurred before his eyes. He couldn't begin to count the number of golden biscuits he had pulled from the two ovens in the corner. Unlike a normal day at the diner that allowed for an occasional lull, today had been nonstop. Today had been the Tammy Dinette's annual *Thanksgiving Feed the Hungry*, when the diner provided a free meal to anyone in need. Apparently, a lot of people in Marathon were in need.

So Marcus had worked hard. And he was tired. And it felt better than anything he had ever known.

Marcus opened his eyes and raised his head as a hand brushed his shoulder. He glanced into the soft blue eyes of Francine Jones, the owner of the Tammy Dinette. She smiled lovingly at him and winked.

"Told you it was going to be a brutal day, Shoe Button," she said and patted him on the upper arm. "Every year the crowd just gets bigger and bigger." She pushed a few strands of her silver hair away from her face before tossing her apron on the table and flopping into the empty seat beside him. "But I cannot stand the thought of a single person not getting a good meal on Thanksgiving Day."

"You know, Francine," Marcus said and chuckled, "if you'd told me a year ago that I'd be thrilled to spend another Thanksgiving slinging plates in a diner, I'd have spit in your eye. But I have to admit, this felt good."

"Oh, really?" Francine raised an eyebrow. She slipped her feet out of her orthopedic shoes and let out a long whistle. "My barking dogs think you're full of it."

"Yeah. Seemed almost normal to me. You know how my mama dragged me from town to town as a kid?" Marcus closed his eyes and leaned back in the chair. "Mama always worked the holidays so she could get double pay. I can hear her now. 'Baby, we need the money more than we need the hoopla.'" Marcus shook his head and chuckled. "I spent most of my Thanksgivings and Christmases tucked in a corner booth of some greasy spoon watching my mama sling plates and sass at customers. A couple of times she let me make a turkey picture by tracing my hand. You know what I'm talking about?" Marcus opened his eyes and mimicked tracing the fingers of one hand with the other.

"Lord, yes." Francine giggled. "I've had more of those damned turkeys stuck on my fridge than I can count."

"Anyway, Mama let me draw them on the back of the paper placemats and hand them out to customers. She made me a black construction paper pilgrim hat to wear, too. Then we'd go home and eat whatever leftovers she stole from the diner." Marcus shrugged and sighed. "Not really Norman Rockwell, but it's what I was used to. I knew other kids got fancier holidays, but I was with Mama, so…" His voice trailed off, and his mouth curled in a half-hearted smile. "Hell, a big old family dinner on Thanksgiving is about as strange to me as Chinese New Year or Ramadan."

"Oh, Shoe Button." Francine patted the back of Marcus's hand. "I'm sorry you never got a real Thanksgiving. Not that today was a real Thanksgiving by any means."

Marcus shook the memory from his shoulders and smiled meekly at Francine. "When I got out on my own, I volunteered to work on the holidays too. By then I'd learned what Mama meant about the extra money. It never really bothered me. You learn not to miss what you think you'll never get."

"But now I feel bad for asking you to—"

"Francine," Marcus interrupted her, "hush. Today was wonderful. I actually felt like I was doing some good. Plus, you know you and your girls are almost like family to me. I wish they'd stuck around for a minute at least."

"Oh, please. As soon as I said they didn't have to help with the dishes, you couldn't have kept them here." Francine shifted her gaze from Marcus to the flickering blue and yellow lights of the jukebox as the song switched to an upbeat two-step rhythm. "Dang-it, Paulette was supposed to switch out the records in the jukebox for the Christmas songs."

"I can do it." Marcus shifted forward in his chair and groaned. "As soon as my feet remember how to work."

"No." Francine grunted as she rose. She shuffled past the row of stools along the counter. "I'll do it. You get on out of here."

"Yeah. I need to get over to Hank's, or he'll think I'm the biggest turkey of the day." Marcus remained seated. "Though I'd be perfectly fine with sitting in this chair until Christmas."

"Well, at least you've got tomorrow off." Francine paused with her hand on the plug of the jukebox and winked at Marcus. "You and Hank can stay in bed all morning if you want." Her eyes shifted over Marcus's shoulder toward a banging sound on the glass of the diner door. "Can't people read? I turned the closed sign over half an hour ago. *We're closed!*" she yelled toward the door.

"Francine," a woman's voice called through the door. "Open this gee-danged door!"

Marcus turned to look through the glass. From the light of the streetlamp, he made out two women huddled close together. One woman was waving her arms in exaggerated conversation, while the other stood with her arms crossed and shaking her head. The women banged on the glass again and looked through the door. Seeing the two faces pressed against the glass, Marcus broke out in a broad grin. "It's Inez and Priscilla."

"Oh, shit." Francine's wide backside wiggled under the tight fabric of her pink uniform skirt as she waddled to unlock the door. "I forgot they were coming by."

The bell over the front door rang, and the two women, deep in a heated conversation, bustled into the room. Priscilla Ellington's towering bouffant of gray hair wobbled above her plump face as she vigorously shook her head. "And I said if you were going to make me park in that spot by the parking meter, then you were going to have to be the one to put the money in it." The pewter cross that hung on a chain around her neck bounced against her large chest as she raised her arm to shake a finger at the other woman. "If that nitwit Deputy Randall gives me a ticket, then I'm *not* going to be the one to—"

"Priss, you are such a pain in my ass." Inez Coffee shoved Priscilla's finger out of her face. She tugged the hem of her dark-blue Atlanta Braves T-shirt back over the waist of her pants and adjusted the lime-green fanny pack that was buckled around her waist. "It's a national holiday. You don't have to feed the stupid meter on a national holiday. I swanee, I should've ridden over here with Helen. At least then I… Oh! Hello, Marcus, Sweetheart! I didn't think you'd still be here!" Inez scurried across the room and wrapped her arms around Marcus's neck. Her overly dyed black hair tickled his temple when she bent to give him a peck on the cheek. "I figured by now you'd be trotting off to Hank's place, ass swinging like church bells on Easter."

"Inez!" Priscilla chastised, "watch your language. Today is about saying thanks to God, not saying filthy words." She patted Marcus on his head and ruffled his hair. "Happy Thanksgiving, Little Man."

"Hey, Miss Inez. Miss Priscilla. Happy Thanksgiving!" Marcus said as he ducked away from Inez's attempt to pinch his cheeks. "I'm heading over to Hank's in a little bit. But I need my daily dose of Do-Nothings first. Speaking of, where's Helen?"

"She's right behind us." Priscilla shrugged. "She probably took the time to find a legal parking spot." Priscilla plopped her ample frame onto a chair and grunted. She reached down to roll the tops of her knee-high stockings toward her bright white tennis shoes. "Unlike *some* people." She rolled her eyes at Marcus.

"Drop it, Priss." Inez shot an angry look at the other woman before turning back to Marcus. "You know Helen has to go do the whole family thing with Raff and his wife. And Skeet got back into town last night. She was just about to spit, she was so anxious to see that grandbaby of hers." Inez jerked a chair out and sat. She unhooked her fanny pack from her waist and tossed it onto the table, causing the sugar dispenser and napkin holder to rattle. A pack of cigarettes poked out of the open zipper, and Inez fumbled it back into the bag. She shot Marcus a guilty grin, then placed her finger over her pursed lips to shush him.

Marcus turned toward the entrance as the bell over the door rang again and Helen Warner swept into the diner. An orange chiffon scarf tossed around her neck fluttered behind her as she hurried to the table. "Oh, thank heavens, you girls are here! If I had to spend another ten minutes with that nitwit daughter-in-law of mine, I'd be calling you to bail me out of jail for murder. She had the nerve to serve dressing made from a box. Can you imagine? Dressing from a box!"

"Oh, Helen." Inez swatted at the other woman's hip. "It's not like Raff would know the difference. He grew up eating your cooking, after all."

Helen stuck her tongue out at Inez and wrinkled her nose. "Why don't you act like a turkey and stuff it?" Her shoulders shook as she laughed. She patted her bobbed silver hair and winked at Marcus.

"Hello, Darling. I didn't realize you'd still be here or I would've brought Skeet with me to see you. He was dying to come up here all day, but his mother told him Thanksgiving was for family and he could see you and Hank tomorrow. I should've made Francine give you today off so you could've joined us Warners."

"Hey, Helen," Marcus drawled as he stood and pulled her into a hug. The warmth of her hug, the soft fabric of her silk blouse, and the familiar scent of her magnolia perfume made Marcus hum in delight into her shoulder. Helen had been the first of his grandmother's friends that he had met, and her doting over him had become one of his favorite things. "Happy Thanksgiving."

"Why are you still here?" Helen twisted her upper body away from Marcus and looked him in the eye. "I'm sure Hank is waiting on you." She turned to Francine. "I can't believe you made this boy work on Thanksgiving and wouldn't even let that absolutely scrumptious boyfriend of his come with him. Poor man has been alone all day." Helen cut her eyes at the other women and tried to hide a grin.

"I tell you what," Inez said and winked at Helen, "no telling what he's up to without you around."

"Girls, don't ruin the surprise," Priscilla hissed and waved the women away.

"What do you dames know?" Marcus knitted his brows in mock annoyance. "Come on. Spill it."

"We know nothing," Helen chirped and raised her eyebrows. "We're just not used to seeing you without him. We thought y'all were joined at the hip."

"With hips like Hank's, wouldn't you want to be attached to them? No, I forbid him from being here today. Marcus here," Francine said as she poked Marcus in the shoulder, "well, he can't concentrate none too well when that man is around, and I needed his mind on work today. And I don't regret that decision for a minute. They kept us hopping from the minute I opened the door until Marcus finally shuffled old Delores Richards out into a cab. Didn't they, Honey?"

"Oh! So it went well? Well, praise God." Priscilla pulled a handkerchief from her oversized black purse and began to wipe the table in front of her. "You know I really appreciate you taking this on. You're earning stars in your heavenly crown with this dinner. I wish I could still do it at the fellowship hall, but after the reverend had his stroke, we just couldn't get the church members motivated to take it on anymore." She pressed harder on the tissue as she scrubbed at a spot on the table. "Plus, you have much better space and equipment for—"

"Priss," Francine interrupted her, "I have asked you to not mention it. Trust me. I'm thrilled to do it. It's become one of my favorite days of the year."

"Was it a good crowd?" Inez snatched the tissue out of Priscilla's hand. "Would you stop that?"

"A record crowd I think," Francine replied. "We served at least a hundred and fifty people."

"Oh, come on." Helen screwed up her lips. "There can't be that many people in this town that don't have the means to make their own Thanksgiving dinner." Helen sat at the remaining empty chair at the table. "Francine, people are just taking advantage of your generosity for a free meal. Delores Richards has more money than she knows what to do with."

"I'll make you a deal, Helen." Francine frowned and shook her finger at Helen. "You come next year and stand at the door and determine who gets in and who doesn't. Remember, not all needs are about money. Some people, like Delores Richards, are just lonely. You really want to turn someone away? You want to be the neediness judge?"

"Well, I just meant… never mind." Helen lowered her head. A deafening silence fell as the jukebox paused between songs and the women all stared at their hands.

To break the awkward silence, Marcus said, "It did feel good to do something that helps the community. I was telling Francine before y'all got here that I never really did the whole, big family thing for

Thanksgiving, and today it felt like half the people in town were my guests."

"Aw," Inez said, "that's sweet, Sugar. And I think you deserve a big old reward for helping out. Girls, let's take Marcus out shopping tomorrow for Black Friday!"

"Lord, no," Francine drawled and turned away from the table. "I had enough of crowds today. Plus, you girls agreed to help me clean this diner tonight so Marcus could get on out of here. And we've got a lot of dishes to wash."

"I'm going to pass too, Inez," Helen demurred. "I don't see the point in going shopping tomorrow. It's not like they're going to have anything on sale over at the Chic Petite that I could get my big-boned daughter-in-law into anyway. Also, you promised to help me start making the Christmas luminaries to put around the streets in the subdivision. I've been saving those milk jugs all year, and they aren't going to fill themselves with sand."

"Priss?" Inez begged. "Here's your chance. Save me from *that* hell and go shopping?"

"No can do." Priscilla shook her head. "I've got to help the women of the church put the Nativity out on the church lawn, and we're starting on the costumes for the children's pageant after that."

"Costumes?" Inez scoffed. "All you need is some old bathrobes, some pillowcases for headdresses, and some tinsel haloes." She turned to Francine and stuck out her bottom lip. "Francine, you'll come spend money with me, won't you?"

"You know I have to put my Christmas decorations up before December first," Francine said over her shoulder as she walked to the jukebox and pulled the plug out of the wall. "It's bad luck to put stuff up after the first." She walked to the swinging door behind the counter that separated the kitchen from the diner. "Now you women quit stalling and get back here and help me wash these pots and pans." Francine bumped the swinging door open with her backside and disappeared into the room beyond.

"No, it's bad luck to leave it up past New Year's Day," Helen called after her. "She gets all those rules wrong. But I plan on starting my decorating tomorrow, too. It takes me at least a week to get the house ready. Plus I have to decorate the law office for the Rotary Club's Tour of Homes. *Gracious Living Magazine* had some really *wonderful* ideas this year, and I've been planning since it came out in September."

"Well, fine." Inez slumped back in her chair with her arms crossed. "I guess I'll just start putting up the lights on the house tomorrow since someone insisted it was tacky just to leave them up all year." Inez cut her eyes at Priscilla and smirked. "You want to help me do that, Marcus? Elbert can't climb a ladder too good anymore."

"Sorry, Miss Inez," Marcus said. "I've got plans for tomorrow, too."

"You and Hank going to spend a lazy, romantic morning in bed? I want all the details tomorrow!" Inez wiggled her eyebrows at Marcus.

"No. Hank's working tomorrow. And I'm going to do some decorating at my grandmother's… I mean *my* house. Make it feel more like home, you know?" Marcus turned to Helen. "And please remind Skeet he promised to help me paint the windows at the garage with Christmas scenes. With Skeet's artistic skills, Hank says he'll for sure win the town decorating contest this year. We're painting a—"

"Oh, Francine will never stand for that," Priscilla interrupted him. "You know she's won that competition for the last eight years. Of course, her daughter Georgette is a regular plate-glass Picasso. One year she painted a baby Jesus on the windows that was so pretty it made several dyed-in-the-wool atheists come back to church."

"Well, Hank and I have a secret weapon." Marcus cast a furtive glance toward the kitchen to make sure Francine couldn't hear him. "We got a little fake tree, and I had Hank save old car parts to hang as ornaments: spark plugs and springs and stuff. I cleaned them and spray-painted them silver and gold. And I've got a big old gear to put on the top for a star."

"Ain't that crafty!" Inez clapped her hands.

"It makes sense," Helen added. "You know your grandmother was a very crafty woman. She made almost all her own Christmas ornaments." Helen snapped her fingers. "As a matter of fact, I have a whole box of ornaments she made. When we were clearing out her house after she died, I found it stuck in a closet. I thought the ornaments were too pretty to donate to charity. Of course, I didn't realize at the time that her grandson was a homosexual who might appreciate the handiwork. I'll bring it over to you tomorrow."

"Girls!" Francine's head poked through the pass-through window between the kitchen and the dining room. "Quit flapping your gums and get back here and help me so I can get home before midnight. Y'all are keeping Marcus from his fella."

"Yeah, I'd better get going." Marcus stood and slid his chair back under the table. "I've got a tree to decorate. And I've got to make something for me and Hank for dinner. Even if I *am* wore slap out. *And* starving. Though after today, I don't ever want to see another turkey."

"Well, that's too bad. Hank's got that turkey in the—"

"Inez," Helen hissed, "that's supposed to be a surprise."

"Hell, I forgot." Inez scowled.

Marcus slapped his palms on the table and said, "All right, old ladies. That's it. Spill it."

"Fine, but don't tell him we told you." Inez raised her hands in surrender. "I know a certain mechanic has spent most of the day holed up above that garage of his making a turkey dinner with all the trimmings. Green bean casserole. Fried squash. The works. And even cornbread dressing."

"And it isn't dressing from a box," Helen interjected. "Hank wanted to surprise you with a whole, big shebang. And he asked us to help. We each made something for him to heat up and serve you."

"The sweet potatoes are mine," Priscilla said, her face aglow. "And tell him I need that casserole dish back."

Marcus watched the women sitting around the table with the joy of their loving mischief beaming from their faces. He was too tired to chastise them for meddling, but wouldn't have bothered anyway. They wouldn't stop, and he wasn't sure he wanted them to. Even though he would never fully understand why, the Do-Nothings had made it clear in his short time in town that helping their beloved, departed friend's only grandchild be happy delighted them. As the women giggled and chattered amongst themselves, Marcus cocked his head and whispered, "Give thanks."

"Oh, Marcus," Inez said in a sing-song voice, "the green bean casserole is Helen's, so, you know, skip that one."

"Inez, shut up about my cooking." Helen punched the other woman lightly on the shoulder. "But, Sweetie, don't ruin the surprise, okay?"

"Girls!" Francine yelled again from the kitchen.

Marcus laughed and worked his way around the table to hug each woman. "Your secret's safe with me. And thank you. Now, y'all better get back there and help Francine before she has a conniption." Marcus ambled to the door and paused with his hand on the handle. He turned back to the women and said, "And Happy Thanksgiving!"

Chapter Two

"IT'S ABOUT TIME," HANK HUDSON said as he opened the plate glass door and let Marcus slip into the darkened lobby of Murphy's garage. The reddish glow from a soda machine in the corner of the room gave Marcus just enough light to see the happy twinkle in Hank's brown eyes and the smirk of a sarcastic grin on his face. "I was beginning to think you'd been killed in some horrible, cornbread-dressing accident."

"What in the hell would be a cornbread-dressing accident?" Marcus asked and laughed.

"Fiat, with your accident-prone self, it could've been anything." Though Marcus no longer drove the yellow Fiat that had led to their meeting six months ago when he'd wrecked it, Hank still used the nickname often. He claimed he remembered people's cars better than their names. Marcus had initially found the moniker irritating, but now the baritone sound of it rolling across Hank's lips made his knees wobble and his tummy flip. He was far too tired and hungry to be frisky, but Hank's broad chest and strong arms in the tight, blue T-shirt he wore made Marcus want to hurry their progress up the stairs at the back of the lobby into the apartment above.

"Nope," Marcus replied as he put his hands on Hank's hips. As he stepped forward and nuzzled into his neck, the other man's soft, dark beard tickled his cheek. "No near-death encounters with a turkey, either."

"Well, let's give thanks for that." Hank ran his hands down Marcus's back and tucked them into Marcus's back pockets. He pulled Marcus tight against his body. "So how was it today?"

"It was a good day, Baby." The warmth of his boyfriend's body soothed Marcus's tired muscles, and he relaxed into the embrace.

Marcus breathed in deeply at Hank's collar bone. The smells of the home-cooked food reheating upstairs that lingered in Hank's cotton shirt mixed with his cologne and filled Marcus with two types of hunger. He satisfied one by turning his face and placing his lips on Hank's. The other man let out a low hum of pleasure as they kissed. Marcus pulled away slightly and looked into Hank's eyes. "I'm going to want seconds of that later, but right now I'm starving."

"Let's get upstairs and get to rectifying that." Hank stepped toward the stairs and pulled Marcus along behind him, only letting go of his hand when they reached the narrow stairway and had to ascend single file. "You can tell me all about how the dinner went. Was it a big crowd?"

"Big doesn't even begin to describe it. I can't count how many plates I fixed today." Marcus concentrated on Hank's backside, which was accented by worn spots on his tight blue jeans, as it bounced up the stairs ahead of him. The sight of Hank's firm body inches away and the scents of food wafting from the apartment set Marcus's two hungers warring inside him. As he clomped upward, a loud rumble from his stomach signaled which desire would win this time.

"Was that your stomach?" Hank paused on the stairs and turned to shoot Marcus a concerned look.

"Yeah," Marcus's answered as he pushed Hank up the stairs into the apartment, "we need to get some food into me." Remembering the Do-Nothings admonition not to ruin Hank's surprise, he added, "I'm so tired I can barely climb these stairs. I don't think I can cook another thing today. Maybe we should just make a frozen pizza."

Hank spun around and grabbed Marcus by both wrists. Excitement danced in his eyes, and he shook his shoulders. "I've got a surprise for you! I made us a whole Thanksgiving dinner. Turkey and everything!" He pulled Marcus into the apartment and gestured toward the folding table beside the kitchenette along the wall of the large, open loft. "You don't have to cook any more today!"

The table was covered with a russet tablecloth and had orange tapers burning in the center of a spray of autumn leaves and berries. Two plates sat on brown placemats embroidered with yellow leaves that Marcus recognized from Helen's kitchen table. He was sure the tablecloth, napkins, and centerpiece belonged to the Do-Nothings as well.

"Oh, Hank. It's beautiful. You shouldn't have." Marcus turned and kissed Hank on the cheek. His stomach interrupted the kiss with a loud grumble. "But, clearly, I'm so glad you did."

"I wanted to make our first Thanksgiving together a special night." Hank beamed as he stepped over to the counter and pointed out bowls of food arrayed there. "And I made all your favorites. Cathead biscuits. Creamed corn. And look!" Hank picked one bowl and thrust it toward Marcus. "Real mashed potatoes. Not from a box!"

Marcus laughed as he walked over and took the bowl from Hank. He set the mashed potatoes on the counter before placing his hands on either side of Hank's hips. He backed Hank against the counter and moved closer to his face. "And it all looks nearly as delicious as you." He playfully nipped his teeth at Hank's nose.

"Easy, Fiat," Hank said with a laugh, "we've got time for that later."

"If I can stay awake. Told you I was tired."

"Look, I still need to put the finishing touches on some things, so why don't you go get cleaned up, and then we'll eat? Maybe that'll wake you up."

"Fine. I do feel pretty gross." Marcus stepped away from Hank and started for the bathroom in the corner of the loft. "But you don't need to reheat the green bean casserole. You know I won't eat anything that Helen Warner…" Marcus stopped suddenly and scrunched his face in regret at his babbling. He swiveled back around to Hank's crestfallen expression.

"They told you." Hank pouted. He tossed the dish towel he was holding onto the counter. "It was supposed to be a surprise."

"Oh, Honey," Marcus said in his most soothing voice. "You know those old biddies can't keep a secret." He walked back to Hank and placed his hands on the sides of his face. "And I don't care who made the food. You're the one who thought of having this dinner for me." He kissed Hank before adding, "That's all that matters."

"I guess so," Hank mumbled. "But I just wanted… I thought… um… I did mash the potatoes."

"And I'm sure they will be the best part of the meal." Marcus turned back toward the bathroom. "Though you know I'd never believe you made all of this. You can barely make a bowl of cereal."

"Yeah. Okay. You're right." Bowls rattled behind him as Hank moved them around on the counter. "Now scoot. I'm pretty hungry too."

"I should've gone home first and changed clothes," Marcus said, as he pulled his sleeve to his nose and sniffed it. "I smell like that greasy grill at the diner."

"You can get some of my clothes out of the dresser and wear those if you want. I mean they'll swallow your bony butt, but they won't smell like an omelette."

"You sure?" Marcus stopped at the dresser. Scattered across the top were Hank's car keys and wallet and random bolts and screws. Tucked in the corner of the mirror was a picture clipped from the newspaper of Marcus and Hank dancing together in front of the gazebo in the town square. Marcus had the same picture stuck to his refrigerator with a magnet. He had been a little mortified when the picture showed up in the town paper, but he had to admit they both looked ridiculously happy. And his suit that night had made his normally wiry body look amazing.

"Yeah," Hank answered. "You know, maybe it's time you leave some clothes over here. Stop having to do the walk of shame when you spend the night. You know how small-town tongues can waggle." Hank concentrated on pouring lumpy gravy from a plastic container into a white ceramic gravy boat. "I can empty out a drawer for you."

"Really?" Marcus asked. "You want to do that?"

"Yeah," Hank said, not looking away from his task, "and maybe I can leave some at your place. Just make life easier. And a toothbrush. Definitely a toothbrush."

"That makes sense." Marcus smiled as he pulled the top drawer of the dresser open and rummaged for a T-shirt that might not be too large. He pulled out a red one and held it up to inspect. On the front was a simple line drawing of a rooster with the word *cock* written underneath. "Where did you get *this*?"

Hank glanced at the shirt and frowned. "Ugh. Skeet gave it to me. He thought it was funny. Of course, I can't wear it out of the house. Can you imagine Myrtle Hawkins seeing that shirt? She'd have me arrested."

"Well, it's not a turkey, so I don't think it is appropriate for tonight, either." Marcus folded the shirt and placed it back in the drawer. As he pulled out another T-shirt, a folded piece of paper fluttered to the floor. Marcus bent to retrieve it.

"I guess I could hang those and let you have that drawer," Hank said from the kitchen. "While we're at it, maybe I should get you a key. Keep me from having to go down all those stairs and let you in every time you come over."

"A key? That would be…" Marcus paused as fancy blue lettering across the top of the paper caught his eye. *Jeffrey's Jewelers.* "…convenient," he mumbled as his eyes quickly scanned the receipt. Two words leaped off the page. *Gold Ring.* Marcus shifted his gaze from the paper toward Hank; his mouth opened in shock. Hank's back was turned. He scoured the receipt and noted it was dated the previous day. At the bottom was scrawled *must be complete before Christmas.*

"Maybe Santa will bring you a key," Hank said with his back still turned to Marcus as he vigorously stirred something in a bowl. "If you're a good boy. Did you find a shirt?"

"Yes," Marcus said in a whisper, the heart pounding in his ears nearly drowning out the sound of his voice. Guilt gnawed at his stomach as he shoved the receipt back into the drawer and pushed it closed as quietly as possible. "I found something."

"Well, hurry up. The food is going to get cold."

Marcus threw the T-shirt over his shoulder and scurried into the bathroom. *Oh, my God.* He closed the door behind him. *Gold Ring.*

Gold Ring. The words repeated over and over in his head, and he had to steady himself against the sink. *Could it be?* He placed his hand against the porcelain and leaned close to the mirror to look into his eyes. *But it's so soon.* He took several deep breaths to slow his beating heart. *We've only been dating…* He pulled his sweaty work shirt from his trim shoulders and let it drop to the floor. *Is he ready for that? Am I ready for that?* He turned on the water in the sink, let it run for a second, and then splashed some on his face. *He did mention keys and moving clothes.* Marcus stared at his reflection. Water dripped from his red eyebrows and the tip of his nose. A broad smile spread across his freckled face. *I'm getting proposed to for Christmas!*

Marcus jumped as Hank pounded on the door. "Everything okay in there? Food's getting cold."

"Yeah," Marcus replied. *A Christmas engagement.* He grabbed the towel from the back of the door and dried his face. *It would be awfully romantic.* He slipped his arms into Hank's T-shirt and pulled it over his head. The large shirt hung loosely around his thin body. *If the setting is just right.* He fussed with his hair in the mirror and then took a deep breath. Gold ring. *Golden Ring. Just like the Tammy Wynette song.* "Tammy Wynette!" he said aloud and pushed himself back from the sink. He fished his phone out of his pocket and began pecking out a text message on the screen.

To Helen: Gather Do-Nothings tomorrow. Emergency meeting. Need help. And bring that Christmas magazine!

He nodded once at the phone and smiled. *My first real Christmas will be the best Christmas ever.*

Chapter Three

"ARE YOU SURE IT SAID 'ring'?" Francine asked as she stepped into Marcus's grandmother's house and let the screen door slam shut behind her. She dropped the heavy cardboard box she was carrying behind Marcus's blue plaid couch in one of the few spots the Do-Nothings had not filled with overflowing bags, boxes, and bins of decorations. "Maybe you read it wrong."

"No. It definitely said 'ring,'" Marcus said over his shoulder as he squatted to open the box. "What's in this one?"

"It's just some old decorations from the diner." Francine braced herself against the back of the couch and slowly knelt beside Marcus. She pulled a huge, red bow out of the box. She shook it back and forth in her hand and tried to mold the velveteen ribbon back into its proper shape. "It got a little squished. I don't know if you can use any of this junk, but it's yours if you want it. If you don't, just donate it to Brother Marty's."

"No offense, but that's kind of tacky." Marcus took the bow and shoved it back in the box. "I'm going for pure class. I want this place to look amazing."

"Wise choice passing on that bow, honey," Helen opined from a bar stool at the kitchen island behind them. Another box lay open beside her, and she had spread yard after yard of glittering gold and silver garland across the counter top. Her diamond earring and a bit of glitter stuck to her cheek sparkled in the morning light as she shook her head. "Primary colors are so three-Christmases-ago."

"I just can't figure out what Hank is thinking. It seems a little soon to me. Y'all haven't been dating that long," Francine said as she pulled the bow back out of the box. "And this bow was very expensive, Helen. Thank you very much."

"What does it matter how long they've been dating?" Inez said as she walked out of the hallway. She tugged at the elastic waistband of her purple Capri pants to pull them farther up her waist. "When you know, you know. By the way, Sweetheart, you are out of air freshener in that bathroom." She walked to the dining table and began pulling glass balls out of another box and sorting them into piles. "Elbert and I dated for less than a year before we got hitched. And Marcus is right; a Christmas proposal would be really romantic. Shit, am I supposed to be grouping these by color or size?"

"You and Elbert knew each other since kindergarten." Francine shrugged and said, "I think Marcus should take a little time to—"

Helen spun around on the stool to face Marcus and Francine. "Just because your first two marriages were disasters doesn't mean everybody has to be as wary as you." She crossed her arms over her chest and grimaced. "Hank Hudson is a good man and you know it. And what a wonderful excuse to do some good, old-fashioned decorating!"

"I'm not saying he isn't a good man. And if y'all are just going to keep insulting me, then I'm going to—"

"Francine, I'm sorry. I didn't mean it that way. I just don't understand why you can't be excited for Marcus." She spun back to the box and rummaged around, humming an off-key rendition of *Jingle Bells*.

"Would you say this is more blue or green?" Inez asked as she held up a large teal ball. "I'm going blue." She dropped the ball onto a pile and reached into the box for another. "You know, Francine's got me thinking, though. Maybe the ring isn't for you?"

Marcus dropped the string of lights he was trying to untangle and stared at Inez. "Who the hell else would he be buying a ring for?"

"Maybe his mother?" Inez shrugged and placed a red ball in another pile.

"He doesn't speak to his mother since she kicked him out for being gay." Marcus picked the lights up and began snatching at the tangle of wires and bulbs. "It has to be for me. Ugh, this is hopeless." He flung the strand of lights toward the garbage can sitting at the end of the kitchen island.

"Easy, now." Francine placed a hand on Marcus's upper arm and rubbed lightly. "Don't blow a gasket. Christmas is supposed to be fun."

"Maybe it's just a friendship ring," Inez suggested. "Do you gays do that? Friendship rings?"

"Oh, good lord, Inez." Helen closed the box in front of her and slid it to the side. She pulled over another box and opened it. "The receipt was from Jeffrey's Jewelers." She began pulling wads of newspaper out of the top of the box. "Everyone knows you buy engagement rings from Jeffrey's. If Hank wanted some cheap little trinket, he would have gone to… Bingo!" she yelled as she pulled an intricate lace snowflake ornament out of the box. "I knew your grandmother's ornaments were in here somewhere!"

Marcus jumped from the floor and took the ornament from Helen. "Wow! Oh, wow," he said in a breathy voice as he held the lacy snowflake up and let it spin on its string. The ornament was made of fine white thread twisted and knitted into a myriad of small lines and angles, spreading out from a simple silver-star pattern in the center. Iridescent thread interspersed with the white caught the light and twinkled with each pivot at the end of the satin ribbon tied at the top. The entire snowflake had been starched to make it hold its shape. "This is beautiful. And you said my grandmother made it?"

"Of course," Francine said as she tried to rise from the floor. She rocked back and forth and let out a groan. "Jesus, my knees. Inez, come help me up."

"Eloise was a whiz with anything that involved a needle," Inez said as she grabbed Francine's arm and pulled her off the floor with a grunt. "She tatted those things way back before your granddaddy died. She'd use them every year."

"Matter of fact," Helen added, "she made by hand most of the Christmas presents she gave people." She pulled another snowflake from the box. "Usually those homemade gifts are a bit *meh,* but Eloise was an artist. I've still got everything she ever made me."

"She'd be so proud of you doing all of this hard work to make her house look pretty," Inez said. "I mean your house. Oh, I wish you could've seen it when she had it all decorated. It was absolutely gorgeous." Her face grew darker, and her lip trembled as she stared at the ornament. She whipped around and returned to her sorting project. She mumbled, "You have to put that on your tree."

"Speaking of," Francine said as she returned to her pile of ornaments on the table, "when are you getting your tree?"

"Oh," Marcus said as he let the snowflake twist and turn from the tip of his finger, "they had some decent fake ones at Ginsberg's pharmacy. That's where I got the one I used in the garage lobby. I'll probably go this afternoon and—"

"Fake tree!" Helen gasped. "You are most certainly *not* putting these beautiful ornaments on a fake tree." She took the snowflake from Marcus's finger and set it gingerly on the counter. "Your buddy Sarge has beautiful trees on that farm of his that he sells at a fair price. Simply *everyone* gets their trees from Sarge."

"But aren't they messy?" Marcus asked. "And kind of a pain to deal with?"

"I insist you use a live tree," Helen said with a firm nod of her head. "Eloise would turn over in her grave if you brought a fake tree into this house. She always used a live one, and you should too."

"Now y'all hush about Eloise," Inez mumbled from the table. She placed another green ball into a pile and stepped away with a sniffle. "You're going to get me crying, and then I'll be no good to nobody. Lord, I miss that woman."

Helen hopped off the barstool and grabbed Inez by her arm. "Why don't you come with me over to Priss's house? She couldn't find anybody to sit with the reverend and she's got a nativity set for Marcus." She began tugging the other woman toward the front door. "We can also get some bunches of magnolia leaves out of my yard, so Marcus can make that wreath for the front door." She snapped her fingers and hurried back over to the couch. "I almost forgot!" She reached into her large purse and pulled out a thick, glossy magazine. "Ta-da! Here it is. The bible. *Gracious Living Magazine.*" Helen handed it over to Marcus with a flourish. "The directions for the wreath are on page ninety-seven. I'm sure you can figure it out."

Marcus was shocked at the weight of the magazine. It appeared to be at least three hundred pages long, far thicker than the Marathon phonebook on his kitchen counter. He scanned the glossy cover, and knitted his brows as he read. A decadent-looking cake with white frosting and delicate decorations adorned the cover under deep-red lettering that read *Gracious Living Magazine: For Southern Homes with Taste.* Glittery ornaments and shiny ribbons curled about the base of the cake. Several headlines promised Marcus "the best eggnog recipe ever with *no* alcohol required" and "proper poinsettia care" and "homemade gift tags that will wow your guests." Marcus dropped the glossy tome onto the dining table, where it landed with a thud and made the pile of glass balls Inez had abandoned there jostle and scatter. Marcus barely caught one before it rolled off the edge of the table.

"You just let that be your guide," Helen crowed, "and you'll have this place whipped into shape in no time. It'll be the perfect spot for your man to get down on one knee."

"Oooh!" Inez squealed from the doorway and clapped her hands in front of her face like an excited child. "I'm so excited I could spit. Marathon's first gay wedding. And right here on our street! We're going to have so much fun planning that!"

"I'll have to dig out my *Gracious Living* wedding issues!" Helen bustled to the door and shoved Inez into the yard. "Let's get moving. Marcus has a lot to do!" The two women trotted down the sidewalk chattering and giggling.

Marcus laughed as he closed the door behind them. He turned to find Francine sitting on a stool at the counter with her arms crossed and a worried look on her face. "Those women are nuts," Marcus said as he sat on the stool beside her.

"Shoe Button," Francine said and placed her hand on top of Marcus's, "don't let those busybodies talk you into doing something you aren't ready to do."

Marcus twisted his face in confusion. "What do you mean? I definitely want to decorate for Christmas. I never had anything like this when I was growing up." Marcus plucked a piece of the garland from the counter and twirled it in his fingers. "You think my Thanksgivings were sad? Christmas was the same thing. Mama always worked. We never had a tree or stockings or any of that stuff. And I always got clothes or *maybe* some book or toy she found cheap at a yard sale—something we could throw in the truck when she decided it was time to move on to a new town." Marcus dropped the garland and frowned. "It sucked."

Francine squeezed his hand. "Honey, that is not what I'm talking –"

"Don't you see?" Marcus cocked his head and kicked at the counter. "I finally have a real home. And I want to have a *real* Christmas. The tree. The lights. The whole shebang. Just think about it, Francine. Getting proposed to in front of a massive Christmas tree with sparkling ornaments and twinkling lights and a big, old, beautiful star on top."

"Sweetie, you sound more interested in the *tree* than the *proposal*."

Marcus scoffed and shot a hurt look at Francine. "No. That's not true." His cheeks burned bright red, and he dropped his chin to stare at his hands as he fiddled with the garland. "But can't I have both?"

"Marcus, listen to me." Francine grabbed his chin and raised his face to look him in the eye. "Christmas is one day a year. Marriage is three hundred and sixty-five. Have you even considered what you're going to answer?"

Marcus stared at her and blinked twice; his confusion at her question clouded his eyes. "I don't know. I'll figure that out when he asks." He waved her question away and spun on the stool to face the piles of boxes in his living room. "I've got other things to think about right now." He hopped down and hurried around the end of the couch. "Like, should

I put the tree over here by the windows or back there by the piano?" He stood in the center of the room and turned back and forth to judge the advantages of each location. "I'd have to stick those chairs in the spare room if I put it over there."

Francine edged herself off the stool and dropped to the floor with a sigh. She glanced at her watch, then back at Marcus. "Honey, I better get going. I promised Georgette I'd help her paint the windows at the Tammy. We've got a contest to win."

"Uh huh," Marcus muttered as he opened a white plastic garbage bag on the coffee table and began pulling fake evergreen garlands out by the handful. He draped one around his neck and flung one end over his shoulder like a feather boa. He shimmied and twirled the ends of the garland toward the mirror that hung over the piano.

Francine shook her head and sighed again. "I'll see you at the diner tomorrow morning." She walked to the front door and paused with her hand on the handle. "Marcus, think about what I said. Only twenty-eight days left."

"To shop?" Marcus asked and giggled as he turned to one side, cocked his shoulder up, and winked at his reflection. "Merry Christmas, Mister President," he sang in a whispery imitation of Marilyn Monroe. He pouted his lips and blew his reflection a kiss. He leaned closer to the mirror to inspect the dark circles under his blue eyes. His excitement over the Christmas decorating had kept him awake late into the night making plans. His face, which he always thought looked too boyish with his freckles and upturned nose, was puffy and tired. *Girl, you look a mess.*

Dismissing the thought, Marcus whipped off the garland and began arranging it around the picture frames that sat on the back of the piano. "Francine, do you think this looks…" He glanced up to an empty room. "Oh, you left." Marcus shrugged and pulled another length of garland from the bag. As he wove the strand of prickly green foliage along the back of the piano, he sang at the top of his lungs, "In a one-horse open sleigh!"

Chapter Four

"FA LA LA DEE DA," Marcus sang, as he dropped a delicate marzipan holly leaf onto a perfect peak of snow-white frosting on top of the red velvet cake that sat on his grandmother's cut-crystal cake stand. He used a toothpick to spear two red fondant holly berries and slid them precisely into place at the base of the green leaf. As he discarded the toothpick onto the kitchen counter, he used his other hand to twist the cake stand and inspect the cake from all sides. The frosting had covered divinely, just as the magazine recipe had promised. He scooped the cake stand off the counter and spun around to the island that separated his small kitchen from the living room. The ties of the emerald velvet apron, onto which he'd appliqued poinsettia flowers earlier in the day, fluttered behind his waist as he gracefully twirled twice. He sat the cake stand on the island beside the dozen small trays of sugar cookies, fruitcake slices, and brownies that were scattered among fragrant boughs of fresh cut pine splayed down the center of the island. He nudged one tray of powdered sugar-covered cookies slightly to the left until it was symmetrical with the other trays. He leaned over the counter and inhaled deeply; the smells of sugar and spice made his head spin. "Mmm," he sighed in contentment.

Marcus untied the strings of his apron and ducked his head out of the neck strap. He flung the apron casually toward a hook on the wall beside the refrigerator. It landed on the hook, spun once, and settled against the wall with a rustle. Marcus nodded his head toward the apron and said, "Good boy. Stay." He giggled as he danced toward the small dining table tucked into the bay window at the far end of the kitchen. As he approached, the flames of the bayberry candles in the centerpiece flickered and cast a slight shadow across the items on the tartan tablecloth. He pulled a pencil from behind his ear and ticked his way down the to-do list lying on the table. "Almost done," he said and drew a quick line through *baked goods*. "And it's all thanks to you," he said to the glossy cover of the magazine lying next to the list, "you glorious little guide to the perfect Christmas!"

He stared at the picture on the cover and then glanced at the cake he had set on the counter. His version matched perfectly the beautiful cake displayed on the cover right under the deep-red lettering of *Gracious Living: For Southern Homes with Taste*. "If it weren't for your help, I don't think I ever could've finished this list in just two weeks." Marcus gestured at the list of thirty-two items. He picked it up and ran his finger along the edge, double checking all that he had accomplished. "Everything is done except the last one!"

He inspected the living room. Since he had inherited the cozy home from his grandmother six months ago, Marcus had not changed much about its décor. He had never met Eloise Sumter and was completely surprised when he found out that her home, money, and belongings were all suddenly his. A sense of not deserving the inheritance and a desire to try to know her better had led him to leave her things pretty much untouched. She had clearly been a no-nonsense woman, as every item in the house had a purpose and a place. Marcus saw no need to disrupt her logic. He had rearranged the kitchen cabinets so that they flowed better for his style of cooking and moved the few clothes he'd shoved in a duffle bag when he came to Marathon into the closet in the bedroom, but everything else in the house was hers and seemed right exactly where it was. Even the photos of the grandparents and father he had never known that were scattered across the back of the piano served to make him feel like part of the family. Though he was forever bumping into the piano and knocking the frames over, he refused to move them. Keeping with his grandmother's family theme, he had added a picture of his best friend, Skeet Warner, and Hank into the honored row of smiling faces. In the center he had placed his favorite photo, a picture of him sitting in the corner booth of the diner surrounded by the Do-Nothings, who had become surrogate grandmothers for Marcus.

But Christmas and the final item on his list demanded he make the place more his own and decorate to reflect the happiness of his new-found life.

And decorate he had.

An eight-foot Virginia pine Christmas tree stood next to the window that looked out on his front lawn. Just as the magazine had suggested, he'd chosen a tasteful color scheme of gold and silver for his ornaments and used simple white twinkle lights to avoid distracting from the beauty of the handmade decorations he had lovingly placed on each branch. Marcus walked to the tree and touched a few of the glass balls dangling from the limbs. He made them spin and send sparkles of light dancing across the blue-green needles of the tree. Tucked between the balls were the delicate, intricate filigrees of the snowflakes his grandmother had tatted and Helen had given him. He used his own hand-crafted ornaments to fill in the rest of the tree—a tow truck, a spatula, drama masks, a peach, a baseball. He had carved and painted these trinkets to represent the new people in his life.

He used his foot to adjust the skirt around the base of the tree so that it swathed the stand in perfect, velvety, green pools. He gazed at the top of the tree, where an angel with hair as red as Marcus's and all Sumters before him spread her stark white wings over the sparkling limbs below. Silk and satin robes billowed from her shoulders, and in her hands she held a rhinestone star-shaped brooch Marcus had found in his grandmother's jewelry box. The angel's face was eerily similar to the photograph of his grandmother that sat on the piano behind him as the angel smiled down at Marcus. Marcus winked at her and said, "You'll have the best seat in the house when it happens!"

He turned from the tree and opened the front door to look at the elaborate wreath he'd copied from page ninety-seven of the magazine. He had deftly wired bunches of broad, waxy magnolia leaves to a ring of straw bound together with tartan ribbon to match his tablecloth and the runner he'd placed along the back of the piano. He had tucked more of the golden glass balls from the Christmas tree between the leaves and topped the whole thing off with an enormous gold lamé bow. Thanks to the advice of *Gracious Living*, the abundance of magnolia leaves in his neighbor's yard, and the wondrous tool called a hot glue gun, it had taken him mere minutes to whip up. Though the article had suggested a plaid or gingham bow, Inez had convinced him that the lamé would give the whole thing a bit of needed pizazz and "add some sparkle."

Marcus glanced from the wreath to the front yard and the soft blanket of glistening snow that covered the ground. "When did that happen?" he asked. "It was eighty degrees yesterday." Before he could belabor the thought, he was distracted by a group of young children bundled in heavy coats, scarves, and mittens standing in the middle of his lawn. Each child stood shivering against the cold and holding a burning candle. Their high-pitched voices wafted across the yard carrying music toward Marcus. Though he made out an occasional reference to an angel or Mary or a sheep, he had no idea what carol the children were attempting to sing. He leaned against the doorframe, listened to their angelic voices, and smiled. "Well, it's lovely anyway." He pushed the door closed to keep the cold air out.

He heard the crackling of a log in the fireplace on the opposite wall. Christmas cards of varying hues and sizes stood along the edge of the mantelpiece wishing happy holidays to any who paused to read them. Long garlands of evergreen branches and lengths of gold and silver ribbon swooped across and dangled from the edges of the mantel, bookended by two velvet stockings—one red and one green. Marcus had used his grandmother's sewing machine to embroider an *H* on one and an *M* on the other yesterday. He crossed the room to admire the fine stitching and enjoy the warmth of the fire against his legs.

"Strange. I don't remember having a fireplace." He stared at the flames and wrinkled his brow. He waved the thought away. "Doesn't matter. It will be the perfect place for the final item on the list to take place." He surveyed the decorations covering his living room again and crossed his arms on his chest in satisfaction. The magical fairyland he had created in his home looked like a page straight out of the magazine. "Everything is tasteful, gorgeous, and… well… perfect!"

Marcus crossed to the dining table and picked up a crystal cup from beside his grandmother's punch bowl. He ladled some spiced apple cider from the bowl into the delicate glass and took a careful sip, fearing the punch might still be hot from being mulled. He didn't remember making the cider, but it was the perfect temperature and flavor, just as *Gracious Living* had said it would be.

"Is there anything you can't do?" Marcus asked as he sat the cup beside the magazine. "Well, I guess you can't do the last thing on the list. Have to rely on Mister Hudson for that one, won't we?" Marcus took the piece of paper and read the last line of his list. *Be proposed to by the man of my dreams.*

"Now where could he be?" Marcus said. "He was supposed to be here by—" The clanging chimes of the doorbell interrupted Marcus. He spun to the front door and broke out in a broad grin. "There he is!"

"Marcus? Are you there?" Hank's voice called through the front door.

"Coming!" Marcus shouted. As he tried to take a second step, his left foot suddenly filled with lead. His leg would not move no matter how hard he tried. "I'm trying at least." He grabbed his thigh and tried to pull his foot off the floor.

"Marcus?" Hank called again, irritation creeping into his voice. "Open the door!"

Marcus's heart raced as he struggled to move to the door. "Hank, something is wrong! I can't seem to…" Beads of sweat burst out across his forehead as he attempted to shift his weight. His right foot had revolted against him now as well, and he stood glued to the spot. A popping noise from the fireplace across the room caught his attention. The logs in the fireplace had shifted and sent a shower of sparks out onto the floor. Small flames began to flicker from the carpet, and the garland and ribbon along the mantel began to curl away from the growing heat of the fire. The two stockings suddenly burst into bright balls of flame. Marcus opened his mouth to scream, but the sound lodged in his throat, and he produced only a strangled croak.

"Hank. Help. Oh, no!"

Marcus's eyes grew wide as the Christmas tree swayed forward and then back. It teetered again and yet again before plummeting to the floor with a crash, sending shards of broken glass ornaments flying across the room. The angel bounced off the top of the tree and landed in the middle of the fireplace; its feathery wings were instantly engulfed in flames.

"Marcus, what was that sound? Is that smoke? Let me in!" Hank pounded on the door; each thud rang in Marcus's ears and made his pulse quicken with fear. "Honey?" Hank screamed through the door. "What are you doing?"

Marcus gagged as thick black smoke stung his eyes and throat. The door zoomed miles away; his knees grew weak. "Hank! Save me! Please, come save me!"

"Marcus! Marcus!" Hank's voice echoed from beyond the door.

"Hank!" Marcus screamed as he jerked his head from the table and gasped in a deep breath of air. Bright morning sunlight streamed through the blinds, and Marcus squinted as his eyes adjusted to the sudden stab of light. He whipped his head about in confusion, as the lingering wisps of sleep and nightmare slipped from his head. A high-pitched alarm screaming from the hallway made his shoulders draw up around his ears, and a pounding noise from the front of the house echoed the beating of his heart in his ears. He shoved back from the table and stood. He gripped the table to steady himself and shook his head. His hand landed in a pie pan full of paint; its bright-red color was cold and thick as it squished between his fingers. "Dammit," he muttered as he yanked back his hand back and wiped his palm down the front of his shirt.

He whipped his head to the left to check the living room. Several bolts of tartan fabric lay draped across the sofa and chairs in the room;

shopping bags spilled over with tinsel, ribbons, and sprigs of greenery. Boxes of hand-me-down decorations that the Do-Nothings had been dropping off at his house for the last few days were stacked behind the sofa. On the table in front of him were a pile of half-painted ornaments, a checklist with nothing marked off, and the mangled cover of a *Gracious Living Magazine*. While the room was decidedly messy, there was no decorated Christmas tree, no well-placed strands of garland or ribbon or lights, nor, thankfully, any tongues of flame leaping from his non-existent fireplace. However, a faint haze of smoke hung over the room.

"Shit! My cake!" Marcus yelled as he stumbled to the oven and pulled the door open. Thick smoke poured into the room, and Marcus fanned it away from his face. He grabbed a towel from the counter and wrapped it around his hands. He yanked the burnt remains of a Bundt cake out of the oven, tossed it into the sink, and knocked the faucet handle on to soak the burnt mess. "Dammit."

"Fiat, are you in there?" Hank's familiar voice called from the front door, followed by loud pounding. "Marcus!"

"Hold on!" Marcus called over his shoulder as he hurried over to the hallway to wave the towel in front of the screaming smoke alarm in a desperate attempt to silence its harpy wail. After several fruitless waves of the towel, he dropped it on the floor. He ran to the front door, unlocked it, and jerked it open.

Hank stood on the other side of the screen door with his dark brows knitted. "What the hell is going on in there? I've been banging on this door for five minutes." He opened the screen door, stepped into the smoky house, and waved his hands in front of his face to clear the air. "I'm going to leave this open to let the smoke out!" he yelled over the screech of the smoke alarm.

"No! You'll let the cold air from the snow in!" Marcus yelled back as he tried to shove the door closed.

"Snow? What are you talking about? It's seventy-something degrees out there." Hank pulled the door open as wide as it would swing.

"I... never mind." Marcus grimaced at the dead, brown grass in his front yard. He checked left and right to make sure no children were standing on the lawn singing.

"If I had a key, I could've just let myself in!" Hank said as he walked into the kitchen and pulled out a folding step stool from beside the refrigerator. He dragged it into the hallway and opened it under the smoke alarm. He climbed on the stool and grabbed the alarm with both hands. With a harsh tug, he yanked the squealing unit from the ceiling and shook it until the batteries fell out. Silence fell across the room, and Hank hopped from the stool. "That's better. What the hell is going on in here?" His eyes grew wide as he looked at Marcus. "Oh, my God. Are you bleeding?" Hank rushed over and grabbed Marcus's face, then turned it to the side to look at the dark-red streak that ran from his eyebrow to his jaw.

"What?" Marcus asked as he looked at his hands and laughed. "It's just paint. I must've smeared some on my face. I was trying to work on some ornaments for the tree." He nodded toward the table and the pile of arts and crafts supplies spread there.

Hank took Marcus's hand and lifted it. He kissed Marcus's knuckles, then flipped his hand over to inspect the palm. "So I caught you red-handed!"

"Har-har," Marcus mumbled and gestured toward the sink. "I burnt my cake, which you probably figured out already."

"The bags under your eyes practically say Samsonite. Did you stay up all night?"

"I couldn't sleep, so I got up and started working on some decorations. I figured I might as well start making my cakes, too. I guess I nodded off and lost track of the... time! Oh, my God, Hank. What time is it?"

"Um," Hank said as he peered into the sink and grimaced at the charred remains of the cake, "nine-thirty. That looks disgusting."

"Nine-thirty?" Marcus gasped. "Oh, no! We're late!" Looking for his car keys, he began frantically pushing things around on the kitchen table. "We've got to go *now*. Help me find my keys!"

"Hold on. Hold on." Hank grabbed Marcus's wrist to stop his shuffling. "I'm driving, remember? Also, I don't think you want to go out there looking like this. Sweetheart, you've got paint and glitter all over your face. Looks like a kindergarten blew up all over you. Why don't I clean the mess in the sink while you shower?"

"No. No time. I'll just throw on a hat. We're going to get dirty cutting down a tree anyway."

"Fiat, you know I think you look hot no matter what," Hank tucked his fingers under Marcus's chin and lifted his face, "but the Do-Nothings will kill me if I let you go out in public looking like this. Ten minutes won't make much difference. There will still be plenty of trees—"

"But not a good one. They'll be all picked over. The tree is the center-piece of the whole room." Marcus picked an ornament off the table and twisted it in his hand. "My whole design is based around getting a very specific—"

"You're just being silly now. Did those old ladies put this idea in your head? I mean if that little tree we put in my lobby is good enough, then I don't understand—"

"No, you don't understand, Hank," Marcus said as he dropped the half-painted ornament onto the table. "For the first time in my life I get a real Christmas and I wanted it to be perfect!" He swept his arm across the table in a fit of anger, sending its contents flying. Several glass Christmas balls skittered across the table, slid off the edge, and shattered on the kitchen's tile floor. Scraps of red velvet ribbon fluttered down amongst the shards as his copy of *Gracious Living* landed on the floor with a loud smack. The bayberry-scented candle burning in the center of the table toppled to one side in its candleholder and dribbled wax onto the ring of holly leaves around its base. "And I can't paint a damned snowman to save my life!"

"Look out, now," Hank yelled as he pushed off the kitchen counter and grabbed for the candle. "You're going to burn the whole damn house down." He fumbled with the taper, dropped it onto the table, and jerked his hand back with a hiss of pain as wax splattered onto the back of his hand. "I don't know why you're burning all these things anyway. It's broad daylight and seventy-five degrees out there."

Marcus jumped from his seat to take the candle; his hips bumped the table and sent more ornaments crashing onto the floor. "I'm trying to make the house feel more... I don't know... festive?" He shrugged. "Nothing feels right. It shouldn't be this hot at Christmas. No one seems to be in the spirit. And I just thought that if I had a good old-fashioned..." His voice trailed off as he shoved the candle back into the holder and noticed the pool of spilled wax on a pile of white feathers scattered on the green tablecloth. "And now you've ruined the wings for the angel on top of the tree."

"You don't have a tree," Hank mumbled as crossed his arms and drew his mouth into an irritated scowl.

Marcus squinted and looked from the pile of feathers to Hank. "Because someone was late coming to cut one down." He scooped the mess of wax and feathers into his arms and turned to the trash can behind him. He stomped on the pedal to make the top open and dropped the wings into the container with a grunt.

"I'm twenty minutes late, Marcus." Hank sat at the table and began picking at the purple wax on the tablecloth. "And you weren't exactly ready when I got here. We can still go get one."

Marcus closed his eyes in an attempt to calm his anger. Light flashed behind his eyelids with each beat of his heart. "I told you Sarge opens the tree farm at ten o'clock, and he said people line up for hours beforehand all up and down the highway so they can pick out the best trees. And now that we're late getting there, all the good ones will probably be picked, and we'll be stuck with some scrawny thing that isn't much better than that pine-scented air freshener hanging in your truck." Marcus jerked his thumb over his shoulder toward the bay window that faced the driveway.

"I don't have a pine-scented air freshener," Hank grumbled. "And I don't know why you don't just go down to Ginsburg's Drugstore and buy a fake one."

"No!" Marcus spun on his heels to face Hank. "It *has* to be a live tree. *Gracious Living* says it has to be a live tree. You just don't understand." He kicked the leg of a dining chair to slide it back under the table, pouted, and stared at his shoes.

"Clearly, I don't." Hank rolled his eyes, dropped the clumps of wax he had picked onto the table, and stood. "But if it makes you feel any better, I was late because I was picking up your present. Not that you deserve anything more than a lump of coal with the way you're showing your ass today. I forgot how obnoxious you are when you're sleepy."

Marcus jerked his head up and stared at Hank. "My present?" He groaned. "See, that is exactly what I'm talking about. Everything needs to be memorable and perfect when you give it to me. I wanted my house to be a winter wonderland when you proposed to me, not looking like a glittery toxic dump with a fake tree and some ticky-tacky decorations flung up."

"Marcus." Hank threw his hands up. "What does it matter what your house looks like when I give you… wait… when I *what?*"

"I'm sorry the surprise was ruined, but I know all about the ring. I found the receipt in your drawer on Thanksgiving. And you were talking about swapping keys and moving clothes, and I just knew what you were up to. And this is a story we will tell the rest of our lives, so I wanted it to be perfect and have really classy—"

Hank ran his fingers through his thick, brown hair and let out a short, frustrated snort. "What are you talking about?"

"I wanted it to be as beautiful as the town square was that night when I finally got my head out of my ass and danced with you. You know, the first night we… But everything in that magazine is a lot harder to make than it looks in the pictures. And I can't get anything done right. And everything is just ruined." Marcus waved his hands frantically around his head.

"Fiat, listen to me." Hank stood and grabbed Marcus's wrists to stop his flailing. "Calm down. I'm *not* proposing to you for Christmas."

"And the Do-Nothings told me I should be sure to use..." Marcus's voice trailed off as Hank's words sank in. He pulled his hands free from Hank's grasp. "You're... not? But the receipt from Jeffrey's Jewelers. I told the girls about it, and they agreed with me that it had to be... well, not Francine. But Helen said everyone goes there to buy... oh, God." Marcus pulled the chair out from the table and dropped onto it. His cheeks grew hot as he leaned his elbows on the table and buried his face in his hands.

"No," Hank said calmly. "I'm *not* proposing. You really want me to propose to you?"

"Oh, shit. I just thought with how close we have grown and the talk of house keys and..." His words trailed off as he lifted his head to the piles of half-finished decorations littering the usually immaculate house. A wreath of wilted magnolia leaves and half-dead fruit rested limply against the wall by the front door. The garlands he had woven around the picture frames on the piano had slipped and dangled askew along the keys. A light haze of smoke still hung through the house. He glanced at his feet and the shards of the broken ornaments lying beside the tattered pages of the magazine. Marcus dropped his head onto his crossed arms on the table. A cloud of gold and silver glitter wafted up and sprinkled down onto Marcus's red hair. "Fine. Just leave, you Grinch. I was trying to..."

Hank took a deep breath and sighed. "Fiat, sit right there. And for God's sake, don't try to decorate another thing."

Marcus groaned and said, "Well, fa-la-la-la, shit." Tears stung at the corners of his eyes.

The front door creaked open and closed with a faint click. Marcus lifted his face in response to the sound and stared out the window at Hank's truck. Hank crossed in front of the window, paused for a moment to look to the sky, and ran his fingers through his dark hair in the way he did when he was in deep thought. He pulled out his phone and dialed. After a short conversation that involved some angry looks and hand waving, he hung up the phone shoved it back in his pocket. He opened the passenger's side door of his truck and snatched something off the seat. He slammed the car door and walked back to the house.

Marcus dropped his head to avoid eye contact as Hank walked back in. A small box wrapped in bright-red paper and a glittery gold bow dropped on the table in front of him. Marcus stared at the package, unsure of what to say or do.

"Merry Christmas," Hank said as he sat beside Marcus.

Fighting back tears, Marcus raised his head and looked at Hank. His voice cracked as he said, "But Christmas isn't for another week. I don't have a gift for you yet. And look at what a mess this house—"

Hank placed a finger on Marcus's lips. "Fiat, just listen to me for a second. Then I want you to open it." He slid the package away and took Marcus's hands in his. He locked eyes with Marcus and took a deep breath. "I'm not too sure what is going on here. I don't know if those old broads of yours put all of this into your head. I don't know if it's because Christmas kind of sucked for you as a kid. Maybe this is some attempt to create a fantasy you've always had. I have no idea where this is all coming from, but I don't think you *really* want me to propose to you."

Marcus opened his mouth to reply, but Hank silenced him with a shake of his head.

"You acted surprised when I suggested leaving a toothbrush and some clothes at my apartment, like the thought of even living together never occurred to you. Hell, just a few months ago, you were seriously thinking about selling this house and running away from here."

Marcus nodded and whispered, "But I didn't."

"No. You didn't. And I'm so glad you stayed. Because I *do* love you, Marcus." Hank lifted a hand and rested it softly on Marcus's cheek. "All of you. Happy you. Sad you. Sexy you. Even the nutjob you sitting beside me right now. And I will still love you even when you explain where all this decorating frenzy is coming from. I will love you even if you act like this every December. Okay?"

Marcus blinked hard, blushed, and leaned against Hank's warm hand. "Okay."

"Good. I want you to remember that I love you when you open that gift and I *don't* propose to you." Hank took his hand away from Marcus's face and slid the box over to him. "Go ahead."

Marcus's hands shook as he grabbed the ends of the frilly bow and pulled in opposite directions to untie it. He nudged the paper away to reveal a velvet-covered jewelry box. He swallowed the lump in his throat and took a deep breath before easing the top of the box open. He peeked inside and gasped. In the box lay a large golden ring. Attached to it were a small gold locket engraved with the letter "M" and a single key. "Oh, my God. It *is* a ring." Marcus threw his head back and laughed. "A key ring." He fidgeted with the locket clasp until it popped open. Inside were black and white photographs of two smiling faces. Marcus moved closer to the box to inspect the pictures. "That's my grandmother and my father!"

"Yes," Hank said. "Those pictures are to remind you that your family is always with you. Even when they aren't here anymore. The key may get you into a house, but a family is what makes it a home. And I really want you to consider me a part of your family." Hank pulled the key ring out of the box. He took Marcus's hand, opened his palm, and placed the key in it. "Look, Fiat, I'm not asking you for forever right now. Just say you want to be in my house more often, okay?"

Marcus stared at the key in his hand until a smile crept across his face. He beamed at Hank. "I do." He leaned forward and pulled Hank into a long, slow kiss. He sat back and rubbed the key between his fingers. "Yes, I do."

"All right. Now about this Christmas madness." Hank bent over to retrieve the *Gracious Living* from the floor. He held it in front of Marcus. "This is not what Christmas is about." He tossed the magazine toward the trash can, and it landed on the tile floor with a harsh smack.

"Christmas isn't trees and wreaths and ribbons and cakes. Christmas is about being with the people you love and remembering the ones who are no longer here. Christmas is about family."

Marcus ran his finger over the picture of his grandmother in the locket. "Family."

"Yes." Hank gestured at the boxes scattered around the room. "All the rest is just stuff."

"Pretty stuff," Marcus said as he set the key ring on the table and lifted one of his grandmother's snowflake ornaments. He let it twirl and sparkle in the morning sun.

"Fine. Pretty stuff." Hank grabbed Marcus's other hand and placed it on his chest, "But this. You and me. Being together is what matters, okay?"

"Okay." Marcus rested his head on Hank's shoulder. He let out a long sigh as he lifted his hand higher to make the ornament catch more light. He shifted his head, looked up into Hank's face, and gave his best puppy dog eyes. "But can we still get a tree?"

Before Hank answered, someone pounded on the door. "That will have to wait," Hank said as he jumped from his chair and went to open the door. He stood with his hands on his hips and forced an exaggerated frown at the people standing outside. "Ladies, how about you get in here and fix this."

The Do-Nothings shuffled into the house one at a time with their heads lowered and faces fixed in sheepish scowls. Helen clutched a large wreath. Inez followed with a tray of cookies balanced on her hands. Priscilla waddled behind with an old CD player swinging by her side. Francine trailed carrying a plastic bucket with a feather duster, several rags, and a bottle of window cleaner poking over the top.

"Oh, Honey," Helen said as she tossed the wreath onto the sofa and threw her arms around Marcus's neck. "Hank called and told us what a mess we might have created." She released Marcus from her hug and bowed her head. "I'm sorry if I made you feel like you had to do all of this stuff. You know me. I just get my mouth going, and my brain gets left out. But don't you worry. The cavalry is here!"

"We forget not everyone has been doing this crap since Jesus was a child," Inez said with a loud laugh. "You know that garland can be tricky stuff." She set the cookies on the counter before rushing over to the piano and rearranging the greenery that drooped from the back.

Priscilla put the CD player on the table. "Nothing will make the work go faster than some good Christmas music." She hit a button on the front of the player, and the room filled with the sounds of sleigh bells ringing and a choir singing. Her bouffant bobbed in time with the music as she wobbled around the table and began to gather the few unbroken ornaments against her chest. "We'll be needing these. Francine called Sarge, and he's bringing a tree a little later."

Francine crossed to Marcus and put the bucket on the floor. She pulled him to her side and rubbed his back. "So? You engaged?"

Marcus shook his head and pointed at the key ring lying on the kitchen table. "No. Key ring. Not engagement ring." He smiled at Francine's confused look. "And it's perfect. I'll explain later."

Francine wrinkled her brow. "Are you okay?"

"Yes, ma'am, I am." Marcus chuckled as Hank and the Do Nothings scurried and danced about the house. Discarded lengths of fabric disappeared into boxes. Decorations found homes. The wreath moved from the sofa to the front door. His home began to transform. Marcus turned up the music and took Francine into his arms. He began to dance her around the kitchen and sang along with the music. Francine's laughter rang in his ears as he spun her out in a careless whirl. "I'm more than okay. I'm going to have a real Christmas." Marcus retrieved the *Gracious Living* magazine from the floor near the trash can. He stared wistfully at the cake on the cover. He shifted his gaze from the picture to his friends laughing and singing in the living room. He tossed the magazine into the garbage. "A *real* Christmas."

About the Author: Killian B. Brewer lives in his life-long home of Georgia with his partner and their dog. He has written poetry and short fiction since he was knee-high to a grasshopper. Brewer earned a BA in English and does not use this degree in his job in the banking industry. He has a love of greasy diner food that borders on obsessive. *Lunch with the Do-Nothings at the Tammy Dinette* was published in January, 2017. His debut novel, *The Rules of Ever After*, is available from Duet Books, the young adult imprint of Interlude Press.

True North

Pene Henson

EVEN FOR LOS ANGELES, IT was unseasonably warm. A winter sunset outlined the balcony railings in gold. Shay Allen leaned against the sliding doors to look out across the city. Beyond her, palm trees and nearby apartment buildings were hazy silhouettes against the orange sky; below, a ribbon of taillights stretched along the street and disappeared.

The evening was flawless. This was what she'd hoped for in spending Christmas at home.

Shay's phone buzzed in her shorts' pocket. Her stomach twisted and twisted again with each new buzz. It was about the ninety-sixth time her agent had called in the hours since they'd landed.

"The man sure is persistent," she said when the buzzing stopped at last.

"That's why you employed him. Persistence makes for a good agent." Shay's closest friend and teammate, Devon Washington, was stretched out to her full six foot five inches on Shay's new faux leather lounge. "Persistence and that face. It's hard for some folks to say no to a man who looks that good."

Shay shrugged. Manny wasn't her type, but he was gorgeous.

"It's probably nothing. Maybe he wants to take you to lunch while you're in town. Chat about the Euroleague championships."

Shay wrinkled her nose. She didn't want to talk to Manny about Europe at all.

With her season as starter for the LA Sparks over, Shay had signed with Ekaterinburg for another well-compensated winter on the Russian Women's Basketball Premier League's foremost team. She liked the club and the fans. She didn't like Russia's stand on LGBT rights, and Ekaterinburg wasn't a safe place to be out, but she didn't plan to hold hands on the street. Plus, it was hard to turn down the salary. Shay may have been a star in the WNBA, but no career in sports was forever. Making enough in salary supplements while she could was crucial.

Shay could have spent this mid-season break seeing more of Europe: Prague's delicate wonderland, Amsterdam's dazzling Christmas lights. She could have visited Santa in Lapland if magic and reindeer and glistening snow were her thing. But the mild Los Angeles weather had called. She'd taken the long flight home, where she could avoid both the snow and her coach.

But she couldn't avoid her agent.

Shay's phone rang again.

"Hand it over, kid," said Devon. "I'll talk to Manny. He likes me."

Shay rolled her eyes, pulled the phone from her pocket and tossed it over. Devon didn't sit up, but simply reached out and plucked it from the air with one hand. It buzzed again as she flipped it over to see the screen.

"That does not look like Manny," she said. She turned the screen to show Shay the picture. "It's your mom."

"God." Shay lunged toward the couch and grabbed the phone from Devon. She sent the call to voice mail. Her mother's anxiously smiling face faded to black.

"Dude," Devon protested.

Shay held up her hands. "Don't 'dude' me. I can't talk to Mom right now. She'll ask me to come home for Christmas. And with all this going on—look, my mama's stubborn, and I'm exhausted. My defenses are down. I won't be able to say no." Shay slid the phone into her pocket and leaned against the door frame again. The sun warmed her shoulder. A horn blared from a car down in the street; a louder honk blasted in reply.

"Your mama's not the only one who's stubborn," Devon said. "Want me to tell you what I reckon?"

Shay folded her arms across her body.

Devon grinned. "That's a yes, then." She pointed at Shay. "You, Shay Allen, star of the WNBA, are in a slump. It's not surprising. You've been on this treadmill for seven years. And slumps happen. You know that, Coach knows that, Manny knows that. Every ball player who's anyone has scoring slumps. Me included. It won't last forever."

Shay chewed her lower lip and met Devon's dark brown eyes. "I'm under twelve points a game."

"I know you are." Devon bent her arm behind her head as a headrest as she considered Shay.

"Under twelve points, Devon. In Russia. The club pays me six times my WNBA salary. It flies us around in charter planes and puts us up in fancy hotels and gives us flashy jewelry I don't even wear. When we were Euroleague champions they gave me a Fabergé egg. They don't give me all that stuff to be decorative. I need to earn my keep."

"It doesn't work that way. Everyone understands that."

"Then why's Manny calling me?"

Devon fell silent.

Shay looked out the window again. The sun was heavy and rust-colored at the horizon. The traffic hadn't dissipated. "I'm gonna lose the contract," she said.

"No, you're not. You're Ekaterinburg's biggest draw. They've invested a lot of money and publicity in you. They want you to succeed. Anyway, this is going to get better. You've made it through bad patches before and you've come back stronger. But it takes hard work. Blood. Sweat. Tears."

Shay raised her eyebrows. "Blood?"

"It's about *work*, Shay. You haven't been putting in the work."

It was useless to protest, but the words tumbled out. "I'm just so tired."

Devon nodded. "Yeah. I know you are. And you know I'm right. Which is probably why Manny keeps calling." Sometimes Devon was more annoying than anyone Shay knew. "Hey. You want to hear what else I'm right about?"

"What?" Shay asked, against her better judgment.

"Before you call Manny back and tell him you're still his best client and you'll put in the hours blah, blah, blah, you need to call your mom. She loves you. And that love doesn't depend on your field goal stats."

Shay groaned. "Devon, I'm really not up for it. If I call home now I'll end up in Montana for Christmas."

Devon met her gaze. "Okay. So you end up in Montana for Christmas."

"We only have fifteen days of break," said Shay. She righted herself from the doorframe and paced the room. "Fifteen winter-free days. We've got it planned out: morning runs at the beach, brunch-time mimosas, clubs with the crew. I don't want to spend the time freezing my butt off on a mountain in Montana."

Truth was, she didn't really want to do all the other stuff either. She wanted to watch Netflix and hide out in sweats in her house so no one would talk about what a letdown she was.

She stopped pacing. "And anyway, how am I going to train up there, genius? I can't get my edge back in Big Timber. The school's closed for winter break, and there're no other basketball courts."

"Big Timber..." Devon was smiling.

"*Outside* Big Timber. You know where I'm from."

"It still amazes me." Devon sat up and shook her head. Her mid-length golden brown twists shifted around her neck. "The little Black girl from Montana."

"I'm not little. And I'm not the only one."

Devon ignored her and went on. "So don't go for the whole break. Have a few days there. See your mom and dad; look at the huge Montana sky. Find a way to clear your head. Then come back to LA, get yourself onto the courts, and we'll get busy. You haven't been home in years, Shay. It might be good for you."

Of course, Devon was right. "Fine. Whatever. Fine." At least in Montana they wouldn't know she was a failure.

Shay pulled her phone out of her pocket. She turned her head to fix Devon with a glare. "But if I'm going to Montana for Christmas, I'll be damned if you're not coming too," she said as she dialed her mother's number.

Devon's open-mouthed stare and perfect outraged eyebrows were almost enough to cheer Shay up.

*　*　*

THE HIRED CAR PULLED UP, shiny black as oil. When the driver opened the door, the scent of faux pine wafted out. Shay climbed in and shrank into the black leather seat. There was plenty of leg room. The car company she used knew who Shay was. They always sent a big car. Shay pulled her cap down to shield her eyes.

The driver recognized her. He chatted to her about basketball as he took West Eighth to South Grand toward Devon's condo.

"Can't believe how many players are retiring. The WNBA's lucky to still have you."

Shay gave a half laugh. "I'm twenty-six. They're not getting rid of me that easily." The guy was being polite, but he probably knew all about Shay Allen and her total lack of current form. "Pull into the driveway here, thanks."

As Devon climbed into the car, she beamed a hello at the driver then swatted Shay's arm as he closed the door. "Here we go. I can't believe I finally get to meet your folks. They're gonna love me."

The driver glanced back as he climbed into his seat. "The rumors are true, then," he said.

Shay raised her eyebrows.

"Don't worry, I won't tell the papers. They don't listen anyway. One time I had this big pop star in here with this English actor. Huge story. Did the papers listen to me? And then three weeks later it's all over the news. I could have given them the scoop."

Devon laughed. Shay frowned. Their relationship gave plenty of cause for speculation online. They were best friends. They went to concerts together and exercised at the same gym. Shay was out as a lesbian but had no regular partner, and Devon didn't date. She was happier that way. The two of them had long ago learned not to answer questions about their personal lives from nosy strangers.

The driver looked at Shay in the rearview mirror. "It's all good. I got no problem with you."

Damn right you don't. Shay resisted making any reply.

Sunlight seeped in through the tinted sunroof. They turned onto West Pico. For a moment the Staples Center was visible off to the right. Shay's stomach dropped. Right there, that was her dream: the WNBA, the LA Sparks, a career, fame. But for the moment it seemed as though she was doing all she could to trash that dream.

Shay found her voice as they slid under a sign for Domestic Departures. "Hey." She looked at Devon. "I'm sorry. You don't really have to come along."

Devon raised one eyebrow. "Uh. What now? Did I hear you right?"

"You can stay here in LA. You don't need to come with me. I can tell my parents you have family commitments."

"You already told them I don't."

"I'll think of something." Shay wrinkled her nose. "I shouldn't have made you join me. You've got better things to do than spend three days of your break shivering in a snow drift with me and my family."

Devon looked out the window as she spoke. "You're right. The weather's pretty good here—"

Shay sighed. "That's fair. I'll call my mom from the airport."

"—but we already bought the tickets. And anyway, I'm looking forward to the things you described: snow as far as you can see; majestic mountain ranges; wood fires and hot chocolate and cross country skiing. It sounds exotic. Plus I want to meet all the colorful Montana characters."

"I was trying to sell you on the place, Dev. Truth is, it's bleak and cold, and the snow goes all the way to the edge of the world. Nothing to see but white. And it gets dark at five p.m. We'll all be inside a lot." She thought of something. "Oh, god. And I bet my parents will throw some kind of get-together with half the town in a room at Neb's saloon."

Devon narrowed her eyes. "Okay. But you told me we'd go for a ride on a dog sled."

Shay shrugged. "Yeah, I mean, I think we can ask Albi for a ride. She had malamutes—these huge dogs."

"And there's Neb and Odette and Teddy and some guy named Mr. Big Ears."

"Yeah. He lives up the river in a cabin. He, well—he has pretty big ears."

"Plus there's a fireplace. And the scenery around your parents' home is beautiful."

"It— Sure. It is. The place has its moments."

"The whole thing sounds incredible. Cold but incredible. I'm starting to think you don't want me there."

"Dev. I want you there. I really want you there. The last time I went home, it was tricky."

"Okay then. I'm glad I didn't buy snow boots for nothing."

Shay exhaled. "Thank you. I appreciate it. Really."

"No problem at all."

The car glided into the drop-off zone. The driver handed over their bags. Shay shouldered hers easily. After years of travel, she was an expert at packing light.

"Thanks," she said.

The airport doors slid open to the noisy lines of people, all with too much luggage, all heading home for Christmas. Shay turned to Devon. "Here we go. You can't leave me alone now."

"I wouldn't want to." Devon patted her shoulder, firm and sure, the same way she did when they were in the middle of a playoff game.

* * *

EVEN IN LOS ANGELES, PEOPLE noticed Shay and Devon. They'd get to their feet after brunch or stride into a nightclub in short skirts and shimmery tops, and people would look up. The attention was rarely welcome. Over the years it had toughened Shay's skin. She would flick a glance the watchers' way and believe she'd won something when their gazes dropped.

One of their teammates, a six-foot white girl named Laura, said, "It's not about Black or white. See, they look at me too." But the attention Shay and Devon received was singular, was everything mixed together: awe, physicality, height, fitness, otherness, being a woman, being Black.

But since this was Los Angeles, it was also about fame. People recognized them as WNBA players, especially when they were out with other teammates. Fans asked for signatures on shirts or napkins or basketballs. That was okay, of course. It might be hard to distinguish sometimes, but that was professional attention and it mattered to Shay.

In Montana, the staring was more pronounced. At Billings Logan Airport, every person they passed looked their way. Shay lifted her face to the light and straightened her spine. She set her shoulders. If she was going to be stared at for being Black and tall, she might as well be even Blacker and taller. She led Devon to the rental car desk.

"Is this what growing up was like?" Devon asked as they climbed into the huge, black Explorer ten minutes later. "Hundreds of short, white people staring at you all the time."

Shay shrugged. "Not at home," she said. "Not in town. They've known me since I was born, so I could be myself there. But look. There were only two Black kids in my high school. Plus I was about a foot taller than anyone. Should've seen everyone swivel their heads to look at me when the history teacher mentioned slavery."

Devon grimaced.

Shay started the car.

The kids hadn't stopped staring when Shay was named the school's athlete-scholar at thirteen and again at fourteen, when she'd scored forty-five points against Yellowstone, when she'd slam dunked the winner at home. But at least then Shay could imagine they were staring at her in awe and adulation. She was fifteen when she was scouted for Santa Ana Academy and left town. There she worked her ass off at ball, learned to play with people as good as she was, and met Devon and a bunch of other talented athletes, most of them Black. At first she fit in at the academy about as well as she'd fit in at school in Montana. Most of the girls came from Los Angeles. Shay didn't talk like them; her hair and clothes were wrong. But her music was on point and, in a school of outstanding athletes, she could play ball.

On an ordinary day, the drive from the airport to Big Timber and on up to Shay's family home on the Yellowstone River took about an hour and a half. But this was a snowy twenty-fourth of December. It would take longer. A plow had carved heavy snow banks streaked gray with dirt.

Shay turned through the city of Billings and drove slowly, getting a feel for the huge car. The Explorer had snow tires of course, but Shay stayed well under the speed limit. There were only a few people on the freeway.

As soon as they were out of town and heading west, the snow stretched out in all directions: silent white fields crossed by fences and punctuated by homesteads and clusters of snow-covered pines and firs. Shay settled her shoulders and let herself breathe. The sky was endless, that achingly clear Montana blue.

Devon opened her window, and a biting wind eddied through the car. The air was crisp. It coiled around Shay's fingers and ears in a way that brought back years of winters like this one.

"Glad my hair's done for Russia. This cold's gonna kill me," Devon said.

"You look good."

"I do." Devon grinned. Her neat Senegalese twists fell to the nape of her neck. Shay's longer, darker braids had the same protective effect. "But shit. My skin's going to be ravaged."

"Don't worry, I've got you covered," Shay said. Years living in this climate had made her and her parents experts on glowing winter skin.

Every mile they drove, the universe seemed bigger. When the mountains swept up before them, Devon whistled, low. Shay understood.

"I love my parents." Shay broke the quiet. She kept her eyes on the twin lines of the road stretching before them.

Devon looked over.

"Obviously, I love my parents. They're wonderful people. The trouble is, the last couple times I've come home… I don't know." She took a deep breath. "My life's really something, you know. People want to be me. I'm in the starting lineup for the current WNBA champions. I get to advertise Gatorade and sports bras and reenergizing pickle juice. People recognize me on the street. They follow me on Instagram. It's a big life."

"You don't need to sell me on it. It's my life too." Devon paused. "Well, not the pickle juice."

"But it doesn't feel like much when I'm home in Montana. When I'm here I feel—I don't know—smaller. It's not their fault. They love me. They're proud of me."

"But that's not enough?"

Shay blinked in the dazzling light. She should have found her sunglasses before they got in the car. "Yeah, of course. Of course. It's everything," she said. Devon was shuffled from family to family as a foster kid until she was scouted and got the scholarship to Santa Ana. Shay was fortunate.

She thought before she spoke. "People here don't see what the rest of the world is like. LA is movie premieres and too much concrete to them. New York, Chicago—those cities are almost as foreign as St. Petersburg. They live here in this desolate space because they want to. And no other place can live up to this one. Everyone I knew growing up was like that. It's cool. But somehow— Look, I have this incredible life. I'm proud of it. I don't want to be pitied for it."

"No." Devon pursed her lips. "So it's not only your parents."

"It's the whole town. They say, 'Shay honey, you've done this basketball thing so long. You've given up so much.' Or they say, 'Don't be lonely in that big city. There's always a place for you here.' Oh, and my favorite, 'When are you going to be like that lovely Candace Parker and settle down to have a family? Then you can move back home.'"

Devon laughed. "Candace is lovely, though."

"She's Candace Parker. She's perfect." Shay sighed. She didn't look at Devon as she muttered, "Last time I came here I might have overplayed how extraordinary my life is."

Devon's "yeah?" was interested. The woman knew when something was up.

Shay's cheeks heated. "Yeah. I guess I wanted to show them that all this work, all the years and the sacrifices—I wanted to show them how much it meant to the big world outside of Montana. I think I talked it up a bit much."

"We all do that sometimes."

"Dev. I sat there at Christmas dinner and told them how many followers I had on Twitter." Shay winced at the memory. She hadn't talked about this to anyone. But here where everything was bright and clean, she wanted to revisit. Devon would tell her how bad it truly was. "I acted all nonchalant about getting into the VIP area at clubs. I don't know, I brought terrible presents. I gave my mom the Fabergé egg."

Devon choked out a laugh.

Shay went on. "My mom— It wasn't her at all. She's into home cooking and hiking. She loves these painters from Ghana. This guy's landscapes with these tall figures. Another guy paints millions of tiny fish. I should have known the egg... I'm not sure it's even beautiful, it's just expensive. Mom loves art that brings the outdoors in. She's at home in Montana now, but those paintings of West Africa— She chose what she loves. As soon as I gave her the egg, it felt wrong." She shuddered. "There were other people there for dinner, too. A local family. My mom didn't know what to say. The whole trip was awful and embarrassing."

The wooden "Welcome to Big Timber" sign loomed on their left. The words were surrounded by romantic pastel sketches of the mountain, of skiers, of the old mill where Shay's parents' fishing and bait business sat on the Yellowstone River.

"Worse, there was this girl, Milla, there—"

"This girl Milla?" Devon turned to look at Shay.

"An old crush. Nothing important. She was nice to me in school. We used to ride the school bus to Big Timber. But she wasn't the problem. The whole place put me on edge. It made me—"

"A bit defensive?"

"A massive asshole."

Devon grinned. "Then nothing's changed."

Shay drove slowly down the main street of Big Timber. They passed Neb's saloon, the library, the drug store. Most of the windows were dark. The trip through town was over within a minute, and they drove on into the open space.

"I'm glad you're heading back, then. You can't keep living that visit over and over. So what've you got your mom this year?" Devon asked.

Shay sighed. "I usually send her soap and stuff. I grabbed something at the airport."

"Well, unless the airport has a set of Russian dolls, it's going to be better than the egg."

Honestly, Shay's mom would have preferred the dolls.

The road narrowed. The sky had turned the palest pink, streaked in grey and darkening for night.

Shay's parents' place was right where the 191 crossed the Yellowstone River. Only a few houses clustered around two intersections.

Shay turned off the main road. She let the car idle at the bottom of the driveway. From this distance everything seemed unchanged: the boxy, painted house, the sharply sloped roof, the big front verandah lit up in welcome, the ceaseless sound of the river as it tumbled by. This wasn't her home any more, but the place was a part of her.

"This might be a mistake," she said to Devon. "I'm sorry."

Devon patted her thigh. "You've got this."

Shay put the car in gear and drove up to the house.

Shay's dad, Anthony, had the door open before they stopped the car. He'd been her dad since she was six months old. She had no other father. Anthony was light skinned and tall, though shorter than Shay. He'd taught Shay to dribble and shoot and play defense. As Shay and Devon climbed down from the vehicle and crunched onto the clear, but frozen, gravel drive, his long face broke into a slow smile. Shay's mom pushed out from behind him and bounded down the stairs.

She glared at Anthony, her eyes fierce in her round face. "Why the heck didn't you tell me they were here?"

"I wanted a minute to see her myself," Anthony said. "You are a sight for sore eyes, Shaylee."

Shay's mother wasn't a short woman, but when she wrapped her arms around Shay's waist, her head only reached Shay's shoulder. Shay held on tight and met her dad's warm gaze. She'd been wrong, wanting to stay away.

Her mom leaned back and looked from Shay to Devon. Her face was the same warm brown as Shay's. "I'm thankful you're here. And Devon too. I've seen your picture, of course. You play center, have I got that right?"

Devon nodded. "Yes, ma'am, most of the time." Their coach refused to refer to the old-school positions, preferring they all play more than one role, but Devon was useful under the post.

"Don't call me ma'am, sweetheart. My name's Michele. Everyone calls me 'Chele. Or Mama. You should too. After all, it's like we're family already, isn't it?" She nodded to Shay's father. "You can call him Anthony. Or Dad, if you'd like."

Michele turned to link arms with Shay and Devon and walked them up the steps. "It's too cold to stay out here talking. We can talk all we like inside. Now, Shay honey, we've just got a few people here."

Damn. Shay should have noticed some of the cars and trucks parked out front were not her parents'. She looked past her mother in Devon's direction. "Sorry," she mouthed.

Michele caught the end of that expression. "Don't be a fool about it. You've known these people all your life, Shay. They didn't want to miss you. Just a small get together tonight and then a big dinner the day after Christmas. And Shay." Michele paused at the top of the stairs. Her eyes shone bright in the light from the door. "I haven't always been as prepared as you'd like. For you." She patted Shay's arm. Shay had no idea what was going on. "This time I've got it."

"Got what?" Shay started as her mother swung open the front door. Immediately a small crowd appeared in the doorway. Flickering light and heat flooded the small front porch.

Michele squeezed Shay's hand and raised her voice. "Everyone, look who's home! And see, she brought Devon. Let's give a warm welcome to Shay's girlfriend, everyone."

"Wait," Shay said, but her mom beamed at her and swept into the house; her dark finger-coiled hair bounced about her head. Shay froze on the porch. Beside her, Devon's shoulders shook with silent laughter.

"You're no help," Shay said and followed her mom in.

From the outside, the room had seemed over-full, as if the whole town was peering through the door at Shay and Devon. But there was only a small collection of visitors. They were mostly the neighbors Shay had grown up with, local ranchers and business owners. Michele said, "You know Albi of course, and Jan and Greg from the climbing center. And you remember Ilie from up at the ranch, don't you?"

Shay nodded. "Mom," she said urgently.

"All our neighbors and best friends. Ilie's brought his niece and nephew. You knew them in school. Oh, and here's Teddy." Teddy had helped in the store for years. His pale, round face broke into a smile.

Shay smiled between gritted teeth. "Hi, Ted," she said. "Mom, I really need to talk to you."

Michele came close. She tipped up her chin, and Shay's own dark gaze was reflected back at her. "Shay. There's no need to worry, you're safe here. I spent years wondering why you don't come home and—I worked it out. I know what it's like to be an outsider. I've been there. When I moved here I was alone. I was carrying you and I was a Black woman in Montana."

Shay had imagined it often. "I know, Mom."

"It took time. I was lucky. I met your father." She smiled. "So as much as I can I thought I'd head off any narrow-mindedness. Make it clear that you are our daughter, and we love you, and your town loves you. This is your home, Shay. We want Devon to be part of the family. She might like it here."

Shay blinked through a sparkle of tears.

"Oh," said Michele. "And look, here's Milla. She's become so important to us."

Milla Dalya. Shay stopped worrying about the crowd of neighbors and her mom introducing Devon as her girlfriend. She stopped breathing too.

"Old crush," she'd said to Devon in the car. "Nothing important." That might not have been the whole truth.

For the first six months of high school, Shay had been first on the school bus each morning. Halfway through freshman year Milla and her twin brother Luka and uncle Ilie had moved into the dilapidated horse ranch up the hill. From then on, Milla and Luka were first on the bus; Shay was second. The three of them rode twenty minutes around the mountain before collecting anyone else.

That first frosty day, Milla had smiled at Shay.

"Oh, no," Shay had thought as she pulled off her thick gloves and shoved them in her backpack. Milla's smile was sudden and waywardly infectious. It balanced the seriousness of the girl's pale, freckled face and silvery eyes.

Shay had managed to smile back and sit four seats away. Not too close, not too far. That was the trip to school. On the way home, Milla had asked Shay's name. By week two they were sitting at the front of the bus sharing Shay's iPod and a set of earbuds. When the bus swung around the mountain, Shay's black, puffy jacket pressed against Milla's sky-blue one.

They weren't friends exactly. Shay didn't have friends. She had goals. She spent any time that wasn't a class training in the gym or on the football field. She had goals.

Anyway, they'd never shared a class or a lunch break. Milla was a year older and a grade above Shay. She was soft-spoken and horse-obsessed, but so were lots of girls in Big Timber. She was quickly surrounded by people. Shay understood that. Milla was pretty and seemed easy with herself—graceful. She fit.

They weren't friends, but however many other kids Milla could have sat with on the bus, she always saved a seat for Shay. They were bus allies. They ignored Luka and his friends and their never-ending noise. With the help of her iPod, Shay took on the development of Milla's musical palate. Now and then, between Aaliyah and Amerie, Milla talked about her horses and the farm. Shay talked about fishing and basketball.

They weren't friends, but every time Shay took the court, home or away, she scanned the bleachers to find Milla among the spectators before the starting whistle blew. And most afternoons Shay would run up the hill beside her house, testing herself on its uneven slope. At the top she'd look down on Milla's blue-roofed farmhouse. Sometimes she'd see Milla walk across to the stables.

She didn't jog down the hill to visit. It was simply reassuring to see the place, always there under the huge, blue bowl of the sky.

The whole brief time they'd shared here in nowhere, Montana, every single time Shay had seen Milla, it was as if she was the only person in the room. She'd always been important.

Then, halfway through sophomore year, Shay had been scouted at a game, and a month later she'd left the school for good.

Her last day, Shay had considered pouring out her heart: telling Milla everything. But any words she thought up seemed too much or too little. Instead she gave Milla a list of songs to listen to, the love songs she'd rationed so she wasn't too obvious, so she didn't embarrass herself while they rode the bus.

As she flew away from home to California, Shay had played Mariah's "We Belong Together." She'd looked down on the mountains through tears and wondered if she'd always regret saying nothing.

Of course, she'd seen Milla now and then when she was home, passed her at the local store or out with her horses while Shay was on a trail run. The most recent time had been that awful Christmas four years ago. Milla and her brother and uncle had come over for Christmas, and Shay had been everything awkward: blustery and brittle and showy.

Shay hadn't forgotten Milla's clear, critical glare across the dinner table. Faced with that look, Shay hadn't felt like a six foot three basketball star. She'd felt tiny.

"Hi," said Milla. "Welcome back." Her smile tipped up at one side the way it always had. She stepped forward and reached out a hand.

Shay shook off the past. She stepped closer to shake the offered hand. Milla's handshake was firm. Her palm was wider than Shay expected and rough from work on the farm. "It's good to see you."

Milla smiled broadly. "I'd started to think you were never coming back," she said. She turned and incuded Devon. "Hi."

"Oh, right, this is Devon, my—" Shay said.

"Your girlfriend. I'm so glad to meet you, Devon," Milla said. "You're remarkable at the post. I was glad they recognized you as defensive player of the year last year."

"Thank you." Devon glanced at Shay, then back at Milla. She grinned. "You must be Milla."

"I am."

"Like a glass of red, girls?" Shay's dad came up behind them. "I don't like to think about it too much, but you're all over twenty-one these days." He poured generous glasses. Shay gulped a grateful mouthful.

Anthony and Michele had produced a table full of food, sorghum-brined chicken and sweet yams and spicy sausages and greens. Everything smelled delicious. People served themselves and sat in lounge chairs or three across on the couch. The house was full of the chatter of people who had known and mostly liked one another for almost thirty years.

Shay and Devon each piled their plates with some of everything, while Michele watched in satisfaction. Devon settled herself onto a low couch beside Albi from up the road.

"I hear you have dogs," Devon said.

Albi beamed. She was an ancient white lady. Her teeth had seen better days, but she was always thrilled to talk about her dogs.

Shay sat next to Devon and listened to Albi list the dogs' names and individual personality traits.

"Now, Sarge. He's a big boy. He thinks he's the boss, but he's too much of a gentleman."

At the table, Milla helped her uncle choose his dinner. Her reddish-brown hair was tied back in a braid that lay heavily down her spine. She took her time as he fussed, but bared her teeth and glared comically as he rejected every kind of vegetable. He laughed at her.

"I'm an old man, Milla. No point trying to change me now." She shook her head at him, then lifted her gaze to scan the room. Shay looked away.

"Sit here, Ilie," called Michele as they crossed the room. She pushed a chair forward for him.

"You're very kind," the old man said.

Milla handed him his plate, then regarded the room.

Devon was quicker off the mark than Shay. "Here you go. I'm ready to see if I can find more of this amazing punch." She stood.

"Oh, no, I don't want to take your spot," said Milla. She eyed the empty space between Shay and the arm of the sofa.

"It's fine. Sit. Eat," said Devon. She strolled away with her empty glass.

Milla lowered herself onto the couch and balanced her plate on her knees. The couch was old; it sank in the middle. Milla shifted her weight, balancing her plate in one hand and holding a glass of wine.

"Sorry," said Shay. "I'll hold your plate for a second if you want to get comfortable. There's a busted spring that you need to avoid."

Once Milla was seated, Shay handed the plate back. The couch tipped inward, and Milla's shoulder touched Shay's. Shay shifted to give her room.

"It's good of you to come," Shay said, the same thing she'd said to a bunch of people.

"Of course we did. Your parents—" Milla shrugged as though there was nothing to explain. "They're wonderful. And they're so excited to have you home. Everyone in town got a call right after your mom hung up from talking with you."

Shay flushed. "It's hard to fit in a visit around games this time of year."

"You're playing in Russia for the off-season again, aren't you? We don't get to see those games the way we see the WNBA." She continued quickly, "I guess it's less of a culture shock now than the first year."

"Hold up a second. You watch the WNBA?"

"Mostly the Sparks." Milla's tone was light.

Shay suppressed a smile, then hoped Milla had missed her more recent games. "Honestly, Russia wasn't ever much of a culture shock. We spend a lot of time training with the team. A third of them are American. The coaches are from Seattle. We're in a bubble of basketball there. I should get out more. The town's pretty interesting. But there's been some violence in the local clubs. And I stand out."

Milla nodded. "That'd be rough."

"Enough about Russia. Tell me about the farm, and the horses, and your uncle."

"Sure. We've expanded since you left. We run a hundred and eighty horses now. You remember Griff and Mer? They sold their land on the valley floor to us. They still advise on our breeding programs, of course. You should see this year's yearlings. We keep up the trail riding and we travel to shows but we've also started horsemanship classes."

"Teaching riders?"

"Riders and trainers. Anyone working with horses. We can raise as many extraordinary horses as we like. But if we don't bring young people up with a knowledge of horsemanship, our industry won't be sustainable."

Shay nodded. Milla's enthusiasm was bright in her face. "You and Luka teach the classes?" Shay had loved watching Milla on a horse.

"Yep. You could have lessons when you've got some time. Or just let me show you around. It's been a while. And Devon, of course."

"I'll come over one day." Shay thought before she spoke further. "It sounds amazing, like your whole heart's here."

"It's my place. The view never gets old, and I love the horses. But I'm not sure I want to teach horsemanship all my life." Milla changed the subject. "So, what are you listening to these days when you sit on the bus?"

"I don't ride the bus too much now."

"Of course you don't."

Shay wrinkled her nose. That had come out wrong.

"You still listen to Prince?" Milla asked. "I cried when he died."

"Me too. A huge loss." Shay had worn a black armband to her game that week.

"I only knew how much of a loss because of you."

Shay smiled. "It wasn't just Prince, Mill. We listened to Ciara and Erykah Badu. And Aaliyah, may she rest in loveliness."

"I haven't forgotten." Milla's silvery seriousness was as lovely as ever. "You ruined local radio for me."

"Sorry to interrupt." Shay looked up to see Milla's male double. "Luka!"

Luka perched on the arm of the couch next to Milla. Broad and freckled and soft-voiced, he was as tall as Milla. "Hey, Shay."

"I hear you're getting married. Congratulations. I can't believe you grew up so much. I can't believe you got anyone to say yes."

Luka beamed. "Have you met my better half?" He gestured across the room to Arianne.

"Not really. She was a junior when I was a freshman." Arianne was solid and strong, with cropped curls and blue eyes. She was very pregnant.

"She fits, you know," Luka said. "She's meant to be here."

The three of them talked about the farm until Arianne waved Luka over.

Across the room, Devon leaned against the wall and talked with Shay's dad. She laughed as he waved his hands, shaping something in the air. Shay couldn't tell if he was talking about fly fishing or basketball or baking. "Wait, wait," he said and made the same shape with his hands. Devon laughed again. Shay should have known that introducing them would open a vortex.

Shay took the opportunity. "I should have thanked you, Milla."

Milla tipped her head. "For?"

"For those times on the bus sharing music every day. They were something to look forward to. That space away from school, it really mattered to me."

Milla took a mouthful of wine. "You know, I never got why you hated school so much. Everyone admired you. I wanted to be you most days. When I saw how you played, how well your body knew what you wanted it to do."

Shay met her gaze as she considered what to say. It was novel and welcome to see herself through Milla's eyes. And sure, she'd wanted that kind of admiration. She'd wanted the whole school to cheer her on. But more than that, she'd wanted friends.

Devon called across the room. "Shay, you should've told me your dad was such a charmer. I seem to have signed up to make gingerbread."

"Of course you have," called Shay. She should never have left them alone.

Milla smiled. "I'm so glad Devon could come. I like to see you happy."

"Yeah, Dev's the best."

Milla looked at Shay strangely. It wasn't really a thing lovers said, maybe.

But before Shay could go on, Devon walked over. "Gingerbread," she said, shaking her head. "I hope he knows I can't bake. I don't think I've ever even opened the oven at my place."

Shay laughed. "You've got this."

"I'd love to see you guys play ball," Milla said unexpectedly.

"Easy. Come visit us in LA." Devon smiled as though this were the greatest plan ever. "Shay has plenty of room and she loves visitors."

Shay couldn't glare at her. "*Or.*" She drew the word out. "If there were courts around here we'd get in a practice session. But we drove past the school on the way in. It's shut and locked."

"Oh, that's not a problem. Arianne has the keys."

"She does?"

"She's a teacher. She teaches high school art and drama and dance."

"Right." So many things had changed.

"Anyway, she has a key to the gym," Milla said. "We could get it from her if you wanted. But you might want a break."

"Nah, Shay's been hanging to get a ball into her hands," Devon said.

Some other neighbors approached. "I won't keep you all to myself," said Milla on a smile. She stood to check on her uncle.

It wasn't late when everyone left, but it had been a long day. In the doorway, Milla grabbed Shay's hand. Her cheeks were flushed. She spoke more quickly than usual.

"Thank you so much for having us. It's good to see you here with Devon. She makes you smile." Shay nodded unsure how to answer. Milla rushed on. "I guess it's easier between you and me too. Not worrying about any—chemistry that might make things awkward. Between us."

Shay was at a loss. She stepped closer to Milla.

Milla blinked. "Were you always this tall?"

Shay was surprised into laughter. "Not when we first met."

Ilie called out from the driveway. "Milla, honey, you have the keys. You'll never forgive yourself if you let your uncle freeze to death out here."

"So, I've made up a bed in the blue room for the two of you," Michele said. She blushed. It cost her something to accept her daughter sleeping with someone under her roof. Even though Shay wasn't.

"Mama," Shay started. But she couldn't tell her mother the romance was something her mother had imagined, especially after the bravery her mom had shown in introducing Devon. "Thank you." She kissed her mother hard on the cheek.

Devon followed Shay up the narrow stairs. The blue room was as advertised: blue, king-sized blue bed, white furniture. There was a blue and gray en-suite.

"Guess we're bunking up, sugar," Devon said. She grinned at Shay.

"I'm so sorry."

"It's cool; it's not like we haven't shared a room before."

"But not a bed."

Devon shrugged. "I think it's sweet. Your mama wants her gay daughter to feel at home." She turned her back to strip.

"It is sweet." Tears pricked Shay's eyes. She turned to hunt through her bag.

"So. Milla's nice," Devon said when they were pajama-clad and lying facing the ceiling.

Shay turned out her bedside lamp. "Yep. She was the first person I ever…" Even in the dark it was hard to speak. "I said she wasn't important. She was. We connected. I was fourteen when we met. Fifteen when I left. It seems silly—I knew what the love songs meant when I was around her."

"I caught that," Devon said.

"Damn."

"You're doing fine. No one else would've noticed." They were silent.

"You should ask her out," Devon said.

"With my girlfriend sharing a bedroom? I don't think so. Anyway, she lives in Montana."

"Right. So she does." They lay in silence. "Christmas tomorrow," Devon said, "Hope Santa comes."

* * *

THE MORNING DAWNED LATE BUT bright with new snow outside. Shay stretched out in her bed. Devon was awake beside her; her long legs were crossed as she sat and read a book.

"Morning," Devon said.

"Merry Christmas, Devon." Shay rolled over and planted a quick kiss on Devon's knee.

"Our first Christmas waking up together. Romantic." Devon smirked.

"It'd be more romantic if you weren't my best friend and a complete idiot."

"Would a complete idiot read this?" Devon held up the book she was reading, Alex Haley's *Queen*.

"Point taken."

"The shelves in here are full of stuff like this."

Shay nodded. Her parents figured she got enough white-guy literature at school. Home was for Haley's *Roots* or Toni Morrison, Zora Neale Hurston, Octavia Butler. "I'm gonna head downstairs." Shay said. "Come when you're ready."

Shay pulled on woolly socks and padded down the carpeted stairs. Her mother was up, sitting at the big table in the kitchen with a cup of tea.

"Is Devon sleeping in?"

"She's awake. She's reading Alex Haley in bed."

Michele smiled. "Oh, she's a good girl. You should read more."

"Mom, you read me everything here before I was twelve."

"True." Michele's face was soft. "Shaylee, I like Devon. Your father likes her too. She's the first girl you've brought home."

"Mom—"

"I'm glad you did. She makes sense here."

After breakfast of soft poached eggs and sweet potato hash browns with cinnamon rolls, the four of them sat in the living room. The fire crackled. Cheeks glowed with food and warmth.

The tree was decorated in red and gold and mismatched decorations Shay hadn't seen in years. At its top was an angel, black with vibrant clothes and gold wings, that Shay had found when she'd first left home. Everyone had gifts to open.

"Guests first," said Anthony, nodding to Devon. "Though you're more than a guest." He fixed Shay with his dark gaze. "You'd better bring her back."

"Now that I know you make cinnamon rolls like that, nothing will stop me." Devon's smile was softer than her words. She took the gift Anthony handed her and opened the snowflake paper. Inside was a teal slouchy beanie. Devon looked from Michele to Anthony to Shay.

"I thought it would suit you," Michele said.

Devon held it up. "You made this?"

"I was working on it when I heard you were coming. It seemed right. Everyone needs to keep their head warm here."

"Thank you. It's amazing." Devon pulled it carefully over her hair.

Shay's gift for her mom was the last. She handed it over.

"You know I don't need anything for Christmas. The only thing that I want is to have you here at home."

"I know, Mom. But I still got you something." Shay's stomach twisted, part guilt, part nerves. "Just something small."

Her mom opened the soap and buried her nose in the box. "Perfect. Lavender. That's my favorite. You're so thoughtful, Shay."

She hugged Shay tightly. It felt as though she meant it.

* * *

THE DAY AFTER CHRISTMAS, ANTHONY, Shay, and Devon piled into the Explorer with a couple of basketballs. Devon had her new beanie carefully pulled over her Senegalese twists.

Shay drove around to the ranch. Milla was waiting at the far end of her drive, stomping snow off her boots. Shay lost track of her breath, same as ever.

"We would have come up to the house to get you," said Anthony from the passenger seat.

"I like the walk," Milla said. "It's peaceful out." As she slid in beside Devon she pulled off her striped beanie and puffy jacket. She kept her scarf. In the cold, her freckles and pretty eyes were more striking than ever. "Thanks for taking me along."

"We weren't going without you," Shay said. She focused on driving.

The school gym's parquetry floor reflected light from above in giant, window-shaped squares. Shay stepped onto the court. In her peripheral vision she saw her dad toss a basketball. She caught it easily. She considered its weight and balance almost without deciding to. The gym was looking the worse for ten years of wear. The floor was dull in parts; the walls needed a new paint. The basketball hoop creaked when Anthony and Milla cranked it out.

"This was it, huh?" asked Devon.

"This was it." Shay passed the basketball to Devon. Her shoes squeaked on the floor.

This was Shay's place. The first place she'd shown she wasn't just another athletic high school student; she was the real thing. This room was as much Shay's as it was the old white guy's whose name ran across the door.

"Let's play then, kid," said Devon.

"You're on."

Anthony clicked the last guidewire into place.

"It's all yours," he said.

"This ain't no exhibition match," said Devon. She passed the ball to Anthony. "Two on two, guys."

Anthony bounced the ball once, twice, then sent it flying neatly through the hoop.

"He's mine," said Devon with a predatory smile.

Shay turned to Milla. "Okay?" she asked.

Milla removed her scarf and placed it beside her gloves on the bench. "Remember, not all of us have your talents."

Shay divested her father of the ball and tossed it gently to Milla.

Milla frowned. "Um. Okay. I'm not a pro, but I have caught a basketball before." She bent her knees to shoot and miss. She blushed. "That would have been cooler if I'd got it in."

Shay collected the ball in one hand and grinned at her. She could relax on this court. It was easy to close the distance between them, easy to reach out and rub Milla's arm in sympathy. Milla's flickering glance in response was difficult to parse.

"Holding!" Anthony said. "Our ball."

Shay turned her mind to the game.

It was instinctive. She gauged distances, knew the height of the hoop. She blocked a shot from Devon, passed to Milla. When her dad checked Milla, Shay was already there at her other side, waiting. Milla passed and bounced happily on her toes as Shay sidestepped Devon and scored a tidy jump shot.

The game was evenly matched. Anthony might be sixty now, but he was a strong player. Milla might not have played much basketball, but she was athletic and had an innate sense of where Shay would need her. Shay and Devon laughed as they tried new tricks on one another.

After five minutes, Shay removed her hoodie and threw it on the pile of coats. Milla did the same.

"It's been a long time since I saw you play," Milla said. "It's as beautiful to watch as I remembered."

Shay shifted her weight and glanced back at the court. "Thanks." Milla was even more beautiful to watch than she remembered.

They played for another twenty minutes. Anthony stopped, and Milla bowed out to sit with him on the subs' bench. Shay and Devon kept at it. The game was more physical without the others, and they pressed into one another and took shot after shot. Shay's skin buzzed with the stop and start of the game and the sense of Milla's eyes on her. Every shot went down more easily.

"I'm not even sure you need a coach to get you back in the game," Devon said when another three-pointer sank cleanly. "You just need her watching." She glanced at the bench where Milla had her legs stretched out.

"Shut up," Shay muttered.

Devon took a shot and missed, but came up with the ball.

"Gotta get those rebounds," Anthony called from the sidelines.

"Love you too, Dad," said Shay.

Finished, they gulped water from the bottles they'd brought along. "I'll fill them up," said Milla. Shay joined her.

The water fountain was in the hallway between the gym and the rest of the school. One side of the hall was lined with trophy cabinets. At least five of the trophies had Shay's name on them. Milla held the water bottle as it filled. "Do you want to check out the rest of the school?" she asked. "It's been a while since you saw it. You could show Devon and your dad."

Shay shook her head. However much she'd owned the gym, the rest of the school hadn't felt safe. It wasn't bullying; it was pettiness mostly. She was always on the outside. She walked alone in the crowded halls. In class she was anxious.

"I don't think so. Not this time."

Milla sighed. "I still don't understand why you hated it here so much."

Shay didn't want to have this conversation. "I didn't hate it."

Milla took a step closer. The only light came through the windows, clear white from the snow. "You never looked back. You left and you didn't miss anything here."

"I missed some things." Shay missed Milla, but she'd never had a handle on that, not enough to put it into words. "There were good times. But I didn't have friends. Not like you did. And plenty of times I felt like I was in everyone's way." She might as well lay it out. "If *you* ran down the hall because you were late for class, Mrs. Jenkins or Miss Talbot or the hall monitor would tell you to slow down, and then they'd smile because you were such a good student who wanted to go to class. If I ran down the hall late, I was too loud and—" She sighed. "I don't know, too intense, maybe aggressive—I was huge and graceless and too much."

Milla shook her head. "But you weren't graceless at all, Shay. God, the way you moved. And aggressive. Honestly, people didn't think that."

Shay looked away. It stung to have to explain. "Listen. I'm not saying I was any of those things. I'm saying how people made me feel. I'm saying that… someone looked at you and saw a kid running late and the same person looked at me and saw—" She sighed. "I'm the one in my body. You can't say you know what it was like."

Milla was still. "Okay. Yeah. You're right."

Shay met her eyes and nodded.

"I'm sorry," Milla said. "I should have—" She didn't finish.

The two of them swung open the gym doors and rejoined Anthony and Devon.

"One more?" asked Devon and passed Shay the ball.

Shay looped it into the basket easily.

"I wish some of the kids from the school could have seen this," Milla said. "It'd be inspiring."

But Shay was glad to get in some time without an audience. For now, the pleasure of playing outranked inspiring anyone.

"It's been a long time since we played with no one watching us," Devon said.

DINNER THAT NIGHT WAS A sit-down meal for thirty-five of Michele and Anthony's neighbors and local friends. They ate in the big dining hall of Neb's Saloon. It was poorly lit, which was probably a blessing, given the carpet, but Neb and his wife Odette were famous for their winter feasts, so the room smelled delicious.

Shay sat beside her mom. Milla was across the table from her. It wasn't possible to talk to Milla. The table was huge and the company loud, but every now and then Shay would look up from devouring her third serving of roast vegetables with gravy and grin at Milla. Milla would smile a sweet, private smile. It was hard to resist staring.

"Michele," Odette said from two seats down. She was curvy and French and everyone's name sounded pretty in her accent. No one had worked out why she'd moved to Big Timbers, but she'd turned up just before Shay left for Santa Ana and three months later had married Neb. She clearly missed city life; she had never quite made herself at home, but she added a touch of something to the town. She raised her voice. "Michele, cherie. Whatever came of that Fabergé egg Shay brought you?"

Michele didn't look at Shay. "Oh, it's in my room where I can admire it."

"You wouldn't believe this beautiful thing Shay brought her mother." Odette scanned their end of the table, eyes wide. "This jewel-encrusted Russian egg. Fabergé. They're Russian, but he was a Frenchman really. You can tell by the craftsmanship. Do you even know what it's worth, Shay?"

Shay reddened. "Not really, no."

Odette's laugh wasn't unkind, but it grated. "I suppose you don't need to figure out things like that when you're an international superstar."

Shay shook her head. "It's not really like that. I mean, I'm very fortunate. But it's not—"

Odette laughed again, this time awkwardly. "I know, I know. Let's not talk about money."

Later, when everyone was distracted by a retelling of Ilie's old life as a talk show radio host, Shay turned to her mother. "Last time," she said and hesitated.

"Yes, love?"

"Last time I was here, I went on too much. I was too much. That egg, it was a terrible present."

Michele put a hand on her shoulder. "No, Shay, I love it."

"It's fine, mama. You have it packed away." Shay was impatient with her mother's endless kindness.

"It's not packed away. It's on the shelf beside my bed. When I look at it I'm reminded that there's a whole world out there with you in it."

Shay shook her head. "I wanted to make you proud of me, Mama. But I got it all wrong. I got everything wrong the last time I was here."

Michele's smile was soft but her words were firm. "We're nothing but proud of you, Shay. Me and your father. So proud. Your drive and your bravery and your talent. You've gone so far. I could never follow you where you've gone. And truth is, I don't want to. I only wish I could be as interesting as all the other places and people you see."

"God, mama. No—" Shay's chest was tight. "You're better than all of it."

Michele dropped her hand to Shay's where it lay on the table and squeezed. "We just want you to be happy."

When she looked up, Milla blushed and looked down at her plate. Through the rest of the meal, every time Shay looked across the table, Milla was just turning away.

The room's heavy, dark-red curtains were drawn so there was no sense of the snowy world outside.

Neb walked in, stamping his feet. "It's still snowing?" Shay asked.

"Sure is, sugar."

Michele turned a worried face to him. "The girls are leaving tomorrow morning."

"From Billings Logan?" he asked Shay.

She nodded. "Yep."

"I doubt it. The I90's closed between Livingstone and Park City. It's gusty down there. From the weather report, I doubt they'll open it till midday. Maybe not even then. Push your flight back, Shay. Stay longer. You only just arrived."

"Really?" Shay eyed Neb.

"I wouldn't lie to you."

Shay turned to Devon. "I'm sure we can get to the airport by late afternoon. If we want."

Devon shrugged. "We've got a court to practice on now. And anyway, we're having a good time."

Shay held her gaze then nodded slowly. The room was warm and full of people who'd known Shay forever. Shay's mom and dad were here. Milla too. Shay hadn't put things right yet, but staying a few more days might give her a chance to sort everything out.

*   *   *

IT SNOWED HALFWAY THROUGH THE morning. But the sky cleared by midday and the afternoon was bright, though bitterly cold. The locals were taking bets on when the warm Chinook winds would come, but it definitely wasn't today. Shay and Devon shoveled the path and drive under Anthony's supervision. Michele and Shay pulled logs from the mammoth pile at the back door and lit a fire. The crackle and aroma brought back every one of Shay's childhood winters.

Shay found the Langston Hughes poetry collection her dad used to read to her and took over the armchair that was once hers. She flung her legs over one arm. Between poems she looked out the window.

At the other side of the room, Devon got caught up in Anthony's gingerbread plans.

"We'll decorate each one differently," Anthony said. "Sporting heroes or something. You want in, Shay?"

Shay looked up. "I think I'll take a walk. It's gorgeous out."

"A walk?" Devon narrowed her eyes. She was true Los Angeleno. "You'll freeze."

"I'll be fine. Come with me if you like. I'll find you a good jacket."

"No, thank you."

Michele spoke from the dining table where she was planning the spring planting schedule. "There are snowshoes in the garage," she said. "Or skis if you want them."

"Thanks, Mom."

"Don't forget, night falls fast in the mountains."

"I know, Mom. I did grow up here."

"You're a city girl now. You're part of a different world."

"I don't think I'll ever be just a city girl," Shay said.

Shay left alone. A glance over her shoulder showed Devon's and Anthony's dark heads bent over the recipe book. Anthony was remarkable at fathering other people's children.

The snow stretched out behind the house and up over the next hill. Shay used to run that way in the mornings, running away from herself, running toward her future. She'd eat up the miles in her favorite shiny silver running shoes. Today she needed cross-country skis.

The hill was steep enough that Shay worked up a good sweat under her jacket. Halfway up, she unzipped the front and shoved her beanie into her pocket.

From the top of the slope, the slope ran down to the Yellowstone River, which plunged, stone-gray and freezing, but mobile, between banks of snow.

Over the next hill was a huge gray and blue house set in acres of farmland. Smoke curled from the chimney.

According to Michele, Milla lived in the cabin beyond the house. The cabin was a new-build of logs with a sloped wooden roof.

It was a quick ski down into the valley. Shay's skis swept clean lines and curved through the snow. She picked up speed toward the bottom of the hill. She would regret this run when she had to tromp back up.

Shay knocked at the cabin door. There was no answer. Sighing, Shay turned to go back toward the slope. She paused when a soft whinny came from the stable.

"I'm going now, Crimson," came a sweet, no-nonsense voice: Milla's horse voice. Then Milla stepped around the stable.

"Oh." She stopped when she saw Shay.

"Sorry. Hi," Shay managed.

"Hi."

"I went for a walk, well, a ski, and came over the hill and—" Shay sounded stupider than usual.

"Hi… welcome," said Milla. "Hey. I'm really glad you're here." They stood as the light and the wind twined between them. "Do you want to see the place?"

"Definitely."

Shay unclipped her skis and leaned them against the cabin wall. Milla showed her the extensions they'd made to the stables and the indoor training facilities. She pointed out the newly acquired stretch of land north and east of the river. The scenery had always been more beautiful when Shay saw it through Milla's eyes.

"Coffee?" Milla asked when they returned to her log-walled cabin.

"Definitely."

Milla stepped past Shay to the cabin door. They left their boots and snow jackets in the enclosed porch. Inside, the cabin was small, but perfectly designed. A spring green two-seater couch with dark wood arms faced a picture window that stretched the length of one wall and opened up to the snowy valley beyond. A wooden kitchen bench divided the living area from a tiny kitchen full of pots and pans and spice jars. There was a log-burning stove and a ladder leading to the loft above. Shay looked up.

"It's warm, sleeping up there," Milla said.

"Yeah." Shay tried not to imagine.

The coffee was ready in a minute. Shay accepted the steaming cup.

"Sorry," said Milla, gesturing with her own cup. "It's not great."

"It's good." The coffee was ordinary, but Shay's face and fingers were cold and the company was excellent.

"You can sit," Milla said. "If you want."

Shay sat. Milla settled next to her and stretched her legs in her well-worn jeans. Through the window, the valley spread out in white. The river broke through the snow, ran into rocks, and tumbled wildly. The sky was dazzling. "Luka and Arianne live up at the house with Uncle Ilie," Milla said. "But down here I feel as though I have the whole valley to myself."

The desk in the corner was piled high with texts titles like *Clinical Anatomy of a Horse* and *Parasitology in Veterinary Science*.

"Is one of the horses sick?" Shay asked.

"No, thank god. I was researching."

Shay frowned. "Hey. Have you ever thought about being a vet? You must have the grades; you were an honor student. And you could bring all that skill back here." Milla began laughing. "Wait— Why are you laughing?"

Milla patted Shay's knee. "Sorry. Yes. I've thought about it. I've applied to some schools. I'm just working out if I can leave here."

They took simultaneous mouthfuls of coffee and looked out at the valley. Shay didn't dare move. She was intently aware of where Milla's hand had rested on her knee.

"You're not with her, are you?" asked Milla out of the blue.

"What?" Shay coughed as the coffee surprised her and went down the wrong way. "What are you—"

"You're not with Devon, are you?" Milla turned her gray eyes from the sky to Shay. "She's not your girlfriend."

There was a difference between lying by omission and lying to the face of Milla Dalya.

"No. No, she's not."

Milla's face closed down. "Why did you tell everyone she was?"

Shay shifted on the couch. "I didn't really. Mom got the wrong end of the stick."

"And you couldn't correct her?" Milla frowned as though trying to understand.

"I tried but… she was so thrilled to be a good ally to me."

Milla narrowed her eyes. "Okay. I can see that." She took a breath. "Your mom's been great since I came out."

Shay's stomach twisted. "Came out. Like came out, came out? She didn't tell me. Came out? You mean—but I remember you had a boyfriend."

"Well, that happens too. I'm bisexual." Milla shrugged as though she wasn't telling Shay anything axis-shifting.

"Right… got it. Sorry." Shay swallowed. "Are you seeing anyone?"

"Nope."

"Right." Shay put her cup on the small table, then didn't know what to do with her hands.

"And Devon?" Milla asked.

"Is my best friend. She came because I forced her to."

"Plus she seems to have found something special with your dad."

Shay nodded. "I know. They're ridiculous." She sighed. "I need to tell my mom about Devon. I hate lying to her. The girlfriend thing just kind of happened. My mom announced it before I knew to correct her. And now it's almost like coming out all over again."

Milla smiled a crooked smile. "Was it bad for you? Was it hard to figure out what you wanted?"

Shay shrugged. "I knew I was attracted to women long before I said anything. Since middle school." She hoped Milla wouldn't notice her blush. "It was another way I felt separate from everyone at school. Things got easier in Santa Ana. A couple of girls were out and so confident. I told my parents during one vacation. They were wonderful." She shook her head. "How about you?"

"Uh, Luka was— He was worried at first, and it made him ask some senseless questions. But he's my brother. My twin. He got it. And Ilie's hardly going to care. He's Ilie. And he'd known and loved you for years. So that helped, I think."

They sat and looked out. There was so much room, but the space between them was electric. It was also impossible. They had different lives. They were hardly ever in the same place.

Shay stood. "I'd better get home before my dad adopts Devon and forgets I exist."

Milla looked up. "Your dad adores you. Always has. You should hear him talk about you every time I saw them. I couldn't have stopped thinking about you if I tried." Milla stood abruptly. "I'll walk to the top of the hill with you. If you don't mind the company halfway home."

At the hilltop they faced one another. In the clear light, Milla was lovelier than ever. Her eyes looked like smoky glass and were fixed on Shay.

"Everything's more beautiful than I noticed when I was a kid," Shay said.

Milla nodded. She turned to the view. "It's an incredible place to call home."

"I'm not sure I've valued it the way I should."

"Well, that makes sense. You're a city girl. You're an incredible athlete. You're not going to settle down somewhere in the middle of nowhere."

"No. No, I guess I'm not," Shay said.

There were about eighty more things that Shay wanted to say, but the words froze and hung like breath in the air before she said them.

MICHELE WAS ALONE IN THE living room when Shay returned.

"You were gone a while."

"I bumped into Milla at the farm. She showed me around."

Michele raised her eyebrows. "Did she?"

Shay took a breath and plowed straight in. "Mom, I need to tell you something. Devon's not my girlfriend."

"I think I was working that out, Shay."

Shay sat on the lounge beside her mother and scrunched up her face. "I'm sorry, Mom."

"I announced you two were together to all those people." Michele looked at her. "Why on earth did you let me do that?"

"I'm really sorry. I tried to tell you." Shay hadn't tried enough of course. "I did try but then you said all that stuff about wanting to show me that you loved me for me, that you were proud of me and would love anyone I loved. And so... look, I really wanted it to be true."

"It is true," Michele said quickly.

"Of course, of course. That's not what I mean. I wanted it to be true that the reason I wasn't coming home was because the town wasn't comfortable with me being gay."

Michele's gaze was unwavering. "Okay. So. That wasn't the reason, then?"

This wasn't where Shay had imagined the conversation going. She rubbed her face. "I never fit in. I was all wrong, Mom. I didn't feel like I could be myself. And that's not your fault, not yours and dad's. You did everything right."

"Maybe," said Michele. "Maybe you shouldn't have had to fight those battles in your home at all."

"Not here at home. I'm not talking about here or with the neighbors."

"The kids at school weren't good to you?"

"It was high school. Is anyone good to anyone?"

"Shay." Her mother was firm. "Tell me."

"Look some of them, some were fine; some were small-minded and horrible. It's not worth revisiting. I decided to bow out. I didn't want to work out who was racist and who was just being fourteen years old. I trained. I played. I made plans."

"You always told us you trained alone because you preferred it."

The faint defensiveness stung. Shay said, "I don't know. I mean, it was partly true. It felt true."

Michele closed her eyes. "I wish I'd asked."

"Mama."

"I should have asked." She looked at Shay. "For me, this place was an escape. It was home the second I got here. I saw the mountain and the river and all the space in every direction. I met Anthony. I felt safe. I loved it."

"I know."

"I shouldn't have made you sacrifice so I could be happy."

Shay tried to find the right thing to say. "I don't know that you get to plan your life so other people are happy."

"You're my daughter, Shay."

"And you gave me this." Shay waved around the room but she meant the whole place. She meant the town and the mountains and the cold and the quirky neighbors and the sky. She meant Michele and Anthony and Milla too. "It wasn't always perfect, but this is my home."

"Always."

"I'm going to come back more, Mama. I don't have to go to Russia every year. It might not hurt to start choosing things that I love."

Michele wiped a tear from her cheek. "I'm sure it won't."

* * *

THE GYM WAS CHILLY. SHAY sat hunched in the bleachers. She'd left the overhead lamps off, so the only light came from the windows high in the wall.

The hoop was still in position. Its shadow on the court was like any other hoop on any other basketball court all over the world.

Soon Shay would be back in Russia with a coach and a team and a crowd all calling for a shot. After that she'd be home in LA with the massive expectations of that stadium. For now she had this court— its bright memories of her parents cheering, her teammates passing the ball, Milla's eyes on her from the bleachers. That focused gaze had been with Shay in every game she'd played since.

But Montana was more than a thousand miles from Los Angeles. However irrefutable her connection with Milla, however much Shay wanted, there was nothing she could do about it. Milla had a life here. Shay had a life in LA. Shay couldn't start something with someone she'd only see a few times a year.

But how would Shay come home at all and see Milla without aching to touch her?

Shay stood and grabbed the ball she'd rested on the bench beside her. She ran through layup after layup, jump shot after jump shot. She shot from the free throw line, took three-pointers, moved close in to the hoop and grabbed every rebound just for her dad. She'd thought she couldn't get her edge back in Montana. She'd been wrong. She couldn't have everything she longed for, but at least she'd leave here with that.

The gym door banged open. A flurry of snowflakes whirled in from outside. Milla stepped through. Her cheeks were pink, and her eyes were brilliant.

"Hi." Her voice echoed. "Hi," she said more softly.

"Hi."

"I— I saw your car outside and thought I might catch a game. But Devon's not here?" She scanned the court. It wasn't as if a six foot five basketball player could hide under the bench.

"Sorry to disappoint you. I was taking some time to myself."

"Oh." Milla hesitated. "Okay. I'll leave you to it."

That wasn't what Shay wanted at all. "I'd like you here, though. If you want to stay."

Milla flashed a warm smile. "You would?"

"I would." Shay took a shot from the three-point line. She missed. "Damn." She collected the ball when it rebounded and bounced toward her.

"I'm pretty sure you don't have to get every single one in," said Milla. Her tone was laughing and fond.

Shay exhaled. "I know. I wanted to get that one."

"Yeah? Why's that." Milla sat on the bench.

Shay focused on the ball in her hands as she thought through several possible answers. She gave the true one. "It'd be nice to impress you."

"Oh."

Shay took another shot. This one slipped neatly through the basket. She left the ball to bounce and crossed to stand near Milla. Milla looked up; her gray eyes studied Shay in the half-light.

"I'm not sure why I came here," Shay said.

"To Montana?"

"To the school gym."

"Well, it's pretty snowy out. I'm not sure where else you were going to get time to yourself."

Shay nodded. "Good point." She bounced on her toes, testing the floor. "This gym could do with some work. The floors should have been redone years ago. Matthias Gunderson will be rolling in his grave."

"Gunderson?"

Shay turned to look at Milla. "Whatever his name is. You know, the white guy whose name's on the plaque on the door. Like every gym everywhere, there's always someone who donated ten thousand dollars to something. I used to read his name about six times a day."

Milla frowned. "You didn't hear the story? The guy, Matt Gunderson, they found him guilty of fraud. They sent him to prison. They took his name off the gym. The school didn't want to be associated with crime."

"Yeah?" Shay strode out the door. Snow dusted her face as she looked up. There was no one's name over the door, nothing but blank space.

Back inside, Shay grabbed the basketball to keep her hands moving. Milla came closer and held out a hand. Shay handed her the ball.

"I could do something, you know. I could get the gym refitted." Shay took a bounce pass from Milla and dribbled the ball. "I could do more than that. If I came back between seasons, I could run some basketball courses or general sports fitness for promising kids."

"There are kids who'd really benefit from that. The school's a bit more diverse than it was when you were here. Not a lot, but a bit."

Shay watched as Milla dribbled down the court.

"You were dazzling here," Milla said from the center line. "On the court. I couldn't stop watching you. I thought people would notice."

She passed the ball to Shay who held it balanced on one hand.

Milla sat on the bench before she continued, "But you know what? When we were sitting on the bus, you and me, and talking about our philosophy of life or sharing a song, or the other day at my place, catching up—that was even more important. You're a remarkable ballplayer. But if you never played ball again, I'd still be amazed by you."

Dust motes moved in the light that streamed through the windows. It took three long paces to be at Milla's side. Milla half stood as Shay came, but Shay lifted one leg over the bench to straddle it and placed a hand at Milla's neck, and they sat again. Milla closed her eyes. Her shaky intake of breath confirmed everything. Shay shifted closer and kissed her. Sensation shimmered up and down Shay's spine. Her heart held still. When she took a breath, Milla lifted her chin. They kissed again.

Shay shouldn't have been surprised that their first kiss was on the basketball court. But here she was, with sunlight angling through the windows and lighting the floor, with the smell of human bodies and sports shoes, the stale sense of everything shut down for the winter. It was unexpected. It was a renewal.

They sat together, slightly dazed. "Honestly," said Shay, "I can't think of anything I ever wanted more than that."

Milla's smile was shaky, "I'm pretty sure you wanted a career in basketball."

"Well, yeah—that and you."

Milla grinned. Her hand traced Shay's cheek. "Shay." She shook her head. "You're so beautiful. I can't believe— Every other person, I've compared them all to you."

Shay kissed her again. "No comparison, right?"

Milla laughed against her lips. "There's no one like you in this whole state."

Probably true.

Shay heart was heavy as she moved away from another kiss. "It doesn't... it doesn't really make sense though, does it? You live in Montana. I live in LA. I want everything. I want to take you out and take you home and hold your hand and keep kissing and talking. Not just now, for a long, long time. Honestly, there are a thousand things I'd do to be your girlfriend, but moving to Montana— I don't think that's one of them."

Milla held up a hand. Her half-smile was charming but inexplicable. "I got a letter last week. An acceptance."

"An acceptance to?" Shay prompted, and held her breath.

"To vet school. At UC Davis. I've been talking it over with Luka and Arianne and Uncle Ilie. We've just worked it out. I'm going to college. We've found a new trainer to help Luka and Ilie. Jan and Greg's daughter Sarah is going to come and help uncle a few days a week. Luka and Arianne want the house. And however much I love them and this place, I don't want to be stuck living in the cabin in the back forever."

"Davis."

"About 360 miles from Los Angeles. Not that I looked it up or anything." Milla's half-smile flashed into a full one.

Shay huffed a short laugh. "No, of course you didn't."

Milla leaned forward on the bench. "Okay. So it's still far. But we'll be in the same state. It's driving distance. It's possible, Shay."

Milla ran her fingertips across Shay's knuckles. Shay shivered and lifted both their hands so she could kiss Milla's palm.

Milla's eyes fell closed. She went on. "You've meant something to me since forever. Since the day we met. Every time you came back I'd hope I wouldn't feel anything. I'd get my mind together, decide I was over you, then you'd reappear and I'd know I was fooling myself. This isn't a fleeting thing. I think it's worth trying." Her chin was up. She was braver than anyone Shay knew. "If you're in, I'm in."

Shay exhaled. "I'm in. A thousand percent." She kissed Milla again.

A week ago Shay had believed that being scouted was the only important thing that would happen to her in Montana. She wasn't sure it was fair that she got this too.

THEY DROVE HOME SEPARATELY. SHAY set her phone to play love songs through the Explorer's speakers. Beyonce's "Halo" faded into Mario and Usher. A new mix for Milla created itself in Shay's head.

The house looked the same as last time, the same as the time before. The wheels crunched over the gravel drive. Milla pulled in behind Shay and they walked to the door together.

At the top of the stairs, Milla placed a hand on Shay's shoulder. "Okay?" she asked. Her eyes were careful and lovely as she searched Shay's face.

"So much better than okay," Shay said and bent her head so she could kiss Milla on the doorstep.

Inside, the television was on. College ball. There was a fire in the fireplace. The room was everything warm and light. Devon was stretched out in one couch. Shay's parents were on the other.

"Hey," said Shay.

"Connecticut's up," said Devon. None of them turned their heads from the game. "This new point guard has some out of this world game IQ. She's like you at that age."

"Um. Guys?" Shay tried again.

Michele looked up. "Oh," she said. "Hi, Milla." She noticed they were holding hands and elbowed Anthony. Devon looked up, too, and smirked.

"Are you here for dinner?" Michele asked.

"I'd like that, if you want me here," said Milla. She looked at Shay.

"We want you here," said Devon. "We definitely want you here. Don't we, Shay?"

"Shut up, Dev," said Shay. Devon twinkled at her.

"Good game?" Milla asked. She nodded toward the TV.

"Absolutely. Pull up a seat," said Anthony. He beamed at her.

Devon swung around from where she was lying and dropped her legs to the floor. She patted the seat beside her. "Plenty of room for you both," she said.

Shay sat next to Devon and pulled Milla down beside her.

Devon gave Shay's shoulder a shove. "I can't believe you broke up with me," she said.

The game was a close one. Anthony and Devon yelled at the TV. Michele yelped at every basket. Now and then one of them would glance at Milla and Shay. Their bright faces assured Shay that this wasn't something she'd imagined.

Shay ran her hand along the seam of Milla's jeans and made her plans. She'd stay here till they had to fly to Russia. She'd spend the week acquainting herself with Milla's mind and skin. Devon might not mind extending her visit too. They could train together. Once the European championships were over, Shay could come back and get local builders to start work on the school gym. Milla would start college in September, but before that maybe she could stay with Shay in LA, come to some training and home games. This was going to be an incredible season.

Milla leaned against Shay. Shay wrapped an arm around her and tugged her closer. It was all so easy. The trouble was, it was going to hurt to leave here, no matter what.

"Hey, any chance you want to come to Russia in a couple of weeks?" Shay whispered.

Milla narrowed her eyes. "You can't miss me already. You haven't even left yet." There was a smile behind the glare.

On screen, a talented young athlete sank a three-pointer. The final whistle blew. Outside, a layer of cloud sat above the dark mountain. Behind the cloud, the sun set the sky on fire in pink and gold. It was the second most incredible thing Shay could see.

About the Author: Pene Henson has gone from British boarding schools to New York City law firms. She now lives in Sydney, Australia, where she is an intellectual property lawyer and published poet who is deeply immersed in the city's LGBTQIA community. She spends her spare time enjoying the outdoors and gazing at the ocean with her gorgeous wife and two unexpectedly exceptional sons. Her first novel *Into the Blue* (Interlude Press, 2016) received a Lambda Literary Award for Gay Romance. Her second novel, *Storm Season*, was published by Interlude Press in 2017.

Last Call at the Casa Blanca Bar & Grille

Erin Finnegan

THE SANTA ANAS SNAKED THROUGH the streets of downtown Los Angeles with merciless, unseasonable spite.

The Devil Winds drove temperatures up and up, and with little else to report, news crews followed the climb toward a Christmas Day record high with unabated zeal. They bumped their usual allotment of predictable holiday stories —the crush of customers at a popular Boyle Heights tamale shop; the rush of Christmas Eve shoppers at the Grove; the hush that fell over downtown as its weekday occupants tried to beat the holiday traffic out of town — in favor of images of street-side thermometers and tourists in shorts and T-shirts.

A veteran of media campaigns, Jack Volarde banked on the fact that the skeleton reporting teams of the holiday had no choice but to report and repeat. The Lakers would play Miami at Staples Center. Surfers would dress in red-and-white neoprene in Malibu. And his boss, the city's mayor, would join a small cadre of B-grade celebrities to serve an early holiday feast to the needy at a downtown shelter.

His only real competition for the lead story on the Christmas night news was the damnable heat, because his boss gave better sound bites than either surfers or power forwards.

Jack stood elbow-to-elbow with actors and corporate volunteers as they served an annual feast of lukewarm turkey, stiff mashed potatoes, and slightly soggy green beans. Through it all, he calculated the odds of who had a better chance to beat the heat—the Lakers on the court or the mayor of Los Angeles on the evening news. The weather story had the good graphics—the kids ice skating in shorts and Santa hats at Pershing Square always made for good video. And for the late news, the likely power outages from the over-stressed electrical grid would offer up B-roll of the carnage at unmetered intersections as power slipped from neighborhood-to-neighborhood.

But Jack had an ace in the hole: a handsome and charismatic boss who knew how to play to his strengths, holding babies and chatting up the constituents as he served their dinners, asking them about their lives, and sharing stories about his own childhood holidays.

"We didn't stop making tamales until we ran out of gossip. That was the rule," the mayor said, repeating the story for more than a handful of guests. Jack had heard it dozens of times and had no reason to doubt its authenticity—he had known the mayor's family for years, since he had signed on as an aide to a community campaign early in the mayor's career. But the story had developed the characteristics of an old Christmas stocking—embellished, and maybe a bit musty. Jack added it to a mental list of items to discuss with the mayor before his next public event.

Jack's family had tried repeatedly to persuade him to come home for the holidays. His mother left reminders on his voicemail that his grandmother wasn't getting any younger. His brother texted promises of a daylong sports extravaganza on his new television, *the one with the sweet curved screen*. His sister, doting and concerned, called him in the midst of the Christmas event in a last-ditch effort to convince him to come home, just for the day.

"You shouldn't be alone," she said.

"I'm literally surrounded by five hundred people right now." He dropped his voice and cupped his hand over the phone to keep the one-sided conversation private.

"That's not what I meant," she said.

He excused himself and stepped away from the mayor's side to speak.

"I know. I'm fine, really."

"No, you're not. Come on, Jack. A day with family would be good for you."

She may have been right. It didn't matter.

He took a moment before answering, as if giving it serious consideration, and brushed away the beads of perspiration that dotted his temples.

"Next year," he said. "Give Nonna a kiss for me and wish everyone a merry Christmas, okay?"

As much as he adored his family—the loud and loving hodgepodge of Italian and Mexican and what his grandmother described as *a dash of who-knows-what*—this was one year that he welcomed holiday work. A knot rose in his throat when he thought about just how much attention would be lavished on him at the family home, when all he really wanted was to curl silently into a corner with a good, stiff drink.

He needed a break, a place of peace, quiet, and privacy—a place with a bar, and a television, and aggressive air conditioning.

It was steamy enough with the kitchen and the bodies and the lack of ventilation at the Fourth and Mission food hall, but an outside temperature of eighty-five degrees translated to sweltering inside the cavernous room. During a Los Angeles summer, it would feel utterly ordinary, but a winter heat wave could turn downtown corridors into saunas, and the event team had been adamant: *Thou shalt wear holiday sweaters.*

To save his life, Jack couldn't figure out how the mayor could stand in a hot kitchen on a sweltering day—wearing a Fair Isles sweater no less—and not shed a drop of sweat. The man was truly blessed with a politician's genes.

The mayor had promised an hour to the event and stayed for close to two. He had planned to be there only long enough for news crews to get video of him dolloping sweet potatoes onto plates, for a collection of sound bites, and a quick side meeting with Jack and a television producer ready to invest in political futures. But the mayor was a chatty man and, without a full schedule, got caught up in the conversations and the stories and the campaigning until his security detail reminded him of the time and hustled him to his Town Car. He paused at the open door.

"Jack, you sure you won't come by for Christmas dinner? Patina's catering. I promise—no campaign talk."

The mayor smiled and pushed his RayBans on top of his head. It was a well-worn move that Jack knew was intended to connect. Jack had seen it a thousand times.

"You lie," he said.

The mayor grinned. *He should know better.*

"True, but we hate the idea of you being alone. And I think Marie wants to fix you up." He shrugged; his eyebrows contorted in approximation of an apology.

Jack knew he should smile. He should appreciate the effort of friends looking out for him. He simply shook his head. Not today, not yet.

"Tell her 'Merry Christmas.' I just want to get a drink and watch the game."

The mayor slipped the sunglasses down his nose and slid into the car.

"Good luck finding an open bar—or at least one that isn't full of purple and gold," he said, and shut the door. The window rolled down as the engine roared to life. "And Jack? Try to have a merry Christmas."

Jack watched the sedan disappear to the north, toward the polished and secured confines of Hancock Park. Safely alone, he tore off the sweater, a ghastly acrylic pullover decorated with reindeer and pine trees, and tossed it in a donation bin. He rolled up the sleeves of his pinpoint shirt and took a moment to let the wind pierce the fabric.

Free at last from work obligations and a gaudy polyester sauna, he pointed himself toward the heart of downtown and walked.

It was a longer hike than he would usually choose for a hot afternoon. Wingtips weren't designed for such a trek, and the concrete seared his soles. But he felt compelled to wander, to clear his head and search for a comfortable bar. Most were closed. Those that weren't—like the Gallery Bar at the Biltmore or the ghastly chain restaurants of L.A. Live—would be jammed with holiday crowds. He didn't need to check.

He shuffled down Figueroa, drawn like a homing device to an old stretch of the boulevard, to an aging Spanish colonial that decades earlier had towered over the street, but was now dwarfed by steel and glass. It was cozily familiar, a place where he would be known rather than recognized, even if he could no longer be considered a regular. They would leave him alone; or at least they wouldn't pry. At worst, he could expect to have a shallow conversation about the Lakers' prospects under new management or whether the Heat would ever recover from losing its biggest stars.

He expected that it, like most of downtown, would be shuttered for the holiday. If it was anything like it had been back when it had been his regular haunt, the owner would grumble about lost revenue, only to send his staff home with a grunt and a modest bonus.

But a far window flickered in neon: Open. Through an unlocked door, a wisp of cool air drifted past him, beckoning.

The Casa Blanca Bar & Grille was never intended to be a trendy nightspot that topped Zagat ratings. It was a neighborhood haunt in the heart of the city, an establishment that evolved over the years as a reflection of one man's devotion to a movie that clung to his soul and to food that stuck to his ribs.

Taking a seat at the Casa Blanca was like stepping out of a time capsule in Morocco circa 1941, by way of Hollywood. Located on the ground floor of an aging hotel, it greeted patrons with the sound of big band music on the stereo and framed photos of Humphrey Bogart and Ingrid Bergman on the walls. Cast on crimson and gold accents, the warm, dim lighting suggested a permanent midnight.

A comfortable oddity compared to its five-star competition up the hill, the Casa Blanca's style was part homage to the classic film, part tequila bar. The owner insisted on a sense of classic style— no jeans or T-shirts for its bartenders, who wore crisp, white dress shirts and black slacks, though he capitulated on the bow ties when the bartenders rose up against wearing the constrictive neck ware.

Admittedly, the Casa Blanca hadn't always been Jack's idea of a great bar. It had been an acquired taste, born of devotion and a willingness to follow. To some, it came across as fashionably ironic: Kasbah décor-meets-Mexican restaurant to a soundtrack from the American songbook. Jack would protest that it was a hipster joint, would try to default to something chic and modern atop Bunker Hill, an elegant spot with a view, but the Casa Blanca's quirks and contradictions grew on him over time.

Like a fungus, he would say.

Like love, he would be admonished.

Maybe it became so much a part of his routine because it was where they had spent many of their best moments together and a few of their worst.

The Casa Blanca was a habit born out of a relationship, a routine that died of unnatural causes one year ago.

Rattan fans swirled overhead, casting erratic shadows across the depths of the near-empty room. Televisions at opposite ends of the bar echoed the play-by-play of ESPN in hushed and reverent tones; the voice of the broadcast team usurped by Peggy Lee.

At the far corner, his back to the entrance, a solitary bartender wiped glasses while glancing at the game.

"You open?" Jack asked.

"So long as you're thirsty," he answered without so much as a glance in Jack's direction, as if anticipating the interruption. "But the kitchen's closed."

"That's all right," Jack said. He made himself comfortable at a table a few feet from the bar and adjusted his chair to face the television. It might not have been sociable, but he wasn't there for conversation.

A napkin floated to the table. A bowl of Chex Mix settled in front of his fingertips. "What are you drinking?"

Jack glanced at the bartender's hands without looking up—the prominent veins hinted at athleticism. The nails were buffed to a soft sheen.

He drank beer at games, but beer was a drink for the sociable, to be consumed among friends. Whiskey had an appropriately solitary feel, but seemed out of place for a warm evening.

"Tequila," he said. "Casa Dragones."

"And here I had you figured for bourbon."

It would have been a good guess. But he'd had too many nights lately when he made the acquaintance of a glass of Kentucky's finest. Besides, the Casa Blanca was known for its tequila collection. Jack had known that as a regular, just as any experienced bartender would.

"You're new here?" Jack asked. He glanced up, finally registering a brief connection with the young face looking back at him. Months before, when the Casa Blanca was habit, he knew all of the bartenders. This one must have been hired in the year since Jack walked away.

The bartender nodded toward the multi-colored Christmas lights strung atop the bar and shrugged.

"The new guy always gets the short straw, right?"

"I had a feeling," Jack said.

"Because I got your drink wrong?"

"On any other night, you would have had it right. I haven't had tequila in months."

The bartender reached for the sliding library ladder that would help him climb to the heights behind the bar. He stretched for the clear bottle with easy, singular grace.

"Lime with that?" he asked, reaching for a short tumbler.

Jack shook his head. "I'll be sipping it."

The bartender winked and set the glass aside. He opened a cabinet where specialty barware was stored, pulled a stemmed tequila glass from the shelf, and spun it between his fingers before setting it on the bar and pouring a generous shot.

He set it on the table and stood, hands on his hips, as if awaiting a compliment.

"Thanks," Jack said.

"No problem," the bartender responded, but he didn't move. If he was waiting for an invitation, Jack hadn't planned on extending one. "Can I ask you something?"

Jack sipped the drink in silence.

"It's Christmas. Why are you looking like you're headed to a business meeting, Jack Volarde?"

Jack scowled at the bartender. Young and clueless. But he carried himself with casual confidence, undeterred by Jack's intimidating glare, a look he had mastered in countless closed-door negotiation sessions.

The bartender nodded toward a television across the room, the only screen set to the local news. On it, the mayor smiled and handed out holiday dinners with Jack at his side.

Jack glanced at his watch. 5:01 p.m. The mayor had won the Christmas night news cycle.

"People recognize you all the time, right?"

In a town that paid its debts in currency of celebrity, Jack sometimes hated the fact that he was considered one, at least in political circles. His face was familiar to anyone who paid attention to city hall or to the mayor's ascension from neighborhood organizer to polished politician. Recognition didn't usually surprise him. Being called out did. He looked back at his drink. He didn't respond.

"You following him to Sacramento?"

Ah, there it was: the question asked by political junkies citywide— the question that obliged Jack to remain mute, at least for another week or two.

Of course the mayor was running for governor. His next decade was carefully charted to place him on the fast track to the US Senate and quite possibly beyond.

"Who said he's going anywhere?" Jack responded, a practiced non-denial.

"Who doesn't?" the bartender answered. He grinned—a warm flash of cheeky smile that said *I'm on to you.* "There are people who think you belong up there, or maybe DC."

Jack chuckled, more a muffled courtesy harrumph than legitimate laughter. It wasn't that he hadn't been solicited: a run for the state legislature or maybe Congress. He had the brains, the looks, the silken voice, and a quick wit that could easily win over hearts and minds. He had allowed himself to consider the possibilities only infrequently, but Jack was married to this life, to this city, and, for all intents and purposes, to the man he had lost the year before.

"I'm not going anywhere," he said.

"A change of scenery can be a healthy thing." The bartender tossed his towel aside and rested his hips against the dark wood of the back bar.

"Is this one of those bartender things, where you get the guy to tell his life story? Because you shouldn't bother. There's nothing here."

"It's what bartenders do," he said. He extended his hand. "I'm Javier, but call me Javi. Javier's reserved for the long, full-name treatment."

Jack allowed himself a muted chuckle. He knew how that worked.

"So, now that we're on a first name basis, let me ask you something. There has to be a dozen places you could be right now. What are you doing alone in a bar on Christmas?"

Because it's better than being home alone.

If he was going to spend Christmas on his own, he had to do it where he could at least distract himself.

"Maybe I just wanted some peace," Jack said, hoping to put an end to the conversation. But there it was again, that cheeky smile, almost a smirk. It reminded Jack of a look he had come to know well over the past half-dozen years.

"And so you came here?"

"You were open. Your air conditioning felt good. It seemed like a good idea at the time."

"Was that all?"

Of course not.

The city and life that once had felt so rushed had stalled into a slow-motion dive over the past year, though the falloff was imperceptible to anyone but Jack. His had kept his calendar booked. His assistant had tried to push off appointments to other members of the mayor's staff. The mayor himself had encouraged Jack to slow down, to take a break.

None of them realized that his life was already slow, nearly a crawl. No matter how frenetic his workload had appeared, it was never enough. To Jack, the world turned at a glacial pace. Breaks allowed him time to think, to dwell on his life—and he wasn't prepared for that.

"Is that all?" Javi repeated. He placed his hands on the back of the chair across from Jack; he was digging in, pushing for more.

The playful tease that had accented his words had evaporated.

Jack looked up and took him in for the first time. The bartender was a few years younger than he, old enough for the earliest hint of laugh lines beside his eyes, but young enough that he had to push back the ever-present fall of chestnut hair. His eyes were focused and inquisitive and trained squarely on Jack. Once Jack would have taken notice sooner and done something about it.

"I used to come here a lot," Jack said.

It had taken some convincing to get Jack through the inlayed doors of the Casa Blanca for the first time.

You'll love this place.

But I made reservations.

Cancel them.

You know how hard it is to get into Bestia on a Saturday night?

Not for you. You'll like this. Take off the tie and live a little. Trust me.

He had been taken aback. He didn't belong there. The Casa Blanca's customers were too young, too self-consciously hip, too aware of the ironic clash of food and decor. But Joey? Joey loved it.

And, over time, so did Jack.

"Let me guess," Javi pressed. "A breakup?"

"Not exactly."

Javi deepened his grip on the chair. Glen Miller echoed through the room, "Moonlight Serenade." Jack couldn't break the interloper's gaze.

He held the stem of the tequila glass tighter and tighter—an agave death grip that secured his confidence.

His conscience told him to stay mute, to shoo this guy away. But something that Jack couldn't quite pinpoint opened the door for him, and he cautiously walked through.

"He's dead."

The room went silent, a simple break between songs that accented an already awkward pause.

"I'm sorry," Javi said.

Jack wrapped his fist around the stem, locking the glass to the table.

"I know what it's like to lose someone—to know that it's over, even though you're not ready."

"You make it sound like breaking up," Jack said.

Javi dipped his chin, looked up to Jack, forced him to meet his eye. There it was again, that look, that light. It was more subdued, but unmistakably and unexpectedly reassuring. Jack's cascading grief started to dissipate, even as this stranger overstepped the lines behind which Jack had so firmly entrenched himself.

"It's *exactly* like breaking up," Javi said. "Getting used to being alone, overcoming that weird guilt when you finally let yourself live again, forgiving them for leaving you?"

"He doesn't need my forgiveness."

He hadn't been perfect, not by a long shot, but Joseph Francis Xavier McCallan had had a way with people, just as he'd had a way with Jack.

They had met at a fundraiser, not that that was Joey's style. He couldn't have cared less about politics. As a substitute teacher and part-time coach, he cared about kids and athletics and the role team sports could play in shaping students' lives. When a pro soccer league sponsor hosted a fundraiser for an up-and-coming politician, Joey took the time to show up and to listen. He also caught the eye of a political advisor who was there as much as friend as he was consultant to the future mayor. And, though his introductory words sounded contentious, they were tempered by flirtatiousness that was undeniably direct.

So, you're one of those guys who serves twenty-year-old Scotch in office meetings and takes people out for five-hundred-dollar dinners, right?

You're thinking of a lobbyist. I'm a consultant to the mayor.

Do you take people out for swank dinners?

I take people out to dinners, sure. Why?

Because I'd love a swank dinner sometime.

Jack wasn't usually drawn to scruffy beards or ponytails, but something about the russet hair and raucous laughter reeled him in like a fish on a hook. It started as casual conversation, continued with life stories over drinks, and concluded on gray thousand-count sheets in Jack's condo.

It took less than twenty-four hours for Jack to realize he was smitten, a week to know that this was something different, something more, and less than a month before he told Joey that he loved him, even if it was while Joey slept curled into his chest.

In some ways, they couldn't have been more different. In some ways, they fit together like a lock and key. It was the first time in his life that Jack realized he needed a contrast to his button-down life.

And somewhere in his hodgepodge blend of priorities, Joey McCarran proclaimed a love of Jack Volarde.

He also declared his love of a methodically poured Guinness, of late-night Australian rules football, of sing-a-longs at the Hollywood Bowl, and of the latest gourmet food trucks to hit the streets of Los Angeles.

"Everyone loved him. He was a regular here… we were. He'd jump behind that bar and help out when it got busy."

"He worked here?"

"Not exactly, but George knew he could mix a decent cocktail, and Joey knew how to talk up a stranger. He could get anyone to open up. He loved it—meeting people, making drinks, telling bullshit stories. He lived for it."

He called it home.

They had all but moved in together after six months, but it never quite felt permanent. Joey had put down roots at the Casa Blanca; his relationship with Jack's home was another story. Joey had insisted on keeping his place in the Valley, even though Jack had plenty of space in his downtown condo with all the clean and streamlined comforts that served as accent points to success.

I can sell it. We can get something that we both like.

And what could that possibly be?

Jack drained the last of the tequila from his glass and raised his index finger as he set it back on the table.

"Uno más?"

Jack nodded. Javi grabbed a fresh glass and returned with the bottle.

"Can I join you?"

Jack let him pour two shots. He raised his glass in a silent toast.

"Tell me more about your man." Javi asked.

"What do you want to know?"

"What do you need to tell?"

Jack glanced behind the bar, to the mirror and the face staring back at him. His hair had become flecked with gray; his eyes were lined with the first tracks of crow's feet. It had started subtly with a hint of salt sprinkled at his temples and through the stubble of a beard, and Joey had treated it as a ceaseless source of mirth, a means of reminding Jack of the years that separated them.

Should I call you Daddy?

Absolutely, fucking not.

As much as he would tease, the jokes were nearly always accompanied by a gentle touch, by fingers that slowly trekked across Jack's scalp as they traced the soft, silver lines.

Not that he considered eight years that much of an age difference, but Jack could feel a pull between them that, while not exactly generational, highlighted a gap that sometimes separated them. The quirks that so many found endearing sometimes wore on Jack's nerves: the persistent scruffiness; the roller-skate key worn on a leather strap around Joey's neck; his damned insistence on riding a bicycle through the unforgiving traffic of downtown Los Angeles, when the subway stop was scarcely a block from his home and a driver was an app away.

Joey had made it clear that he hated Jack's suits, or at least that he liked taking them off. His elaborate shopping trip as part of his *Make Jack Human Again Campaign* resulted in bags full of color-washed jeans and skin-tight, short-sleeve shirts Jack wore only in private.

And always, always there was the hair. Joey, with his wavy mop that fell to effortless perfection, couldn't let it go. That wouldn't be any fun. He would slip behind Jack in the shower and run his hands through the emerging slivers of silver.

I know someone who can fix this.

You know you like it.

You're kind of hot for an old man. If I squint a little, it's almost like sleeping with Clooney.

"For what it's worth, it looks distinguished."

"What?"

"Your hair. You're one of the guys who just looks hotter as he gets older, aren't you?"

Jack shook his head and chuckled. It was the closest he'd been to a laugh since he'd heard the substitute weathercaster try to explain the origins of downslope winds that morning.

"Was that too much? I can't help myself. Silver foxes are my kryptonite." Javi shot him a look that was at once intense and playful. It had been so long since he had been attracted to someone that Jack almost didn't recognize that he was being hit on. Against his better judgment, he did nothing to stop it.

"You want to tell me about your man? What was his name?"

"Joseph," he said. He sipped the tequila, letting it coat his lips. "Joey."

Jack traced the line of Joey's spine with his fingertips, detouring at his hips. He braced his chin on Joey's shoulder and whispered in his ear: Joseph Francis Xavier McCallan.

I only hear that much name when I'm in trouble.

You are trouble. And I like your name.

"He had these damn dimples. You could see them straight through the beard. They were his tell, a sign that a big grin was about to break out, and laughter, so much laughter. That man loved to laugh. He said that the dimples were 'happy creases.'"

"Like this?" Javi grinned, and his smile folded into a cheerful repetition of folded skin. "I hear they're my best feature."

They're not bad.

"I just keep smiling. I figure if they're good, put 'em on display, right? That's why people with dimples smile so much."

"I smile."

"Yours is practiced," Javi said. "It's a tactical smile."

"Maybe I just need a reason."

"To smile?" Javi said. "I'd say that this tequila is reason to smile."

"Cheers to that," Jack said. He raised his glass again, and the muscles in his face loosened and lifted without so much as a voter in sight.

"That's a little better," Javi said.

"Contrary to what you might think, I do smile."

Mmm. Scratchy.

Sorry, weekend scruff.

I like it. You should let it grow.

I don't look good in a beard.

Not a beard, just scruff; just enough to hint at the man beneath the suit.

Joey had pushed, early and often, for Jack to loosen up, to present a more casual appearance, something more edgy than the close shave he had sported for so many years. But his moustache grew faster than his beard, and Jack hated the look and feel of it.

It's a porn 'stache.

You look hot.

It's easier to shave.

You look like you just got back from a week off—and I like how it feels.

They compromised, as they had on so many things—the stubble that Joey swore made Jack look worldly, and a trip to the barber to keep the edges sharp and the length consistent. Jack could live with it.

But he wasn't so sure that compromise was a two-way street.

Joey had resisted becoming part of Jack's professional life. He hated political events: the rubber chicken dinners at the Hilton, the election night marathons. He could be convinced to go along for the right event, the right cause. Jack had bought him the suit, had it tailored to show off Joey's athletic build, and sprung for the hair appointment that controlled the volume of dark waves that Joey so often contained with a ponytail. He'd grimaced through the haircut, but bit his lip. It's not every day that you're a VIP at an inaugural dinner. But Jack felt the distance through the night: the aloof manner, the dead eye—the sense that Joey would rather be anywhere but in that hotel ballroom.

"He thought I was trying to change him."

"Were you?"

Jack shook his head and raised the glass to his lips. He muffled his words with a sixty-dollar shot of tequila.

"He changed me."

You should get off the bar.

The Dodgers are in the Series, and I'll shake it if I want to. Get up here, Mr. Volarde.

I'll just sit here and enjoy the show. No need to risk a drunk and disorderly.

You love the Dodgers. Dance with me. No one's going to stop you.

Only if you get off the bar.

Behind it, then.

"Do you dance?"

"What?"

"The song—George's rule. Gotta honor it."

The Casa Blanca's owner had programmed the music mix himself, proudly creating what amounted to a mixed tape of Glen Miller, Benny

Goodman, Louis Armstrong, and Billie Holiday. But one song, the signature piece, had its own set of house rules: When "As Time Goes By" cycles through the rotation, hit the dance floor with someone you love.

"You know the rules, Volarde."

"I'm not in love."

There was that damn smile again, accented with the slightest of winks.

"Yes, you are."

Javi nodded his head to the side, toward a tiny space that doubled as a dance floor.

"Let me stand in."

He held out his hand. As if compelled, Jack took it and followed him toward the dark corner. Javi turned, wrapping an arm around Jack's waist. "Ready?"

Jack responded by slowly falling into the embrace and letting it support him.

They swayed in the glow of the multi-colored string lights. The moon slipped through the leaded window, casting shadows of ethereal dancers across the floor. A strong palm drifted down Jack's back to settle into the notch above his waist, as if the spot had been carved specifically for this hand, these fingers so comfortably at home against his spine. How long had it been since someone had touched him there? Joey always teased him that this was his *magic spot,* like when you rub a dog's belly until it kicks with uncontrolled joy.

Jack shut his eyes and let the sensation wash over him: the warm comfort of being held, the cool breeze of the overhead fans. He rested his head on a welcome shoulder until he felt the tactile shift of a body delicately turning, adjusting, and of lips caressing his neck.

The sensation stopped him cold. Jack pulled away.

"I'm sorry," he muttered.

"Too soon?" Javi asked.

"Too familiar."

Jack rested his forearms against the bar, and lowered his head into a cradle of pinpoint cotton. Javi stepped alongside and placed his hand back on his shoulder.

"Have you considered that maybe you need a little nudge; that maybe it's time to move on?"

That was the last thing he needed. He'd already tried giving in to the whims of an unsentimental body in an unsettling attempt to clear his head, if not his heart. He had convinced himself that was all he really needed—an anonymous moment to take and not give, time to tune out his mind and his heart and listen instead to the amplified cries of his libido. He was free to do as he pleased; no one would blame him. For god's sake, friends were *urging him* to hook up with someone. It was nothing more than a release of a pressure valve, an anonymous blowjob that would be forgotten the next day as he tackled the unsettling work of moving on.

But it wasn't.

There was a time when he was comfortable with casual sex. But that had changed with Joey. Jack had driven home after the encounter as if a police cruiser had followed him home from a bar—too cautious, too self-aware, and too anxious to get the hell home and slam the door shut behind him. Two months later, the lingering guilt still haunted him.

"It's not like I haven't tried," Jack said, his voice a whisper, a soft murmur of regret.

Javi stepped behind the bar. He poured an ice water and set it in front of Jack, then pulled up a bar stool.

"No more tequila for you."

"Am I going to get a lecture?"

"No, just hydration."

Jack took a long, slow swig from the glass, then wiped his lips dry with the back of his hand.

"Why are you doing this?"

Javi smiled. *Those dimples.*

"Because you need it," he said. "Call it a Christmas gift, if you like."

"You're about to give me the 'Isn't this what he would have wanted?' speech, aren't you? I've heard it before."

"I'm sure you have, and that's why I'm not."

The smile was back, with a certain restraint; the smirk was replaced by a soft expression that urged Jack on. He covered Jack's hand with his own.

"When people tell you that, maybe you should think about what they're *not* saying, you know?"

"What do you mean?"

Javi looked straight ahead, avoiding Jack's gaze and letting his words make the contact.

"No one's saying you have to rush into anything. No one's saying you have to get married. No one's even saying you've got to get laid. You just need to get yourself into a place where that's a possibility again—and no one's going to judge you for it."

Jack pushed the water glass across the bar. Hydration was all fine and well, but he was having an evening that required something stronger.

Javi raised an eyebrow and reached for the tumbler.

"No, I don't need more water," Jack said. "Make it a red wine."

"You're not going to like how your head feels tomorrow. But if you insist…"

"I insist."

Javi grabbed two Bordeaux glasses, stepped behind the bar, and returned with a dark green bottle. He turned it in his hands, showing Jack the label.

"That's a nice Cab. You sure George won't mind?"

"It's Christmas, and I'm tending this place by myself. Yeah, it's okay."

Javi uncorked the wine and poured a sample for Jack.

"Oh, please," Jack said. He took the bottle from Javi and poured two full glasses.

He tapped their glasses. "Cheers."

"To moving on," Javi said.

Jack nodded and sipped. Lingering over the wine's aroma, he kept the glass poised at his lips.

"Thanks," he said, "and I'm sorry. I don't know what's gotten into me today."

"What? Because you're talking about him?"

"Talking to a stranger... about him."

"Maybe that's what you need."

The grass wasn't as lush or green as the fields in the suburbs, but that was kind of the point. After cutting the ribbon on the urban field, the mayor spoke of the importance of inner city soccer, how the sport's suburban nature had essentially locked urban kids out of participating. This park would be the first step in changing that, the mayor said.

Jack may have written the talking points, but they were largely of Joey's making. He had come up with the proposal and, in his own way, lobbied for it by sharing the idea with the mayor's wife at a dinner party the year before. She had become its champion—and his. When the park opened and a new inner city youth soccer league began, Joey was invited to stand alongside the politicians on the dais. For this cause, Joey would play politics.

Jack stood off to one side, next to Marie. She looked at him and winked.

"He's a keeper."

"You've kept this all bottled up, haven't you?"Javi said. "My mother used to say that grief was like breathing. You have to breathe to keep living, and you have to grieve to let someone go. You can't free yourself until you free *them*. You understand?"

"Not really."

"You have to let him go. You have to give yourself a chance to live."

"Is this standard bartender patter?"

"This is common sense."

Jack stood up, walked to the window, and looked out at the empty streets of the central city. Out of the corner of his eye, he could see the Library Tower. A bank had bought the naming rights years before, but

Joey had always insisted on calling it by its original name and reminding him that it was the building the aliens attacked in *Independence Day*.

You would have been up there on the top with one of those Welcome to Earth! signs, wouldn't you?

No way. I would have been Will Smith, punching out the alien and lighting up a stogie.

Except you don't smoke.

Except I don't smoke.

He also got married before the final battle.

It's a metaphor, Jack.

The Library Tower had style, even for a skyscraper—full of layers and fine details so lacking in many of the city's high-rises. Panels illuminated its peak: a red and green luminescent crown for the holidays.

Javi stepped alongside him and quietly took in the Los Angeles skyline.

"It's beautiful, isn't it? It has an old aesthetic, a personality. And I like how they change the colors for the season—the red-and-green for Christmas," he said, nodding at the tower. "But mainly, I like it when they just have the white lights. It's like a beacon pointing to the heavens."

Jack nodded his agreement, but said nothing. He took the building in and held his fist to his mouth as if holding in the words that finally burst free.

"We fought that morning," he said. "Last Christmas. The day it happened."

It should have been a little thing, a spat, but Jack wouldn't let it go. He wanted an answer. He wanted certainty. He wanted to get married and to announce an engagement among family at dinner that night. But it didn't go according to script.

Joey brushed it off, as though it was a simple suggestion, or maybe a joke, but certainly not a proposal. He laughed and said that he was allergic to rings.

Don't you love me?

Do you need a ring to prove it?

Maybe a conversation would be nice.

I'll make you a deal. You'll know that you have my undying love the moment I give you my skate key, but please, no rings.

A Christmas Eve proposal spilled into a Christmas Day argument.

"We were supposed to have dinner with my family, but Joey said he was going to a friend's place across town."

"He needed to get out?"

Jack shrugged. "I guess—He went to see his old girlfriend."

"Oh." Javi went silent, as if considering the possibilities. "Did you trust him?"

Jack bit his lip. He knew the answer. He knew that Joey had always been faithful, even during rough patches. But a small, stubborn corner of his mind chose to believe the worst.

"He was monogamous," Jack said. His tone was guarded. Though he could speak convincingly on any number of policy issues he didn't believe in, when it came to Joey—no matter how much he knew he should believe in him—he also knew that he lacked conviction.

"It just didn't feel right. I know that sounds bad, but we'd just fought, and then he up and left. He said if I wanted him to go to dinner with me, I'd have to go to her place and pick him up. And he grabbed that fucking bicycle and took off."

Jack stared off at the tower. Usually, its crown created a hazy glow as the soft evening fog rolled into the city, but the heat wave kept the lights at its peak oddly crisp, creating colorfully defined stripes along the top of the building.

"I thought he'd call, but nothing."

"Didn't you go look for him?"

Jack shook his head.

"I thought he needed space. I thought he'd be here when I got home." His voice drifted off.

He turned his back to the window and rested his weight against the wall.

"I found out the next morning. They ran a check on his license. The address came up with my name. Someone recognized it and sent it up the ranks. My boss woke me up with the news."

A knock on the door at such an ungodly hour for a holiday—it could only be Joey.

He must have forgotten his keys.

But he opened the door to the mayor, alone and grim.

Jack, I don't know how to tell you this…

He folded his arms across his chest, closing in on himself.

"I should have gone after him. He never should have been riding that bike in the dark."

Javi pulled Jack into his arms, held him tight, whispered in his ear.

"You can't blame yourself. It was just a fight. He shouldn't have left you like that."

Pressure built behind Jack's eyes—*That's how tears should feel*—yet the dust kicked up by the winter winds still scratched at his corneas. He inhaled and held his breath, suppressing tears, but Javi pulled back and gripped his forearm.

"Don't. Let it out."

The words willed him to cooperate, permitting his body to surrender its grip on his grief. He may not have had The Good Cry that so many people had told him he needed, but the pressure finally found its release. A tear, and then a second, rolled down his cheeks. For now, it was enough.

Jack let the arms that he had pushed away minutes before enfold him, support him. He held on for dear life while "Stardust" played, and slowly calm overtook him. He exhaled and released the pressures and demons that had shadowed him.

Ever-so-slowly, Jack let the music carry him in a hesitant step-ball-step. He wrapped his arms around Javi's shoulders and swayed in slow syncopation with the ballad, in no hurry for the song to end.

"If George was so determined to have Big Band era music in here, he should have used the Bing Crosby version. Nat King Cole didn't record 'Stardust' until the fifties," Jack said.

"But Cole's version is the best," Javi said. He paused, resting his hand on Jack's chest, near his heart. "You're going to be okay, Jack Volarde."

Javi paused and angled his face to Jack's. The kiss was brief, comforting, and gentle. Jack hesitated, but didn't pull away.

"Mistletoe," Javi said, smiling. "I had to."

He laced a hand through Jack's hair, and kissed him again. It was more determined, more certain—a cool, electric rush that started at Jack's lips and rushed to his fingers and toes. It felt like life itself.

He'd forgotten this feeling—a sensation not so much of want, but of need—and once reacquainted, Jack embraced it. His senses awoke as he gave in to lips, hands, and tongue.

How do you tell a stranger that they know you better than they should, that they've pinpointed your tells and weaknesses and have zeroed in on the things your soul knows need to change?

"When's closing time?" he murmured into Javi's neck.

"Whenever I'm done."

"Then maybe you should close up," Jack said.

Javi loosened his hold.

"You sure?"

Jack nodded.

"Is this the same guy who wandered in here wanting to be left alone with his memories?"

"Maybe you were right," Jack said. "Maybe it's time to let go. It doesn't mean I don't still love him, but maybe it's time to move on."

Jack let his hand drift to Javi's hip.

"Come on."

"Jack…"

"Close up the bar. Let's get out of here."

Javi stepped aside, creating a gap between them. He turned toward the window and looked out on the city lights.

"I wish I could."

"What?"

"I have to be somewhere."

"In the middle of the night? On Christmas? You're just going to walk away?"

Javi turned to Jack. The flirtatious smirk had been replaced by a half-smile that looked wistful, maybe even remorseful. He kissed Jack's cheek; the sensation lingered against his skin.

"I'm sorry."

"But…" Jack waved at the room, at the dance floor, the string lights, and the mistletoe.

Javi kissed him again, a quick brush of the lips that gently ended any hope of the night ending anywhere other than the Casa Blanca. "This was a good night, but we both know that it's a bad idea."

"Can I at least get your number?"

"You know where to find me." He grinned. "I'm the guy serving cocktails from here to eternity."

"Wrong movie," Jack muttered. "If you're going to end the night on a pun, at least make it from the right film."

Javi took his hand, entwining their fingers. "I think this is the beginning of a beautiful friendship."

He kissed Jack again and then stepped to the front of the bar. He turned off the neon light that welcomed the outside world and held the door open.

"I haven't paid," Jack said. "What do I owe you?"

Javi smiled.

"Nothing at all. Merry Christmas, Jack."

AFTER A YEAR OF SLEEPLESS nights, Jack's nightstand played host to a menagerie intended to see him through the night. His phone doubled as a sleep machine, though the sound of traffic on the downtown slot of the 110 freeway was more soothing to him than an app of croaking frogs. The books were well worn and constantly cycled in and out of the nightstand pile. The laptop computer never really shut down and had become his reliable if somewhat unsatisfying surrogate bed partner. If the nightstand collection couldn't cajole him to sleep, it could at least amuse him during his restless hours.

He shuffled into his bedroom shortly after midnight, pulled back the bed covers, and picked up a book. His mind had been racing when he left the Casa Blanca, but by the time he climbed into bed, the rush had subsided. He set the book aside, turned out the light, and slept.

He awoke far later than his usual routine allowed, thanks no doubt to a Christmas dinner of tequila, Cabernet, and Chex Mix. He flipped on the television just as the local news ended.

Boxing Day? Who does a story about Boxing Day in Los Angeles?

He opened his laptop to cycle through the Christmas news coverage and measure the success of his work. It was routine by this time in his career. He could wait for Monday's evaluation, complete with impressions and analytics, but he liked the immediacy of looking up coverage and rating it *positive, negative* or *neutral.* It was old school, the Jack Volarde method, but it worked.

The mayor's stint atop the news cycle began and ended at five on Christmas evening. A series of power outages across the city caused by the heat and an unexpected drain on the electrical grid settled that. *Fair enough, lead with the breaking news.* After that, it was a toss-up. The network affiliates covered the event on their Christmas night broadcasts. It had slipped by morning, when crews were sent to shopping malls to cover the early rush for discount gift wrap and electronics. He'd still score it in the win column.

He could dig deeper if he logged in to his metrics, but he folded his laptop closed. He'd do it later. Better yet, he could let his assistant do it. She had wanted to create the media impact reports for ages. Maybe it was time to let her.

Habit told him it was time for a run, then a shower, and then a suit. But this was a day off, and the office would be locked tight. He had a speech to write: a career-changing announcement that could keep him tapping at his keyboard most of the day, even if he wasn't supposed to be working.

But something told him to set it aside, to take a break, to rest through the *not-quite-a-hangover* grogginess of a morning after. He got up and opened his bedroom blinds. The sun was already beating against the towers of the downtown financial district and, off to the west, the coast.

It would be another unseasonably warm December day, and the malls and movie theatres would be filled with holiday crowds. Maybe he would join them. He couldn't remember the last time he'd watched a movie that wasn't on either Netflix or a seatback monitor.

Go, get out of the city center. Get in your run; put in your miles. No one's going to be in a bar at nine a.m.

Jack's workouts were usually cursory. Do what you have to do; just get it done and get to work. He would run through the city, or on a treadmill at the gym down the street, solely for the sake of efficiency.

Not today, not on a day off.

He grabbed his gym duffel, running shoes, and car keys. He could jog along the waterfront in Santa Monica before the beach crowds set up camp and could shower at one of the stalls on the sand when he finished. He could change into jeans and a shirt at one of the beachfront hotels, maybe grab lunch.

He followed wherever the day led, from beach to al fresco lunch to movie, without a laptop in sight; a day without a plan, or a map, or a strategy, at least not a conscious one. As the sun set, he found himself back where he was before, standing on a hot sidewalk, waiting for the cool air of the Casa Blanca to welcome him back once more.

The Christmas lights and mistletoe were still up, but the bar's owner was struggling to hang a Happy New Year banner. George was quick to tell people stories of his days as a college fullback, but age and knee injuries left him teetering awkwardly on the stepladder as he tried to string up the letters.

"What's a guy got to do to get a beer around here?"

George turned toward Jack so quickly that he nearly fell.

"Jack Volarde, as I live and breathe."

He scrambled across the bar and wrapped Jack in a bear hug. "I wasn't sure I'd see you again."

"It's been too long," Jack said.

George motioned him to a bar stool and pulled out a pint glass. Jack eyed the assortment of novelty beer taps that advertised a range from local craft brewers to international brands.

"I'll have a Bohemia," he said.

Daylight breathed life into the Casa Blanca. A few customers sat at the bar watching football, and a few more claimed tables, waiting to order bar grub for a happy hour dinner. Los Angeles may have rolled up its sidewalks for the holidays, but the downtown dwellers knew where they could always get a good taco.

George shared restaurant duties with longtime bartender Brenda, a surly veteran mixologist to whom he had once been married. They had separated years before and might have divorced—the story was a bit fuzzy around the edges and changed depending on who told it—but they continued to work the Casa Blanca together.

"Just the two of you today?" Jack asked.

"It's a slow one today," George said. "I really should send her home. Better yet, I should send myself home and let her handle it."

"I heard that!" Brenda shouted, a disembodied voice from the kitchen.

The air was thicker, warmer than Jack remembered from the night before, when the air was chilled by persistent air conditioning. George must have been stingier with the electric bill than his employees.

"Mayor keeping you busy?"

Jack rolled his eyes. "You could say that."

"Yeah, I figured," George said. He angled the glass to the tap, methodically aerating Jack's beer as he poured, then leveling it off near the top, creating a picture perfect head. Jack smiled. He'd been on the receiving end of the "pour is an art form" lecture many, many times.

George slid a coaster toward Jack and set the beer on it. He sank down, locked his elbows against the wood, and offered Jack his full attention.

"So how are you really doing?"

Jack raised the glass to his lips and stopped.

"Better," he said. "It's getting better."

"Good. We worried about you when you stopped coming round."

"I guess I just needed some time," Jack said.

George reached across the bar and patted him on the arm.

"Understood, my friend. No hard feelings. I'm just happy to see you again. What finally brought you back?"

Was there a good answer to that question? Was it auto-pilot, or did the Casa Blanca trigger some sort of magnetic pull?

"I stopped by after the mayor's thing yesterday for a drink, but you'd taken the day off. It got me thinking that I should stop by and catch up, I guess."

"Yeah, good thing we were closed. That blackout would have forced me to shut down, anyway," George said.

Jack stopped, mid-sip. He set down the beer.

"I just meant you weren't here. The bar was open."

George slapped the bar and laughed, turning away.

"You wish!"

"You were open. You didn't really have any customers, other than me, of course. The new guy was working—Javi?"

George turned back toward Jack and tilted his head.

"Who?"

"Javier? The new guy. Dark hair, kind of young?"

George smiled as if he had heard a joke.

"I don't know any Javier, but if he makes a decent mojito, let me know. I've been looking for an excuse to sack Brenda for years."

"I heard that!" Brenda was uniquely skilled at hearing her name from any location at the Casa Blanca, only to tune out everything else.

"You're pulling my leg, right?" George asked.

123

"Dead serious," Jack said. "I stopped by yesterday afternoon. Didn't leave 'til late. It was just me and the bartender."

Wiping her hands on a towel, Brenda emerged from the kitchen. She nodded at Jack. "You're back." She had little patience for niceties or small talk. "George, I think there's something in the lost and found that belongs to Jack. I found an envelope with his name on it when I was opening up this afternoon." She pointed at the drawer, making it clear that George should investigate, and then turned back toward the kitchen. She didn't wait for a response.

"Good seeing you, Jack," she said with a half-wave, and left.

George rummaged through the drawer and pulled out a small manila envelope. He rolled it between his fingers and then looked at Jack. He lowered his voice.

"We were closed yesterday, and I haven't hired a new bartender in over a year. You okay, Jack? Have you been drinking already?"

"I haven't been drinking. I was here yesterday. No one else came in. We watched the game and talked until closing time."

George wiped his hands on a towel and stared at the floor. He spoke in a deliberate monotone.

"Jack, if you need someone to talk to... I know it's been a rough year."

"I'm telling you the truth."

"We were closed on Christmas. Locked up tight. I gave everyone the day off."

When George lowered his voice, Jack countered with an increasingly determined tempo.

"I sat right there, had a couple of drinks after work. Check your security camera. I swear."

George shook his head.

"There was a blackout last night. The power went down and took the camera with it." George wiped his forehead with the back of his hand. "The A/C was already shaky. Now it may be down for the count."

He looked at the envelope again and put it down on the bar in front of Jack. It was a small jeweler's envelope, thick with its contents, and sealed shut. In red letters, someone had scrawled, "Property of Jack Volarde."

"Recognize this?" George asked.

Jack shook his head.

"Not my handwriting, and Brenda wouldn't have bothered. Must have been in there a long time, eh?"

Jack stayed mute, his eyes fixed on the envelope. It was small, maybe two-by-three inches, like the one in which a jeweler had placed a ring after Jack had it resized a little over a year ago.

George pushed the envelope toward him.

"Have you thought about taking a vacation? I know they run you ragged in that job of yours."

"I think I'll just be going," Jack said. He stood up, over-paid his tab with a twenty-dollar bill, and placed the envelope in the front pocket of his jeans. George tried to push the cash back to him, but Jack waved him off. "Keep it."

"Jack? Don't be a stranger, okay? We've missed you around here."

"I promise," Jack said.

He left, confused; his head throbbed. He stepped into the twilight heat and walked up the street to a curbside planter, which was just tall enough to rest against. He reached into his pocket and pulled out the manila wrapper.

He tore it open and poured the contents into his palm. The leather strand spilled out first, followed by the pendant that was strung on it—an old roller skate key turned brown with age.

Jack gripped the token and shut his eyes.

Breathe, Jack.

He opened his eyes as he inhaled, and looked up to the early evening sky. The setting sun cast tangerine shadows across the cityscape. Rising above its neighbors, the Library Tower's panels had been switched from the red and green of Christmas to soft white for the New Year.

It's okay. Breathe.

He slipped the key around his neck, covered it with his palm, and pressed it hard against his chest. He looked again at the tower's peak, and cool breeze slipped past him: a gust of relief as tears flowed unfettered down his cheeks.

Overhead, the lights of the Library Tower flickered to life, a beacon to the heavens.

About the Author: Erin Finnegan is a former journalist and a winemaker who lives in the foothills outside Los Angeles. Her novel *Luchador* was named one of Publishers Weekly's Best Books of 2016, and along with her 2014 debut novel, *Sotto Voce*, received both a Foreword Reviews INDIES Book of the Year award and a PW starred review.

Halfway Home

Lilah Suzanne

Chapter One

AVERY PUCKETT HAS NO PERSONAL items on her desk to pack away. The woman from Human Resources offered her a box, along with a small severance package, while she stood, her face struggling to convey sympathy, at an uncomfortable distance from Avery's tiny cubicle. She'd fired a dozen people that day alone, the HR lady whose name Avery never learned, with Avery gone today in round three of a never-ending cycle of layoffs at the company. Avery doesn't blame the HR lady for her lack of sympathy. Such are the cold, churning cogs of corporate America. So no, she doesn't need a box. She leaves the high rise building in glossy Uptown the way she came: empty-handed, unaffected, and wearing the same tan blazer with a mustard stain on the sleeve.

The traffic on her way home is bad, because it always is, and the radio plays one song for every seven commercials, but it doesn't matter. It's all noise. Avery inches along the commute that's become second nature over the past year and two months. It's mostly city streets, which is better than her last commute, which was highway. Avery slows to a stop across from the red glow of a traffic light. Maybe the highway commute *was* better. It doesn't matter; a commute is a commute is a commute. The light turns green. Headlights flash in her rearview mirror, charging too fast and too close.

A tow truck takes her home.

"Sorry I'm late," Avery calls, entering her apartment and being surprised, once again, to come home to lights on and the TV murmuring. Mary Anne moved in three months ago. Avery still isn't sure if she likes it. She doesn't dislike it, which is close enough. "I got into a car accident." Avery sets a plastic bag on the kitchen counter as Mary Anne emerges from the bedroom.

"Oh, my god, are you okay?" Mary Anne likes vintage eye glasses, high-waisted A-line skirts, and NPR. She knows a great deal of 80s pop culture trivia, which is how her team won trivia night at the bar where she and Avery met—where Mary Anne walked up to Avery and announced they were a good match and should go out. Avery couldn't find any reason to object.

"Hmm? Oh yeah, I'm fine." Avery removes a carton of ice cream from the bag; it's gone a little soft in the time it took to get home. She should have eaten it right away. No matter, melted ice cream is still ice cream. "Is vanilla okay? The store didn't have a lot to choose from."

Mary Anne sighs. "I don't like vanilla. We have this conversation literally every time you buy ice cream." Behind her vintage, pink, cat-eye glasses, Mary Anne squints.

"Oh," Avery says. She opens the spoon drawer, grabs one spoon, then hesitates. "So, you don't want any?"

Mary Anne's mouth sets into a tense line, shifting into a mood that Avery can't read. Anger? Annoyance? Regret? Is one year and three months with one person long enough to know exactly what the tense set of their mouth means? Avery slowly closes the spoon drawer.

"What is with you?" Mary Anne says. "You're mopier than usual."

"Um," Avery says. *Usual?* "Well. I got fired."

"Oh. Shit." Mary Anne frowns and follows Avery into the living room. They bought all the living room furniture at Ikea together; they piled heavy boxes onto a pallet and then had a snack in the Ikea cafe. Mary Anne had a cinnamon roll and coffee, and Avery had a vanilla ice cream cone. Did Mary Anne tell her then that she hated vanilla ice cream? Avery can't recall.

"You liked that job," Mary Anne says, perching on the far end of the Ikea couch.

"It was okay. Did you DVR *I Love Lucy*? It was the one where Lucy gets her foot stuck in a bucket of cement. With John Wayne?"

Mary Anne swivels to face her. "Avery, aren't you upset about losing your job?"

"Um," Avery says, eating a spoonful of ice cream to give herself time, because she's pretty sure the answer *should* be yes. "Someone usually brought doughnuts on Monday mornings. I'll miss that." Avery stabs her spoon into the lumpy mostly melted ice cream and risks asking again. "So… did you DVR—"

"Forget about stupid TV shows, Avery! *God*. Feel something!" Mary Anne shoots up from the couch with her hands clenched at her sides. Her skirt has little cartoon foxes printed on it; it swishes and twists around her legs from the sudden movement.

Avery glances at the TV, then back at Mary Anne. She feels sad that she missed *I Love Lucy*. But then, it'll come again, or she can watch it online. And her car can be fixed, and there will always be more boring, pointless jobs, so she's not really sad at all, actually. "Um," she finally says. "Sorry?"

Mary Anne throws her arms out at her sides; her skirt ruffles and sways. "You know what, Avery? I can't. I thought moving in together was the solution. That maybe you needed to be in your own space to come out of your shell, but clearly you *are* a shell."

Avery frowns and replies, with a mouthful of ice cream, "What?"

"You—" Mary Anne flaps her hands in Avery's direction. "Are dead inside. And I am not going be sucked into your vortex of— of— of *nothing*, anymore. It's over. We're done." Mary Anne stomps away down the hall. For several minutes the only sounds are drawers slamming open and closed, closet doors squeaking and then being thrown shut, loud rustling in the bathroom and kitchen, and then Mary Anne returns with her two matching suitcases: the big one that looks like a bumblebee and the small one, a ladybug.

"I'll get the rest of my stuff in a few days. Don't be here."

She leaves. Avery sets the ice cream carton on the Ikea coffee table and turns on the TV. Finally, something goes right: There's a different episode of *I Love Lucy* on, the one with the grape stomping. It's one of her favorites. She's seen it dozens of times, but tonight it's not as funny as it usually is. In fact, Avery doesn't laugh at all.

Chapter Two

"A M I DEAD INSIDE?" AVERY wonders out loud, to no one in particular. The idea has been haunting her for days now.

She's surprised to hear a response.

"You are eating peanut butter from a jar while sitting on a park bench."

Avery frowns at the open jar clutched between her hands, then looks up at the children running through the open field of the small neighborhood park. "That's a good point," she concedes.

Mary Anne came to pack the rest of her things and demanded that Avery leave, and she didn't have time to make anything for dinner. She doesn't have an excuse for eating the same thing for lunch.

"I'm just a stranger on a park bench so you don't have to answer me, but— Are you okay?" The man arrived at the park with his kid, or more likely his grandkid, and sat next to Avery. He kept an eye on the kid while he scrolled through his phone.

Am I okay? Avery, immobilized by the idea that she no longer feels anything and didn't even realize it, has been going over and over that very question for days. "I don't know."

Avery took so long to answer that the man, who has white hair and patchy white facial hair and whose cheeks are flushed red from the cold, appears startled that she spoke. He shuts off his phone, glances at the playground, then turns to address her. "Listen, uh…"

"Avery," she fills in.

"Avery. I think if you were dead inside, you probably wouldn't be worrying about it, right?"

Avery shrugs. *Maybe.*

She had a job that she didn't hate; it was fine. Her apartment and her car are nice enough, or the car was until the rear bumper was crushed. She and Mary Anne were— Well, she thought they were okay. But now that she's lost her job and Mary Anne and her car, she's not angry or sad or worried. She's not even numb; she just doesn't care. Was she ever happy at all?

"I wasn't worried about it. I just think I should be."

The guy rubs his whiskered chin. "You look young, so from someone who's been at it for a while: I get it. Being numb is the easiest way to get through life sometimes. But you gotta find moments of joy where you can. Then hold on to that joy, as tight as you can."

What was the last moment of joy she had to hold on to?

They sit quietly until the man and his little grandson start to leave, and Avery thanks him for listening. If *she* had been sitting next to herself—a woman with unbrushed hair, who was wearing pajama pants and a poncho she found on the floor three days ago and has been wearing ever since, while eating peanut butter from a jar and mumbling to herself—Avery would have chosen another bench.

"Happy to help," the man says. "You look too young to be so world-weary."

Considering what the world is like, Avery doesn't see how she *couldn't* be weary.

Back home, Avery discovers that Mary Anne took all of the Ikea furniture from the living room. There is just the TV and a pile of throw pillows on the floor. "Well, that sucks," she says to the empty, quiet apartment. They paid fifty-fifty for that furniture, Mary Anne doesn't get to just take it. She sighs and drops onto a floor pillow. It's not worth it. Avery lived in this apartment before Mary Anne came along, and she's fine living here without her. But she has to admit, sitting on the floor in the silence, that it's lonely in a way that it never was before.

It rains on and off the next few days, and, of course, it's a downpour during Avery's Uber ride to the mechanic, where her car is ready and waiting. The always-bad traffic is even worse in the blinding rain, so she barely makes it before the garage closes for the night. They aren't happy that she's there so late, but are happy enough to take her money, and then she's directed out back to a gravel parking lot. Avery drapes her poncho over her head as a makeshift umbrella and carefully but quickly makes her way through the parking lot that's turning into a cold, muddy bog. Once safely inside her car, she tosses the damp poncho on the seat and shakes herself off, as if she's shedding the doldrums of the last few days. A fresh start, that's what she needs. Avery flicks on the headlights, puts the car into gear, and allows herself to be a little bit optimistic for the first time in a long time.

And then she screams and clutches her chest in sudden terror.

A demon blocks her way—a tiny demon with glowing eyes standing in the beam of her headlights. Or… Maybe it's a gremlin—a soaking-wet gremlin that refuses to move even as Avery's car creeps closer. She stops her car. The demon stares her down. She beeps at it, and the demon-gremlin doesn't blink. She honks the horn longer. The demon ferociously barks back.

"Oh." Avery hops out of the car and throws her poncho over her head. "It's a dog."

A scrawny, skinny little thing, its coat matted with mud and rain, ears flat and tail tucked under its body, shivers violently. Avery's never had a dog, never wanted one; she finds their exuberant energy overwhelming. But she is still a human being with a heart— Or at least she hopes so. She shouldn't just leave it here to freeze to death. Avery glances longingly at her warm, dry car. Someone else will probably help the dog. Like… someone in the office. She makes her way to the office to get help, but it's locked and dark, as if they took off the second she paid them. The adjacent garage is also closed. There isn't a soul around, just Avery and the stray dog in the parking lot. If she just left, no one would know. And it's because of that, the fact that what she really wants to do is nothing, that she decides to act.

"Okay." Avery glances around for a box or cage or something. A giant net would be nice, but she finds nothing in the dark, flooded parking lot. As she approaches the dog, it growls and barks frantically, spins around and bounces up and down with the force of its yelping. Perhaps her initial assessment of it as a demon wasn't entirely off the mark. "Okay. Okay. Okay." She chants to reassure both of them. She twists the poncho into a sort of net, tries to scoop the dog up, but drags the fabric through a puddle.

"Come on. It's cold and wet. You don't want to be out here do you? I sure don't." Avery throws the fabric out again and misses again. The dog doesn't cease its barking and growling, but it isn't lunging for her. It isn't attacking. It's backing up, terrified. Avery wipes freezing cold rain from her eyes. She's shivering now, too. The poncho is completely waterlogged and useless. They could play this game all night or, she could be bold for once in her passive, apathetic life. "I'm sorry, dog. I promise this is for your own good." She drops the poncho right on top of the dog, and scoops it up like potatoes in a gunnysack.

Chapter Three

AVERY AND THE TINY DEMON-DOG have a chat on their way to the only shelter out of the dozen she called that was still open this time of night and had space. "I found a place for you. I'm gonna let you out of this poncho, and you're gonna chill out, okay?"

The dog doesn't move or make a sound, so she takes that as a good sign and untwists the still-damp folds of fabric. The dog, to her immense relief, does not flip out. He shakes himself off, then stands shivering on the passenger seat, even though heat blasts from the vents. In the light of a streetlamp, Avery gets a good look at him. He's filthy; his black and white coat is grimy with dirt and motor oil. He smells like wet garbage. His ears are too large for his head, and one sticks straight up, while the other flops over at an odd angle, and his eyes are big and brown and look out in two wonky, bulging, opposite directions.

"Yeah, I still think you might be a gremlin."

Even if she wanted to keep the weird little thing, which she doesn't, she has no idea how she can keep a dog. She doesn't like them, or she thinks she doesn't like them. She certainly can't take care of a dog; she's not doing a great job of taking care of *herself* right now. A shelter is the best choice.

"Halfway Home" is the name of the rescue center. She enters a lobby bright with harsh white lights and white linoleum floors and a long gray desk off to one side. She tucks the dog against her chest and fills out a stack of paperwork. "Should I put 'dog' even if I'm only eighty percent sure?" she asks the front desk person, while the dog snarls and barks and thrashes in her arms like the possessed thing that he is.

The front desk lady does not respond. Avery hands the clipboard back, and the lady calls for someone to take the dog. Avery's mind is already on going home, wrapping herself in a blanket, and relaxing on the pile of pillows that make up her living room furniture now. She even has some ice cream left. So she's only sort of paying attention when the shelter worker reaches to take the dog. The shriek of rage and terror that the dog lets out makes Avery twist away and instinctively curl around him.

"Uh. Sorry I—It—Um—" Avery stutters.

"No problem." The woman smiles the most beautiful smile Avery has ever seen. Her name tag says "manager" and beneath that, "Grace." She picks up the clipboard with the paperwork Avery filled out with as much information about the dog as she knows, which is very little. "So he was a stray? It was really kind of you to help him, especially in this weather." She smiles again. *Grace.*

It dawns on Avery that she's supposed to say something in response, but she suddenly can't remember how to speak or move or do anything but cling to this terrified and funny-looking dog who keeps snapping at *Grace*: Grace, with dark, wavy hair pulled into a messy ponytail, and a smile that lights up her whole face and the entire sterile lobby and Avery's pathetic numbed heart.

Grace reaches for the dog again. He growls and lunges and starts a new round of hysterical, high-pitched barking. "If you wouldn't mind," Grace says, with her smile slightly dimmed, "I think I'll have you take him to a kennel, since he's so aggressive right now."

Avery nods, wills her feet to move, and trails Grace down a hallway lined with metal cages. Most of the cages hold small dogs, some who bark and some who cower and some who watch quietly with nervous, sad eyes. Grace opens an empty cage, and Avery deposits the dog inside. Her T-shirt is wet where she held him. It smells terrible too.

"Thanks for your help," Grace says, then pulls a pen from one of the pockets of her blue cargo pants. Her gray T-shirt reads: Halfway Home Animal Rescue and Rehabilitation. "More paperwork," she says with an excited, teasing gleam in her eyes. "Any ideas for a name?"

"Oh." Avery points to herself—how rude of her. "I'm Avery."

Grace laughs. It's even more beautiful than her smile. "I meant the dog. But it's nice to meet you, Avery."

Avery's face warms with a blush. "Oh. Um. I don't know. I found him at Rudy's Garage— "

"Rudy it is." Grace writes on a little card attached to the cage: Rudy. Chihuahua mix. Male. Stray. She gives him an ID number and marks the date of intake, then fishes a red pen from another pocket and puts an ominous red slash in the corner.

Avery points to it. "Um. What does that… Is that bad?" It seems bad.

Grace caps the pen. "It just means that he was initially aggressive so other employees and volunteers know to be cautious." Avery glances at the dog— At Rudy, who is doing a pretty good job of making that clear on his own. Grace laughs again, a husky little *hah*. "Yeah, pretty obvious, right? Barking doesn't always mean aggression, though."

Avery wants to find out what it does mean and she wants to know more about Grace and mostly she wants to see her smile again and maybe a million times after that, but Rudy has gone quiet in his cage, pressing himself against a back corner and trembling harder than ever. "What happens to him now?"

Grace's smile is sympathetic. "Tomorrow he'll have a health examination and then a basic behavioral assessment, and we'll go from there. He's in good hands, I promise."

Avery glances again at the red mark. "Okay."

As if reading Avery's mind, Grace adds, "Truly aggressive dogs…" She looks sadly at Rudy in his cage. "Are a bigger challenge," she finally says, diplomatically. And then she gently squeezes Avery's arm. "Don't worry. I like a challenge."

Avery's breath catches; she swallows heavily. "Okay."

"Okay." Grace says. Then her face draws tight. "You are freezing cold." She rubs her warm hand up and down Avery's arm and tugs her wrist. "Come with me."

Avery composes herself, then follows Grace down a different hallway, past larger kennels with larger, louder dogs, into an office that is as barebones as barebones can be with a plain metal desk, gray cement walls, gray cement floors, and a poster with a graph that reads: "Fundraising Goals." Only twenty of one hundred marks representing needed money are filled in. Grace tosses Avery a hooded sweatshirt with the shelter's logo.

"Oh. I can't—"

"Please take it," Grace says. "I'll worry about you catching pneumonia otherwise." Then she smiles, so Avery puts it on. It smells at first like the rest of the shelter, like animals. But as Avery zips it up she catches the sharp, sunny scent of citrus and wonders if it's the smell of Grace's shampoo. Avery tugs the loose sleeves down over her hands. It's too long, but snug on her chest; Grace is taller than her with a slim, muscular body. "Thanks," Avery says, looking down bashfully after Grace catches her staring just a moment too long.

"Sure. And thank you for helping Rudy; most people don't bother."

Any other day, Avery would have been one of those people. "Well, I should..." Grace cuts in, "Yeah. Right. Yes, have a great night." Avery waves awkwardly, hustles out of the office, and stops to say a quick goodbye to Rudy. He's in good hands. She is sure about that, though she hates that he's stuck in that cold cage, terrified and alone.

In the dark of her car on the drive home, Avery catches the whiff of dog on her poncho and citrus on the sweatshirt and she feels... She *feels*: warmth and excitement, concern and regret. She thinks about the man on the park bench with the kind eyes who told her to find joy. It's a flicker of possibility, of something that could be something. That's a start. Isn't it?

Chapter Four

AVERY BEGINS THE NEXT DAY with a renewed sense of purpose. She makes herself a balanced, healthy breakfast. She showers and puts on clean clothes that she did not find on the floor. And then she searches for job openings that actually spark her interest, instead of being merely tolerable like her last two jobs. She also washes and dries the sweatshirt from Halfway Home and goes back to the shelter to return it. She's holding on to that tiny spark of hope in her heart that perhaps there is joy to be found in the world and that maybe one hopeful bit of joy is named Grace.

"Uh, hello, Deb." Avery stands at the tall desk waiting for Deb's reluctant acknowledgment, just as she had last night, but now with a folded sweatshirt in her arms and not a terrified demon dog. She hopes he had an okay night, Rudy. "I'm here to see Grace."

"Grace is out on calls today," Deb says, brusquely. The rescue center is busy, with an adoption event filling the lobby and phones ringing off the hook.

"Oh. Okay, well, I wanted to return this sweatshirt—" Deb deposits it behind the counter. "... And if you could tell her Avery dropped by? She probably mentioned me. I saved a dog's life last night, no biggie." Avery all but dusts off her shoulders with pride; she actually *did* something, something that mattered.

"She didn't mention you. I'll give her that jacket, though. Have a nice day." Deb turns to address one of the many people waiting at the counter as the phone starts to ring again and two dogs bark at each other. And then, a flash of hope, Grace walks in. She's smiling and laughing just as she did with Avery, but with someone else. She doesn't even notice Avery.

Avery's ember of hope grows cold. Of course Grace wouldn't notice or mention her; Avery is one of thousands of people Grace interacts with here on a regular basis. Why would she remember Avery, of all people? Dejected, she heads home without even stopping to check on Rudy.

This is why, she reminds herself, now wrapped in a blanket and hunkered down as comfortably as possible on her living room floor pillows. This is why she doesn't bother, because hope leads to disappointment, which leads to despair, which leads to Avery being completely dramatic about a beautiful woman who smiled at her a few times. The doorbell rings. Avery answers it still wrapped in her blanket.

"Got a medium mushroom and green pepper."

Avery peers at the delivery guy from the hood of her blanket. "I ordered a large pepperoni." He double-checks his receipt and the address. "Says medium mushroom and green pepper." Avery sighs and reaches for the pizza with her blanket-covered hands. "It's fine. It doesn't matter." She plops the pizza box onto the floor and doesn't bother picking off the toppings. She hates mushrooms. It doesn't matter.

Her phone rings with an unknown number while she's searching for something to watch. It pings with a voicemail after she gives up and turns the TV off.

"Hi. Avery? This is Grace, from Halfway Home. I was wondering if I could ask you something. If you could call me at this number…"

Avery doesn't even finish listening to the message; she fumbles the phone to call back immediately, then kicks herself for so easily getting her hopes up over nothing, *again*. Just because Grace remembered her after all doesn't mean anything. When Grace answers, Avery pushes her expectations way, way down.

"Are you there? Hello?"

"Yes, this is Avery Puckett returning your call." She is, after all, accomplished in the neutral-but-pleasant corporate employee business tone.

"Avery, hi! Thanks so much for calling me back!"

141

Grace sounds so genuinely excited that Avery badly wants to respond in kind, but no. Friendly and sweet is Grace's necessary business mode; Avery needs to remember that. "Of course," Avery responds, mildly. "Was there something you needed from me? More paperwork?"

"Oh." There's a pause, then a squeak in the background as if Grace sat in the metal chair of the rescue's office. "Not paperwork, no. But it is about Rudy."

"Is he okay?" Avery responds, annoyed at the concern in her voice. It's just a dog and not even her dog. She doesn't care; she *can't*. "I mean. Is there a problem?"

"Sort of?" Grace hedges. "The thing is, he's acting about the same: aggressive and snapping at anyone who comes near him. It took three of us to hold him down just so the vet could look him over, and, for a dog who weighs eleven pounds, that's impressive." She laughs, and Avery is not strong enough to resist the musical sound, can't stop herself from imagining Grace's beaming, bright smile.

"I did think he was a demon at first," Avery says.

Grace laughs again. "He trusts you, though. So I could use your help."

"Oh. Really? Me?" Avery unwraps from her blanket cocoon.

"Absolutely," Grace says. "We have this program called 'Pen Pals,'" Grace explains. "A special volunteer comes by as often as they can, once a week if that's all they can manage, and they spend one-on-one time with our more difficult cases."

"Just, like, hang out with him?"

"Sure. Spend time with him. You have a calming presence that will really be good for him. And then I'll spend time with both of you to get him to a point where he can be adopted."

Avery barely hears what came after "*I'll spend time with you*" and, breathless and eager, says, "yes." She squeezes her eyes shut and winces. "I mean. I'll, uh, look at my schedule and check if I have some free time."

"Great! Thank you, Avery. Seriously, you're incredible." And there's that stupid flicker of hope again. She's never felt this giddy and excited around someone; it's ridiculous and bound to lead to disappointment. She has got to rein this silly crush in.

"It's— Yeah. I'll see what I can do."

She can hear the confusion in Grace's voice when she replies, "Okay. I will maybe see you around then, I guess."

"Maybe," Avery says, before hanging up the phone and pulling the blanket all the way over her head. She wasn't totally lying about being busy— She does need to find a job, and a couch, and to figure out how to be around Grace without acting like a besotted idiot. And she definitely needs more ice cream.

Chapter Five

AVERY SPENDS THE NEXT DAY putting in online application after online application and even cold-calling a few places. Dead ends everywhere. Job hunting is so demoralizing that she wants to retreat into her blanket cocoon. No, she should get out of the house. A change of scenery could do her some good. What she needs is a mall pretzel.

The mall isn't busy at all, to Avery's surprise. But it is a weekday, in the early afternoon when most people are working. Most people haven't been recently fired and have nothing better to do in the early afternoon on a weekday. Avery is surprised, too, at the Christmas decorations everywhere and the holiday music piped over the speakers in the food court. Is it that time so soon? She's always liked Christmas, but it only takes a few years of working through the holiday to start thinking of it as just another day, like all the other days that blend together as one long, slow, pointless slog through life. Same old crap, just with lights and tinsel.

Across from the food court, there is a Santa's Village going up: a snow-dusted North Pole with small workshop buildings and posed reindeer and a huge artificial Christmas tree. A woman with long, black dreadlocks and an ugly Christmas sweater rushes around, obviously managing the employees who are assembling the village. Avery finishes her soft pretzel and sweeps salt into a little pile. A packet of papers drops, scattering the salt pile beneath it. *Lutz Events: Making Magic! A leader in event programming.* Sprinkling salt like snow, Avery picks up the packet.

Would you like to be part of a magical experience?

Avery spots the woman in charge of the fake North Pole construction, who is busy dropping the applications onto other tables. Her criteria for hiring must be adults who have nothing better to do than be at the mall food court on Tuesday afternoon. Avery does need a job and doesn't want to go through the torture of job hunting. On the other hand, she isn't fond of kids or Christmas. But on the *other* other hand, she would be in daily proximity to the soft pretzel stand. Avery hops over miniature train tracks to address a man who is arranging huge teddy bears and gold-wrapped presents next to Santa's throne.

"Got a pen?" she asks.

As it turns out, the ugly, light-up, jingle-bell-festooned Christmas sweater is part of a uniform. It comes with a matching ugly, light-up, jingle-bell hat. Tracie, the manager with the dreadlocks, apologizes when she hands the uniform to Avery, along with forms to fill out and an employee handbook. She starts in two days, after the village is completed and her references are checked, so she does indeed have time to stop by the shelter the next day to see Rudy—and Grace.

"Can I help you?" At the front desk, Deb looks up at Avery as if she's never seen her. "Who are you?"

"Avery Puckett? Here to volunteer? Grace asked me?" With every question, Avery sounds and feels more unsure. Deb is right, who is Avery, anyway? How can she help a dog? She doesn't have any experience with dogs; she has no couch; she eats peanut butter directly from the jar and calls it dinner. And Grace will be able to tell what a mess Avery is right away and realize she made a mistake and ask Avery to leave, and that will be that. It's not worth the humiliation just to see Grace smile again. But, she doesn't want anything bad to happen to Rudy. She did go to all that trouble to catch him, ruining her third favorite poncho and everything.

Deborah hands her a clipboard. "Fill this out." Avery has filled in her personal information on so many forms lately she's starting to get existential about it. When Avery pushes the clipboard back to Deb, she tosses a volunteer badge onto the counter. "Tino will show you what to do."

Tino is a tall, brawny man with a tattoo of a tiger covering half of his neck, who is busy spraying the concrete floor of a large kennel with a high-powered hose. When he spots Avery he points the nozzle of the hose at her; water drips down his beefy arm and onto his scuffed combat boots. Avery steps back.

"You the new volunteer?"

Avery looks at the plastic badge clipped to her sweatshirt. She doesn't want to point out the obvious, because Tino is a large man who is pointing a high-powered hose at her face.

"Yes?"

Tino drops the hose with a sudden *clack*. Avery startles. "Come with me." He takes a still-jumpy Avery to the large kennels in the back. Rudy got an upgrade since she dropped him off; he's now in a large pen outfitted with a little, blanketless cot, metal food and water bowls, and a door flap to an outside enclosure. "He's been goin' after everyone," Tino says, gruffly. "Can't get near him unless you wanna lose a finger."

Avery starts to apologize, as if it's her fault Rudy hates everyone. She's particularly worried that Rudy has made himself an enemy of Tino of the tiger neck tattoo. But then Tino crouches outside the pen, pitches his voice high, and croons, "Poor widdle baby boy's so scared. Sweet angel boy, it's okay." Avery stares at him. Tino looks up. "You can go in."

"Yes. In. Right." She enters the pen, and Tino closes the door, latching the metal handle securely. Rudy is cowering in a corner, growling and baring his teeth and shaking like a leaf. He's even more funny-looking cleaned up and in the light of day. "Um," she says, standing stiff and awkward as Tino waits. "Hey... Rudy. Uh, how's it going?"

Tino narrows his eyes, seeming to clue in to the fact that Avery has no idea what the hell she's doing. Tino points to a clean patch of cement floor. "You sit down there, and I'll get some treats. He hasn't been eating, but maybe you can get him to."

When Tino leaves, Avery lowers herself to the cold, hard floor. She doesn't know what a dog expert would do, but if she were in this chilled, dark pen with all kinds of scary noises and gross smells and people poking and prodding her while she was already scared out of her mind, well— She'd probably just want to be left alone. So she doesn't talk to Rudy, doesn't call him over or touch him or tell him he's okay. When Tino brings the treats, Avery puts them down nearby and doesn't try to entice Rudy at all. She just sits with him. And maybe he can tell she's giving him space, or maybe he just needed a minute, because he does creep closer. After a while he's sitting near her—close, but not too close.

It's a start.

Chapter Six

GRACE APPEARS OUTSIDE OF THE kennel door; she crouches down, with a smile for Avery. Avery's heart flutters. Rudy barks and charges at Grace. "I know, I know." Grace stands, moving back, and Avery nearly reaches for her. "I'm glad you were able to come by," Grace says, after Rudy retreats to his corner and settles for growling at her.

"Not like I have anything better to do," Avery says. Grace's face falls, clearly disappointed. Avery may have overplayed her whole "cooly unaffected" vibe. "I mean," she tries, "I'm not just here because I have nothing better to do. I mean. I have things. To do. That I... Also... Want to do?"

Grace gives her an amused chuckle. "I need to make rounds, then I'll be back to help you, okay?" She stands, reaching up to pull her loose hair back in a ponytail. Her forearms and biceps flex with the movement; her T-shirt pulls up and tight across her stomach and chest.

"Sure, yeah, yep, yeah." Avery winces and snaps her mouth closed and then, for some reason, waves cheerfully until Grace is out of sight. She covers her face with her hands and groans. Grace is just a girl—a cute girl with the most beatific smile in the world and nicely toned arms, and she smells like sunshine and laughs like sunshine and overwhelms Avery completely.

Rudy is still in the corner, still trembling with just a bare cot and no blanket in his cold cement cage. "I'll go find you a blanket, stay here," Avery tells him, as if he can understand her or has any choice in the matter. Avery tracks Grace down at the row of kennels nearest to her office, where she's filling out a kennel card for a white-muzzled golden retriever lying at her feet.

"Oh, hey." Grace glances up. "I just have this intake to finish and then I'm heading back to you."

"Actually I was hoping to find a blanket..." The golden retriever sighs heavily and closes his eyes. He looks well cared for, not dirty and starving like Rudy looked when she found him. He even has a collar with happy little snowmen printed on it. "Is he lost?"

"She," Grace corrects, tugging the plastic shelter leash clipped to the dog's festive collar. "And no. She's an owner surrender. They're moving out of state." Grace clicks her tongue and says gently, "Come on, Pepper."

Avery follows Grace and Pepper's slow stroll to the large kennels. "Wait. They just left her? Just like that?"

Grace opens an empty kennel and guides Pepper inside, then bends down to pat her head. "It happens more than you think. I'm sure they had their reasons. On the plus side, we have a lot of information about her, so it should help get her adopted." She crouches down to hug and pet her, whispers encouragement, then closes the door and turns to Avery with a determined look. "I try not to judge." Grace's decisive tone and the determined set of her mouth makes it clear that she is now finished with the conversation. Pepper curls up on her shelter-issue cot and sighs. Avery's heart aches; she can't imagine how Grace does this every day. After giving Pepper one last glance, Grace claps her hands and strides down the hall to Rudy's kennel. "Shall we?"

Avery scrambles to keep up. "Grace, uh." When Grace throws a smile over her shoulder, Avery trips over her own feet. "Do you have any blankets?"

Grace stops at Rudy's kennel. "Why, do you need warming up?" Avery's mind supplies an image of Grace warming her up. "I'm kidding," Grace says with a laugh. "I know, he's cold. Unfortunately, we had a horrible flea infestation last summer and had to throw away all the bedding and..." She unlatches Rudy's kennel, then pulls another nylon leash from one of her cargo pockets. "We are completely out of funds, currently. Actually, behind on funds."

So that's what the chart was about. Avery clears her throat, finding her voice again. "And what happens if you don't get more funds?"

Grace's usual bright smile is strained. "Gotta be optimistic," she says, not answering the question at all. "Now, we are going to attempt to get a leash on this guy. Care to join me?"

They're completely unsuccessful at the leashing attempt, but Avery gets to spend nearly forty-five minutes in an enclosed space with Grace, listening to Grace talk about dog behavior, and some of the other animals that have come through these doors, and how every case, no matter the outcome, no matter how difficult, has made her more sure that this is her life's purpose. Forty-five minutes goes by in the blink of an eye, and Avery leaves the shelter certain that Grace is the most incredible person she has ever met.

Chapter Seven

IN A STROKE OF LUCK, Avery gets assigned to the Santa's Village cash register instead of wrangling sticky toddlers on and off Santa's lap. However, she had not counted on the endless dithering of parents who want a photo of their child screaming on Santa's lap for a bargain basement price and in sizes they don't offer as if Avery, the lowly cashier, is trying to grift people on behalf of her corporate overlords.

"If we get the largest photo pack, then we can give them to everyone as gifts," one dad points out, as Avery waits slumped against the register with her cheek smashed against her fist. They've been at this for a while, as the line stretches on behind him: a beast growing larger with every indecisive back-and-forth.

"But," says the other dad, "If we get the five-by-sevens like we said, that won't be enough. And how do we decide who gets the eight-by-tens? And the one eleven-by-fifteen?"

"Cage match," Avery mutters, not as much under her breath as she intended.

Both parents look at her and demand, "What?"

"I, uh…" Avery stands taller, then points out options on the display screen, yet again. "I said, you can add key chains to the five-by-sevens and make it even. And then keep the portrait size for yourself." Either they think that's reasonable, or else their kid incessantly kicking the cashier stand is finally irritating them, too, but they agree to Avery's suggestion and go on their way.

"Nice up-sell," Tracie comments between customers.

"Thanks," Avery says. She's sort of good at this gig, and it's even kind of fun sometimes. Too bad it's temporary.

When the line finally starts to dwindle, Santa takes his lunch break, and Tracie puts up a sign notifying everyone that Santa is off to "feed his reindeer." Avery finishes the last handful of parents waiting to purchase pictures, then takes her break, too. One of the "workshops" is the breakroom, which houses a card table and some folding chairs and a block of cubbies for employees' personal items. The man who plays Santa is inside, munching on gingersnaps and sipping a cup of coffee. He's authentic looking, that's for sure, with a real, snow-white beard and round, ruddy cheeks and a spot-on, jolly, *ho-ho-ho* laugh.

"No milk with your cookies?" Avery jokes as she sits across from him.

He winks at her. "If Santa's going to make all these children's wishes come true, he needs a little fuel." He laughs his Santa laugh.

It's a weird reply, and it's weirder still that's he's keeping up the Santa schtick in the employee breakroom. He must be one of those method actors, taking himself way too seriously. Avery pretends to be occupied by her phone, and eats her pretzel in silence until he leaves.

After she goes back to the register, Tracie bustles past, dragging a ladder. "Will you steady this for me?" She nods to Avery, who doesn't have any customers and spots Tracie as she climbs up to fix a garland that's come undone over Santa's throne.

"What are your Christmas plans, Avery?" Santa says.

Avery frowns. She doesn't remember introducing herself. He must have overheard Tracie. "Not much. I'm not a big Christmas person."

He looks heartbroken, then leans forward and directs his kind, twinkling eyes at Avery. "Now Avery, just because you've grown up doesn't mean you shouldn't celebrate. There's still plenty of joy to be found."

Avery whirls to face him, releasing the ladder. "What did you just—"

"Avery!"

She snaps back to attention just in time to stop the ladder from leaning dangerously to one side. "Sorry, sorry."

Tracie fixes the garland and makes it safely down, then Avery helps her carry the ladder away. A long line of excited children and frazzled parents starts to gather, so they hurry as much as they can.

"Where did you find that Santa?" Avery asks, stumbling backwards with the heavy ladder.

"Why, at the North Pole of course!" Tracie says, much too loudly for Avery alone, then purposefully glances behind Avery and juts her chin. Avery looks; the line has curved all the way around to the back of Santa's village, and little ears are listening to their conversation.

"Right. Of course! Where else but the North Pole?" Avery says, just as loudly. These kids will grow up and grow jaded like everyone else soon enough, but not because of Avery, not today. Back at the register, she tries to inject a little more holiday cheer into her cashiering.

Santa's Village shuts down before the stores do, so the mall is still busy with holiday shoppers when Avery grabs a food court dinner to go and walks on aching feet toward parking deck H. She passes by a store advertising "gifts for your pet," and, in the window, they have little fleece blankets on sale: two for the price of one.

The shelter is only open for emergency drop-offs by the time she gets arrives there; Avery doesn't think Grace works that late; she hopes Deb will at least be there.

"Can I help you?"

Avery squints at her. "It's Avery. Puckett. I volunteer here. I was just here working with Grace." Deb looks at her for a long, skeptical minute, then rummages in a drawer, and finally pushes Avery's volunteer badge across the counter.

Tino is in the back fixing a latch on one of the small kennels, but the shelter is hushed otherwise; most of the dogs are asleep on the cement floors of their cages or on those hard, bare cots. Avery stops by Pepper's cage first. Pepper heaves herself off the cot as soon as Avery enters, wags her tail and snuffles Avery's hands. When Avery squats to unfold one of the blankets, Pepper gently kisses her face. The blanket is blue with snowflakes; it matches Pepper's snowman collar. Pepper sniffs the blanket, then looks up at Avery with her warm, brown eyes as if to say thank you. Avery, for a moment, thinks seriously about taking her home.

"There you go," Avery whispers when Pepper settles back onto the cot with a heaving sigh. Avery rubs her soft ears and silky tummy. "You're a good girl. I'm sorry people suck."

Rudy cowers and shakes, as usual, and investigates the blanket only after Avery has moved back into the walkway. Then he sniffs it all over, climbs onto the cot, turns around in a circle five times, and settles in. "Two down," Avery says. Two blankets for two dogs out of all the dogs here waiting for a home. It doesn't seem like much; in fact, it doesn't seem like anything. An infinite number of dogs could come through the doors of Halfway Home looking for another chance at happiness. That is, if the shelter can stay open at all.

Chapter Eight

BRIGHT AND EARLY SUNDAY MORNING, Avery is back in Rudy's kennel, working on attempt number thirty-seven or so of trying to wrangle Rudy onto a leash. When she does finally get it around his neck, he throws himself onto the floor and writhes in agony. "See? Demon."

Grace laughs and continues to wait outside Rudy's kennel while he thrashes and flings himself around and yelps. "This is new for him, and it's scary. Just do what you normally do, and he'll be fine."

Avery observes the dog's hysterics and frowns. "What do I normally do?"

"You have a very calming presence. It's a nice balancing energy for someone who's more intense." Grace's eyes are soft and hold Avery's gaze long enough that Rudy's temper tantrum peters out. "Okay, now," Grace, steady and commanding, instructs quietly. "Stay calm and relaxed, just like you were before. Walk forward and give the leash a tug and, if he panics again, just stop and wait. Repeat."

Rudy's freak-outs get shorter and less violent with every attempt, and eventually he does walk with them to a wide outdoor pen that has a few toys scattered inside. "I'm hoping he'll feel less threatened in a neutral environment," Grace explains as she closes the gate behind her. Indeed, Rudy doesn't bark or charge at her. He does sit trembling in a corner.

"Come sit with me," Grace says, patting a spot next to her. "Let's see what we can make happen." She rakes her hair back into a half-ponytail; her back bows inward and the still-loose strands of her hair brush her neck. Avery swallows thickly and kneels. It's a waiting game then, hoping that Rudy will approach one or both of them for treats, hoping that he can trust them. If he can, maybe he'll find a home in time for Christmas.

Avery's usual laid-back demeanor is important, or so Grace says. Unfortunately, Avery's finding it very challenging to be calm when she's sitting close enough to feel the warmth emanating from Grace's body and smell the hints of Grace's citrus shampoo in the chilly breeze, and with the way Grace keeps glancing at her.

"Can I ask you something?" Grace says after a stretch of quiet minutes.

Avery heart thumps too hard. "Yes? I mean. Yes." Grace flashes a beaming smile, and Avery is now barely clinging to the panicked edge of calm, cool, and composed.

"You don't have to answer if it's too personal, but..." Grace pauses to form her question, tilts her head, and sucks in her bottom lip. Avery can't tear her eyes away until Grace says, "Do you not like dogs?"

Avery shudders out a breath; her shoulders sag. *Oh. That.* "I— Uh—" How to explain to this beautiful, kind woman who has dedicated her life to helping dogs that Avery finds them obnoxious? That the problem is really her, and not the dogs at all. "No, not really. Sorry."

Grace just smiles, though, a small, patient-seeming one. "Don't be sorry. I mean, the fact is, you're here to help him anyway." She pauses, then her face morphs into delighted surprise. She nods to Avery's left, then puts her finger against her lips. The only reason Avery can look away from Grace's fingertip pressed into the bow of her top lip is the surprising press of something cold and wet on her hand.

"Oh!"

Rudy flinches and backs away from her. Avery turns her hand over, opening her palm slowly and offering a toy. He sniffs the air, creeps closer, slinks back, creeps closer. Then he takes the porcupine toy from her hand and trots off to play, wagging his tail and romping around like a normal dog and not a terrified goblin demon.

Grace's grin is so wide and jubilant, and Rudy seems so happy, that Avery gets swept up in the moment, clapping and cheering and taking Grace's hand, forgetting all about her need to be cool and distant to save herself from disappointment.

156

"We did it!" Avery says.

Grace looks at their joined hands, and her cheeks bloom pink. Avery releases her hand immediately. They both speak at the same time.

"Um."

"It's o—"

"Just got excited—"

"I really don't—"

They stop speaking. Avery rubs at her neck, and Grace's cheeks grow a deeper pink. Rudy squeaks and squeaks the purple porcupine toy. Then the alarm on Avery's phone rings, startling them both out of the moment. "I have to get to work," Avery says, grateful for the excuse to escape this awkward moment. She's shocked at her own behavior; she never makes the first move—or any move. If that was even a move, which it wasn't, because Grace doesn't like her like that, Grace is just nice to everyone because she's nice. Avery scrambles to stand up and yanks open the gate.

"Okay. Bye."

"Wait!"

Avery pauses. Maybe Grace didn't mind holding hands. Maybe she wants to hold hands again. Maybe she wants to do more than hold hands, and Avery can find out if her lips are as soft as they look. "Can you help me get him back to his kennel? If you don't mind."

"Oh. Yeah. Yeah, yeah, yeah, yeah," Avery rambles, as if she's *trying* to make things even more awkward. They get Rudy back to his cage with only a few hysterics, and he goes right to his bed, exhausted from the effort of being calm and reasonable.

"Oh, hey," Grace says. "Do you know where that blanket came from?"

"Oh. I picked it up for him," Avery says, "Pepper too. They were on sale." It really was no big deal, but Grace gives her a warm look.

"So this may be a weird proposition…" Grace bites her lip, then smiles, then asks, "Would you maybe want to come by my place sometime later this week—"

"Yes," Avery interrupts, not needing to hear anything else.

"… and meet my dogs?" Grace finishes.

"Oh," Avery says. Right. "Sure that sounds… Sure." Or maybe she could get in her car, drive down I-40 until she runs out of gas, and start a new life, in which she doesn't keep embarrassing herself in front of Grace. "It's a not-date," Avery adds as she walks away, just to keep the awkward streak going.

Chapter Nine

Rudy, enticed by treats and the porcupine toy, makes slow and steady progress the rest of the week and grows braver bit by bit. Meanwhile, Avery has made progress in accepting her hopeless crush on Grace and sometimes even manages to be slightly normal around her.

"A shelter is tough for any dog," Grace says as she leads Avery and Rudy outside and opens the gate to the wooded property surrounding the shelter. "We do what we can to keep them comfortable. A dog belongs in a home, though." She shrugs, then glances down Avery's body and moves closer. "Here. Like this." Grace sidles up behind Avery and slides one palm up the curve of Avery's spine to straighten it. She takes Avery's arm in her other hand—the one holding the leash—and tugs it to hang loose at her side instead of clenched anxiously against her chest. "Calm and confident. He's insecure, so he's looking to you for assurance. If you feel safe, he'll feel safe."

Avery struggles to release a calm breath. Grace's close presence makes her feel many things: Heart-fluttering nervousness, yes, but the more time they spend together, the less that's true. She does feel safe with Grace. Still, being around her is exciting and exhilarating for Avery in a way that being with Mary Anne—or anyone—never was.

"That's good," Grace says, low and warm in Avery's ear. "Just like that."

Avery shivers. Step by step, they move forward into the quiet grove of pine trees. Rudy relaxes, freed from the kennel. He trots beside Avery; his giant, goofy-looking ears bounce. He's kind of cute, now that Avery is used to him.

"I just love taking walks in the woods." Grace sighs. In the chilly afternoon her cheeks are flushed, and her eyes are bright. She's beautiful, achingly so. Avery wants so badly to kiss her. Avery can't be imagining the chemistry between them, what if she makes the first move, just once? Avery stops, faces Grace, and steps forward. Rudy sprawls, content in a patch of sunlight. Grace smiles her brilliant smile. It's a moment of joy. This feeling, this warmth and brightness, this is what Avery's been missing.

"Grace, I—"

Grace's phone trills, shattering the silence of the woods. "Shoot, I have to go out on a call. Can you get him back by yourself?"

Avery feigns being unbothered. "No problemo."

Grace hustles off. Avery mentally kicks herself for saying *no problemo,* because it's not only a dumb thing to say, it's also her not being honest about her feelings, again.

Avery deposits Rudy in his cage and stops by Pepper's kennel to say hello. She's sleeping, as she so often is, but drags her weary, old body, tail wagging, to greet Avery. She may be "pen-palling" Rudy, but if there was ever a dog that could capture her heart, it would be sweet, gentle, gray-muzzled Pepper.

"'Sup, Avery."

"Oh. Hi, Tino." He's dragging a long folding table behind him. The horrible scraping noise of metal on cement causes a chain reaction of equally loud barking from the kennels. "Need some help?" Avery takes the dragging end, and they waddle it to the office and set it against one bare wall.

"Thanks." Tino rubs a spot on his arm that took the brunt of the table's weight. "Trying to get an adopt-a-thon going."

Avery remembers the one that had been going on when she first started coming by and how chaotic it was. "How often do you do those?" Rudy isn't ready for adoption yet. He hates everyone but Avery and Grace, and even Grace sometimes—soon though, maybe.

"Usually once a month, outside of the shelter as much as we can." Tino opens a drawer in the gray metal desk. "We have these pop-up events, adopt-a-thons in a box sorta. Just need a location and we're good to go. If we don't make our budget by the end of the year, we're toast. So we've been trying to do those more often." He pulls a stack of adoption forms from the filing cabinet. Avery glances at the poster chart keeping track of the funds needed with the very small amount of funds raised filled in. She nods at it. "That budget?"

"Yup." Tino's expression is not optimistic. "Toast."

Avery works that afternoon and evening. She's warmed up to the job, even finds it fun. It's hard not to get caught up in the exuberance of the kids, in the magic they can still see. Tonight, though, she's distracted. Tomorrow is her maybe-a-date, no, not-a-date, definitely not-a-date, but maybe it *could* be, at Grace's house.

During a lull, Avery plucks a candy cane from the oversized stocking hanging next to Santa's throne. "What do *you* want for Christmas, Avery?" Santa asks as she snaps off a pepperminty bite. What does she want? A couch. A permanent job she actually enjoys, love, happiness, peace on earth, a lifetime supply of vanilla ice cream. But mostly... What will happen to all the dogs at the shelter if they aren't adopted? What will happen to Rudy? To Grace?

"Is a miracle too much to ask for?"

Chapter Ten

AVERY HAS ONE DATE OUTFIT and, much like her one beige work blazer, it has a stain: spaghetti sauce on the elbow of her off-white blouse and the knee of her jeans that are too skinny for normal wear. This date with Grace is *not* a date. Even still, Grace deserves better than Avery's one spaghetti-stained date outfit. So she stands at her closet until she annoys herself enough to just pick already and finally puts on nicely fitted red jeans and a polka-dotted button-down she'd shoved in the back of her closet and forgotten about— too bright, too peppy. But tonight the outfit is perfect. Tonight Avery wants to be bright.

Moving on to the second stage of her pre-date, not-a-date prepping, Avery stands in front of the mirror staring hopelessly at her hair. If she stands there long enough, perhaps it will transform into glossy, tumbling waves. Stage three of her pathetic routine is trying and failing to put on makeup. Mercifully, her phone rings with an unfamiliar number.

"Hi, Avery. It's Tracie from Santa's Village."

"Yeah. Hey, Tracie." Avery scrutinizes herself in the bathroom mirror and frowns; maybe she should start over. "I hate to do this," Tracie says, "but I've got three of my Santa's elves out with the flu today. Do you think you can come in and cover a shift?"

She isn't going to Grace's until later tonight; work will be a welcome distraction from hours of aimless waffling. "Yeah, I can come in."

Tracie sighs. "Thank you. See you in a bit. Oh, and please do not make out with anyone on staff, I can't afford to lose more people."

Avery pulls a face at that, making out with the college-aged Santa's elves was not high on her list. "Uh, won't be a problem."

It's getting closer to Christmas, and the mall and Santa's Village are hopping. Avery soon finds that helping kids get to and from Santa Claus' lap is quite a bit more exhausting than running the cash register, even more so today with the smaller-than-usual staff. By the time she's off for the evening, she's dead on her feet and is running late to her date, not-a-date at Grace's house. Still, when she passes by the upscale store where she bought the dog blankets, Avery is drawn in by the promise of a forty-percent-off-everything, one-day-only sale. She buys as many dog blankets as she can afford, and, at two-for-one and forty percent off, it's a decent number, though still not enough. "You must know some cold puppies!" The woman at the cash register says, in exactly the sort of cheery, booming voice Avery expects of an upscale gift boutique worker in a suburban mall.

"It's for an animal shelter," Avery mutters, struggling to get her wallet out from beneath the drape of her ugly Christmas sweater. "I'm volunteering there." She hands her card over the counter.

"*Well.*" The boutique lady sets both hands over her heart and shakes her head. Avery works as a cashier, she doesn't mean to be annoying, but she's already running late, *come on.* She flicks the card with subtle impatience.

"Hold on." The lady strides into the storage room behind the checkout, and Avery grunts in frustration. She's officially standing up Grace now, her feet are killing her, and the lady behind Avery is making irritated noises, as if Avery is the one holding everything up. She just wanted to buy some dumb dog blankets.

"Okay. No charge." The manager bursts back into the store. "We're always looking for ways to give back to the community here at Sweet Chics Boutique." She places more blankets on the counter in front of Avery. "Happy holidays!"

"Oh." Avery blinks, overwhelmed with the store's generosity and her own guilt at being annoyed. "Wow! Thank you."

When Avery finally gets to the front door of the cute little house that's fully decked out in Christmas lights, she braces herself for Grace to be upset, and rightfully so. Grace answers the door beaming that bright, wide grin.

"You made it!"

"So sorry," Avery rushes to say. "I got called into work, and it took me longer to get out than I expected. I should have called. I suck; I'm sorry."

Grace tilts her head and frowns. "You don't suck. It's fine. Things happen." She glances down and tilts her head the other way. "Great sweater."

She's still wearing her blinking Christmas tree work uniform, including the matching pointy hat, which she snatches off her head. She forgot all about it. "It's for work— Santa. At the mall. Not really— Fake Santa, I mean. Obviously," Avery blathers.

"Well, I love it." Grace pushes the door wider and steps back so Avery can enter. "I *love* Christmas, as you can probably tell."

The house is cozy, with a fire crackling in a brick fireplace. It smells like evergreen and cinnamon; holiday decorations fill every wall and corner and nook. The little house is crammed so full of holiday cheer that it's impossible to take it all in. To top it off, four large dogs sit patiently in front of a picture-perfect Christmas tree as if posed for a holiday card.

Grace says with a laugh, "You look terrified."

"Um," Avery hedges. The dogs are wearing candy-cane-striped bow ties. A miniature train comes chugging across train tracks hung from the ceiling. "Coming from someone who's wearing a light-up Christmas sweater and works for Santa Claus: Yeah, it's a lot."

And Grace doesn't say, "You're such a wet blanket, Avery," or, "Why don't you ever like anything, Avery," the way Mary Anne did—and everyone she dated before Mary Anne. Grace, with her boundless, determined positive energy, beams at Avery. "See? This is what I need in my life. Someone sensible." She turns to Avery and lightly grips her elbow, which sends a thrill up Avery's arm. "You're such a mellow, calm spirit. That's why Rudy responds so well to you. Speaking of." Grace releases Avery's elbow and snaps her fingers— the dogs come right over.

The dogs. The reason Avery is here. "This is Ethel, Ricky, Fred, and Lucy."

Avery sort of… waves, unsure of what else to do. The dogs once again sit patiently, after a hand signal from Grace. "Hey," Avery says. "I like your names."

"They're very well trained, so I promise they won't jump up on you or sniff you in any unwanted places—" Grace sends Avery a cute wink that's likely supposed to help her relax, but most definitely does not. "You're doing so great with Rudy, trying so hard. But I can tell you aren't totally comfortable and I do want you to be comfortable."

"Comfortable…" Avery mumbles. At the moment, being comfortable with Grace is impossible, with her hopeless crush growing more intense by the minute.

"Are you hungry?" Grace asks, then adds without waiting for answer, "I have cheese and crackers and wine. If you want to sit, I'll be right back."

Avery sits on the couch while the dogs hang out nearby, curious but not bothering her. They all look to be mixed breeds: one with short brown hair and one with shaggy brown hair, one all white and another black but for a single white paw; Avery reaches toward the black one, and he gently sets his head beneath her palm.

"That's Freddy. Throw a ball for him and you've got a friend for life." Grace sets a tray on the coffee table and sits next to Avery. None of the dogs give the food a single glance.

"Four dogs," Avery says, stating the obvious. She stuffs a cracker and a cube of cheese in her mouth.

"Mmm," Grace covers her mouth as she chews. "I'd adopt more, but five would probably be the start of a hoarding problem for me." She takes a sip of wine, then leans back, draping her arm across the back of the couch behind Avery's shoulders. "I do have a cat, too. A huge Persian named Petunia who bosses the dogs around. You won't see her though; she likes to keep to herself."

Avery nods, considering that perhaps she could join Petunia in whatever dark corner the cat is hiding in. *Conversation, Avery.* She can do this. "Have you always—" Avery starts, trying not to choke on her cracker when Grace tucks her leg up on the cushions and leans closer. Avery stares at the crook of Grace's bent knee, trying to remember what she was asking. "Um. How did you get into animal rescue?"

Grace sips more wine; her lips against the glass are damp. "I grew up as a military kid. We were always moving, so it was hard to make friends. But that was okay because we always had the animals with us. I wasn't lonely or sad because of them. I guess, in a way, I was just trying to return the favor, and then I realized it had become a calling, like I know that's what I was put on Earth to do."

"That's— Wow," Avery says. "I wish I was passionate about something like that."

There's no mistaking the glance Grace casts at Avery's mouth. It lingers there, then comes up to hold Avery's eyes. "It's not too late."

Avery does choke then, a bit, and, needing several gulps of wine to move the stuck clump of cracker down her throat, finishes off the large glass. One of the dogs, the brown one with short hair, saunters over to investigate. Once she can breathe normally again, Avery gives her head a pat.

"Ethel is a caretaker. She doesn't leave my side if I'm sick." Grace calls the dog over; she rubs her face and ears as Ethel's tail wags. Avery wishes she had that kind of companionship, that kind of loyal, true love. As if she's unthawing with the help of the wine, Avery's awkwardness and self-doubt melt away. She *can* see herself having that kind of love, not settling for close enough, but finding something real. Finishing a second glass of wine, Avery finds that somewhere along the way she has ended up tucked tightly beneath Grace's arm. It's nice: her and Grace hanging out on this cozy couch, drinking wine, eating cheese. Suddenly she recognizes the couch, pats it, and smiles. "I had this very couch."

"Oh? What happened to it?" Grace says. "Don't tell me it fell apart. I can't afford a new one right now."

"Mm-mmm." Avery shifts even closer, drawn into the heat of Grace's body. "My ex took it when she moved it. Just—" Avery makes a swiping motion with her non-wine-glass hand. "Took it, even though we bought it together." Grace moves her arm away and into her own lap.

"Moved out? So you were living together?"

"Yep. And it's been a few weeks now. I guess I should get a new couch."

"A few weeks?" Grace moves away fully, making Avery tip to the side before she catches her balance. "So that's pretty major."

"Not really." Avery pushes herself up. Somehow things have gotten weird between them. She tries to fix it, clarifying, "We weren't that serious."

At that, Grace crosses her arms over her chest; her expression goes stony. Avery can tell, even from their brief time spent together, that expression means Grace is closing off to the conversation. "You weren't serious with someone you lived with?"

"Um." Avery picks at the couch cushion, unsure how to explain without making it sound even worse. "Yes?"

"Right." Grace says, short with her now. "Let's just take the dogs outside to run through some exercises. It's getting late, you should probably go soon."

Chapter Eleven

"MA'AM? EXCUSE ME?"

Avery blinks back into awareness, unsure how long she'd been zoned out while slumped over the cash register stand. "What?"

"I said," The woman juggling a squirmy toddler and fussing infant says tersely. "Are the photo packages really worth the price?"

It's Christmas Eve eve. She hasn't seen or spoken to Grace since their not-date that could have turned into a date-date until it went terribly wrong. Avery can no longer muster the energy to care about photo packages.

"Not really," she says flatly; her attention drifts and vision goes unfocused. "Just jump in and take a picture with your phone for free. What are they gonna do, put you in mall jail?"

"What?" The woman sputters as her baby begins to cry in earnest.

From behind her Tracie says, "Why don't you take a quick break, Avery?"

Avery shrugs. *Fine.* The baby was giving her a headache anyway. She wanders past the Orange Julius, the pretzel stand, and the massage chairs and keeps on moving. She isn't in the mood. She just wants this pointless holiday to be over.

"What's up with you?" Tracie finds Avery slumped over the breakroom table.

"Nothing," Avery says. "The world is garbage." Her words are garbled into the hard surface of the table. "The usual."

"Does this have anything to do with that girl you're always talking about? Grace?"

Avery lifts her head, scowling. *Always talking about?* She does *not.* "I don't always talk about her."

Tracie's mouth curls, and she crosses her arms. "Oh, you do so. 'Grace says most dogs' bad behavior is caused by people.' 'Grace wears cargo pants because she has seven different types of dog treats on her at all times.' 'Grace *loves* Christmas.' 'Grace *loves* dogs.' 'Oh my gosh, Grace said the funniest thing.' 'Grace—'" Tracie's arms drop, and her face seems sympathetic. Avery's expression must show exactly how shaken she is. Oh no, she's got it *so bad*. It's not just a hopeless crush, she's totally head over heels in love with Grace. That makes everything so much worse.

"You didn't even realize, did you?" Tracie asks.

"I— It's not— I can't—" Avery tries, then deflates and drops face down onto the table again. "We're just in different places right now. It's fine."

"Oh, Avery." The bells on Tracie's sweater jingle merrily as she walks over to Avery and places a kind hand on her back. "It's okay to care."

Avery shakes her head against the table; it smashes her nose sideways. "It's not just Grace. They're gonna close the shelter, and all those dogs won't have anywhere to go, and Rudy is still nuts but he's *trying*. I tried *so hard*, and it's just like, what was even the point?"

"I don't know. Sometimes trying is the point."

Avery frowns into the table and contemplates this. "Well, that is terrible."

"Yeah," Tracie says with a soft laugh. "I suppose it is. Too bad Santa can't just find them homes, huh? That'd be convenient."

Avery sits up so fast that Tracie jumps back.

"Wait, why can't he?"

Tracie glances around. "I know we work really hard to make all of this seem real, but you know that's not actually Santa, right?"

Avery flaps her hand at Tracie. "Yes, yes. I mean, an event with Santa for dogs. People take pictures with him like with their kids, but they bring their dogs instead. That's a thing, right? But a portion can go to the shelter. Oh!" Avery stands, knocking her chair backward in her excitement. "And we do an adopt-a-thon. The shelter does these pop-up ones. We could totally do it on short notice. A 'Home for The Holidays' kind of thing, right? People love to do charitable stuff on Christmas, right?"

Tracie hesitates; her eyes scan Avery's face. Avery presses her hands flat together, tucks them under her chin, and gives Tracie her best pleading smile. If things are hopeless with Grace, at least she can give Rudy, the other dogs, and the shelter a fair shot at some hope.

Tracie relents, tentatively warning, "I'll have to talk to a few people—"

Shocking them both, Avery cuts Tracie off with an enthusiastic hug. She is not dead inside. She is *not*.

It takes a lot of fast-talking and finagling, of quickly working out logistics and the possible promise of someone's firstborn, but the "Pet Photos with Santa and Halfway Home Adopt-a-Thon Extravaganza" is a go on Christmas Eve. Dog crates stack up behind Santa's Village, volunteers mingle with customers, pampered pets and shelter dogs take turns getting photos with Santa. It's happening. They're really pulling it off.

And then there's Grace, arriving at the mall to coordinate volunteers and wrangle dogs. Avery swallows her disappointment and sets aside her feelings.

"I guess a mall isn't the ideal venue," Avery apologizes when Grace has to yank a dog away from passing shoppers who are uninterested in the event. If Christmas Eve isn't crazy enough, some people hate the mall on not-crazy days.

"Are you kidding?" Grace says. "Santa Claus, soft pretzels, and massage chairs? I *love* the mall."

"I think we're soulmates," Avery mumbles, just as the shepherd mix Grace is wrangling lets out an exited bark.

"What?"

"What?" So much for setting her feelings aside. "I said, uh. Great turnout!"

"Oh, yeah. This was such a great idea, Avery." She smiles her huge smile that turns Avery to goo. There's no time for all that. More dogs need to see Santa, and Avery needs to get back to taking donations and ringing up pictures.

Not only is the turnout great for pet photos with Santa, but people are also extra-generous on the day before Christmas, or else just desperate for a not-awful last-minute gift. They're stuffing the donation jars with bills and checks and picking dogs for adoption at a fast clip. They just may save the shelter and get every single dog chosen in time for Christmas morning.

"Someone wanted to say hi you." It's Grace again, approaching the cashier stand where Avery has been completely focused on staying calm in the chaos.

"Pepper!" Avery crouches to wrap her arms around Pepper and press her cheeks against Pepper's silky-soft neck. "How's my good girl?" Avery hopes the day hasn't been too tiring for the old girl.

"Great news," Grace says as Avery stands back up. "Pepper found a home." Grace indicates an older couple standing just to the side. They wave, and Grace calls them over.

"Oh that is... Wow. That is great." Avery reaches down to pat Pepper's head. "You're going home, Pepper!" For some weird reason, Avery's voice is strained, and her eyes water. "Sorry, I don't know what I'm—" Avery swipes at her eyes and sniffs. Pepper is going home, which is amazing. And that also means that Avery will never see her again. Avery gives Pepper one last pat, crouches, and tells her she's such a good girl and that now she gets to have a soft bed again.

And then she's gone.

"I see a lot of really awful things happen to dogs," Grace says, kindly allowing Avery to compose herself. "You'd think that would be the hardest part, but it's not. This is. You know they're going to a good home; it's exactly what you've been working for. But it breaks your heart." She hugs Avery, a solid, strong embrace that she soaks up like parched earth. When Grace pulls back, her eyes scan Avery's face, and she presses her lips flat, then takes a deep, steadying breath. "Avery. About the other night—" Suddenly, a familiar frantic, high-pitched bark rings out. Grace laughs, looks away and drops whatever she was about to say. "It sounds like it's Rudy's turn to sit with Santa."

Chapter Twelve

IT HAPPENS SO FAST. AVERY has only turned halfway around after
setting a very nervous Rudy on Santa's lap for a lightning-fast picture
when there's a yelp—then a gasp and a shout and a scuffle. Avery turns
back to see blood and snarling sharp teeth. Someone yanks Rudy away,
and someone else gives Santa a paper towel, and Avery rushes to follow
him to the breakroom workshop, apologizing in a frantic stream of
babbling. "He's just so afraid of everything. Oh, god. I'm so sorry. I'm
so, so sorry. He's not a monster, really. Or a demon. Even though he
kinda looks like one? He's just afraid and he lashes out. I am *so* sorry."

"Avery." Santa uses his non-bloody hand—*oh, god*— to pat her
shoulder. "It's okay. Barely a scratch, really."

"You're bleeding," Avery points out, still panicked. "He bit you!"

"It's not the first time. Occupational hazard." Santa *ho ho ho's.*

"But—"

Santa gives her shoulder a steadying squeeze. "There's a first aid
kit next to the cubbies. Why don't you help me clean up and put a
bandage on?"

Avery nods and goes silent. She finds the first aid kit and latex gloves,
cleans Santa's hand with an alcohol wipe, dabs on antibiotic ointment,
and carefully secures a wad of gauze to the puncture wound right below
Santa's thumb. There's a knock on the door as Avery is putting the
items back in the metal case; her hands shaking just a little less. Grace
appears in the doorway.

"Just wanted to let you know we're all packed up and heading back.
Every dog was adopted, except for…" Grace pauses, then smiles sadly,
and that's enough to tell Avery exactly who didn't get a home; his teeth

marks are in Santa's left hand. "We raised easily three times what we usually do at an adoption event."

"Was it enough?" Avery asks. "Did we save the shelter?" Grace's face once again says all Avery needs to know. "Of course it wasn't."

Grace steps closer. "Avery..."

She doesn't want comfort or platitudes. She doesn't want to hear that they tried their best and that's all that matters, because it's not true. Trying won't save the shelter. Trying won't save Rudy. "What will happen to him?"

Grace presses her lips flat, and casts her gaze away from Avery. "I will try to do everything in my power to help him."

"And if you can't?"

"I don't like the situation any more than you do, Avery." Grace replies. "I'm not in charge of these decisions. I have to follow protocol."

Avery's jaw tightens "Which is?"

Grace sighs. Her expression is stony, but her eyes are sad. "Sometimes aggressive dogs have to be put down." She glances to Santa and back. "Especially if they've bitten someone."

Avery's stomach lurches; she turns away. "Okay."

Grace steps forward. "There's still a little time. We– We can try some other things with him, maybe."

Avery stares at the floor and shakes her head. "There's no point. It's over."

Grace leaves. Rudy is gone. Things can't be fixed with hope alone. She tried so hard, with Rudy, with this adopt-a-thon, with Grace. All it did was hurt and disappoint her. She'd be better off numb.

"What was your favorite Christmas, Avery?"

Avery stares at him blankly, so twisted up in her own head she forgot that Santa, whoever he really is, was there. "My what?"

"Your favorite Christmas. Just one."

They always travelled somewhere, usually to somewhere warm. It was nice enough. "They were all the same. Nothing special."

"Really?" Santa gives her a knowing look. He's angling at something, but she doesn't want to talk to him, or anyone, right now—maybe ever again. But he did suffer a dog bite without complaint—or a lawsuit—and it was her fault, sort of, so she probably owes him a conversation, at least.

There was that year when she begged to go somewhere with snow as if she'd gotten it into her head that it wasn't really Christmas without snow on Christmas morning. "Well, this one Christmas we rented a cabin in the mountains. It snowed the whole time—this perfect fluffy snow. Not like the ice and freezing rain crap we get in February around here. I got to go sledding and make cookies with my grandmother and hang out with all of my cousins. Everyone actually got along the whole time. I got a Furby! Remember those?"

Santa gives a hearty *ho ho ho.* "I do remember those."

Despite her sullen mood, she smiles at the memories. She hasn't thought about that year in so long. "We built the perfect snowman. And then sang Christmas carols. Just like a cheesy holiday movie. But then, on the way home, my parents argued in the car the whole way. My Furby broke. Then the car broke down, and my parents argued on the side of the road. So that ruined it."

"Why?"

Avery squints at him. "Why what?"

"Why did that ruin it?"

"Because," Avery says with an incredulous laugh. Isn't today proof positive that everything always gets ruined? "Nothing good lasts! It just tricks you into happiness and then goes back to being awful again." She holds up a finger. "But I figured it out. If you're never happy *or* unhappy, then nothing ever hurts."

"Hmm." Santa strokes his beard. "Do you find that to be true?"

Avery opens her mouth to say *of course I do* but it sticks in her throat because the truth is that she's been unhappy for a long time, except for this last month or so, up until it all went wrong. "No," Avery answers, truthfully. "It still hurts."

Santa nods, adjusts his hat, and turns to leave, saying as he goes. "All we have are moments, Avery. Good and bad. Hold on to the good moments. Joy is out there, you just have to go and find it and hold on to it. Just like that one perfect Christmas." Avery tips her head and takes a good long look at this so-called Santa Claus. She's heard that sentiment somewhere before—

"Avery," Santa says, interrupting her thoughts before they can get very far. "Don't you think there's some joy you should be going after right now?"

Chapter Thirteen

IN THE DARK OF THE shelter's parking lot, Avery takes several bites of morale-boosting vanilla ice cream and waits in her car for the right moment. The lot is empty except for the truck used for stray-dog pickups and Deb's car. Grace is not there. But Avery isn't there for Grace. Deb appears in the lonely yellow glow of the shelter's door, locking up for the night; it's now or never. Avery races to the front door, getting there just before the last deadbolt slides into place. "Just one quick thing!" Avery says through the glass. Deb's face pinches with clear annoyance, but she does open the door.

"I have a last-minute donation, wanted to get it in before Christmas." Avery tries to scurry past, but Deborah shoves a clipboard at her.

"Name and donation amount?"

Avery blinks, incredulous. *Seriously, still?* "Avery. I am *Avery*."

Deb scribbles the name. "Avery…"

"How about I save you the trouble and drop the donation off in the back office myself," Avery says, already walking away. She ducks around the corner, calling, "Just finish up what you were doing; pretend I'm not even here."

The shelter is quiet and empty, eerily so. All of the dogs but Rudy are in homes, and, with the shelter's closing eminent, no new dogs have come to fill the kennels. What will happen to them, the dogs who need this halfway point to get another chance at a happily ever after? Avery reaches the office, determined to complete just this one mission. She can't save every dog, can't save the world, but she can do something. She can try.

The donation chart in the office has been filled in to reflect the amount earned at today's Santa fundraiser. The meter is noticeably higher, yet still far from the goal. Avery pulls one-hundred-and-fifty dollars from her coat pocket, all of her Christmas money from her family, plus the little bit she set aside from her paychecks to get a couch. It's not enough to make up the difference in the amount needed, not by a long shot, but it's not a donation, so it doesn't matter how short the amount falls. This money is for an adoption fee.

Searching the filing cabinet until she finds the folder of adoption forms, Avery fills one out quickly and attaches the cash with a paper clip. She hopes it's enough to absolve her from what is technically dognapping. Creeping in the dark to Rudy's kennel, her heart races, her footsteps echo, the kennel door screeches open. *No Deb.* No one to there to stop her. Of course, Rudy greets her with his usual frantic yapping. She shushes him and slips inside, then crouches at his cot.

"If you can understand anything I say at all, please let it be this," she whispers, shaking out his blanket and covering him completely. "Zip it," she tells him. "Not a sound." Clutching the blanket-bundle to her chest, Avery walks at a steady, non-suspicious, confident pace out of the kennel, around the corner, past the office, almost to the lobby, just a little farther—

"Avery."

She winces at the deep voice calling her name and turns around. Rudy squirms in her arms. "Oh, hey, Tino!" she says, wincing at how fake-cheerful she sounds. "I'm gonna take this blanket home and wash it. Um. For Rudy? Because. It smells. So."

Tino looks rightfully unconvinced. He says nothing and doesn't move, just stares at Avery while her heart pounds so hard she's sure it must be audible in the quiet between them. Tino stretches his arm out to Avery, as if to take Rudy away, then he opens his palm. In his hand is Rudy's favorite squeaky purple porcupine toy. She takes it, then Tino nods. Avery nods. For a moment, standing in the dark of the shelter, they're two outlaws doing what needs to be done. Then Tino calls out to Deborah, "Deb! Go on home. I'll finish locking up."

If Avery weren't hoping to kiss someone else soon, she'd plant one right on him. "*Thank you,*" she whispers. Tino winks, giving her the all-clear.

She drives to Grace's house next, even more anxious than she was about staging Rudy's escape. "Just be glad you don't have to date," she tells Rudy, scooping out a bite of drippy ice cream. "You'd be dead inside after a while of that too." Avery holds out the ice cream lid for Rudy to lick. Can dogs eat ice cream? It's probably fine. "See? Who doesn't like vanilla ice cream, right? It's like all other ice cream owes vanilla its existence. Rocky road. Cookie dough. Moose Tracks. Cookies and cream." Rudy looks plaintively up at her, so she sets the now-empty carton down on the seat for him. "Okay, yeah. I'm stalling."

Covering him with the blanket again, Avery cuts the engine, promising to be back quickly before the cold seeps in, then runs up Grace's driveway before she chickens out. Grace answers with two of her dogs at her heels.

"Hi," Avery says, clouds of steam puffing out as she speaks. "Sorry to drop by."

"It's okay, I'm glad you did." Grace smiles, and Avery shivers.

"I um, had a weird, yet inspirational, talk with Santa. I mean not real Santa. I don't think he's real; you know what I—"

Grace laughs. "I get it, yeah."

Avery exhales a cloudy breath. "Okay. The thing is, I've been settling for feeling nothing because it was safe, or I thought it was, but I don't want to feel numb anymore. Even though my nose and fingers do actually feel numb right now." She rubs at her nose. It's so cold; she has to wrap this up and get back to Rudy. "I just wanted to tell you that I really, really like you a lot. Like I haven't liked anyone as much as you… ever, actually. Yes, including the person I lived with because— because I was afraid to speak up and say how I really felt. But I'm not anymore. Grace, meeting you was fate. And I don't even believe in fate, but I don't know what else it could be. If you need time, then I can give you time. But this is real, and it's worth the risk to me." Avery turns and jogs down the steps, not giving Grace a chance to respond. She said what she had say, she did what she needed to do and she's proud of that, whatever happens or doesn't happen. "Merry Christmas, Grace."

Grace calls her name, just once, soft and hesitant. Avery doesn't turn. The timing isn't right, and that's okay. It will be. Avery tucks this moment away, an ember warm and steady in her chest: hope.

Chapter Fourteen

AVERY WAKES CHRISTMAS MORNING WITH her legs pinned under eleven pounds of stubbornly snoring mutt. It turns out that Rudy, once off the streets and freed from the pound, is extraordinarily lazy. As soon as they got back to Avery's apartment, he immediately curled up under the covers on Avery's bed and hasn't budged other than shifting positions a few times. So far, he's the best roommate she's ever had. They don't have anywhere to be today, Christmas morning, so Avery nudges Rudy off of her legs to shift her sleeping position; he grunts and resettles by her hips, and Avery curls around him. When her phone rings some time later, she yawns and reaches blindly behind her, squinting one eye open to hit the answer button, then closing it again as she says, "Hi, Mom."

"Merry Christmas, honey! Wish you were here!" *Here* is Key West, a favored holiday retreat.

"Merry Christmas," Avery replies sleepily, and, for the first time in a very long time, means it when she says, "I wish I was there too."

"Well, I hope you're not alone anyway," her mom says. It sounds as if they've arrived somewhere, with a sudden whip of wind crackling through the phone.

Avery gives Rudy a pat on his head. "I'm not," she says. "Not alone."

In the background now, Avery can hear water splashing, the excited chatter of tourists, and an unintelligible loudspeaker announcement. "We're getting on the glass-bottom boat now, chat later? We love you, honey!"

Avery promises to join them next year and smiles as she imagines Rudy on a boat somewhere warm and tropical, wearing a little doggy life jacket, soaking up the sun, and barking at everything. He'd probably love being somewhere warm in the winter. They doze again until Avery gets another call, this time from Tracie.

Avery sleepily answers, "Isn't Santa back in the North Pole getting ready for next year by now?"

"Ha," Tracie says. "I think Santa's gone back to being a retiree."

"Mmm, that's the life," Avery says, as if she hasn't been in bed all day.

"Actually, speaking of the off-season, I am calling to offer you a job. Aside from Easter and Christmas, the company provides costumed characters for festivals and parades and birthday parties, fun stuff like that. And we need a coordinator, someone who makes sure everyone gets where they need to be and everything goes to plan."

"And you want me for that? Really?"

"Yes, Avery." Tracie's tone is firm. "You're cool under pressure, you're a hard worker, and you really try to make the best of any situation. *Usually*. I think you'd be a great asset… If you're interested."

Is she interested, or is she just agreeing to something that's falling in her lap? "Actually, yes. I am interested. It sounds really fun, and like something I'd be good at. So, yes."

"Great. I will send you the paperwork," Tracie says.

"I look forward to it."

She's just closed her eyes again when the phone rings for a third time. She groans, grabs for the phone to see who it is, then sits up, wide awake. Rudy lifts his head. "Grace? Hi. I, um. I wasn't expecting to hear from you. Hi."

Grace hums warmly. "It's been a day full of surprises for me too."

"Um?" Is Avery's confused response.

"I was hoping…" Grace starts, "Can you come to the shelter? I hate to ask on Christmas, but maybe you can clear up some stuff for us."

Avery's stomach churns. She's in trouble. They found out about Rudy, and she has to give him back, and they want to charge Avery with dognapping. "I left money!" She protests. "I left— I had to— I couldn't—"

"Avery. Relax." Grace's commanding, assertive tone halts Avery's nervous babble. It also sends a thrill down Avery's spine and spreads warmth across her belly. Grace continues, "Why don't you come in and we'll clear up what happened, okay?"

Before heading to the shelter, Avery takes her time walking Rudy and feeding Rudy and struggling to dress Rudy in the Christmas sweater she bought at the pet store when she stopped in to buy him food last night. Then, of course, she has to send a picture of Rudy in his sweater to her family—and one of the two of them, which she saves as her phone background.

In the shower, Avery practices what she'll say to stand her ground. "I filled out the paperwork. I paid the adoption fee," she tells her shampoo bottle. "I know you said you'd do everything you could, but he's mine. He's been mine from the very first moment in the rain when I almost ran him over. I needed to do something…" She shakes her head; that's not quite right. "No. I finally did what I should have done a long time ago."

The roads are nearly empty, so Avery makes it to the shelter in record time. She gives herself one last pep talk in the vanity mirror and strides purposefully into the lobby with her speech ready on her lips.

Inside there's… a party?

"Avery!" Deb sweeps her into a hug as soon Avery steps inside, to Avery's immense bewilderment. She pulls back to hold Avery at arm's length, beams at her, and says, "I can't believe you did this!"

"Yeah, me either." Avery glances around once Deb releases her. The shelter's lobby has been decorated for Christmas, with lights and garlands strung across the ceiling and the front desk, red and green stockings stuck onto the wall, and a little tree tucked in one corner. "Wait, I— Avery starts to explain the mix-up, but she's interrupted by Tino.

"I knew you were sneaky, man, but this is next level!"

"I didn't—" Avery says, then she's interrupted by Grace. Her hair is in loose waves, and she's wearing a worn thermal shirt and soft flannel pants as if she'd come here fresh from bed. Her eyes are bright, and her smile is impossibly brighter. Avery's heart clenches at how beautiful she is, and, as much as she wishes she could take credit for decorating the place so festively—because she so badly wants to be the person who makes Grace smile like that—it's not true. Avery swallows and looks away.

"Grace, I didn't do this." She gestures around the lobby.

"What? Oh, no! No, I decorated. Would you believe that I have even more Christmas decorations in storage because they wouldn't all fit in my house?"

Avery glances up to give her wry grin. "Yes."

"Well," Grace says with a chuckle. "I'm glad, because of course we had to celebrate the shelter staying open!"

Avery's face shifts through several stages of confusion. "Wait, the shelter is staying open?"

"Yes, because of you!"

"My adoption fee for Rudy was all you needed?"

Grace's expression goes on the same journey of confusion that Avery's did. At least they're both confused, and it's not just Avery being dense. "Okay, you adopted Rudy. That clears that up. Tino was being really cagey about where he went." She seems relieved, then confused again. "I'm talking about the huge anonymous donation you made?"

Avery flounders for a response and finally comes up with, "No?"

"So you didn't..." Grace crosses the lobby to duck behind the front desk and comes back with a snow globe that has an envelope attached to the bottom of it. "Deb said you came by last night with a donation." She holds up the envelope. "This isn't it?"

"No. I came here to bust out Rudy— I mean, adopt Rudy through the appropriate legal channels that definitely won't get me in trouble. I left enough money for that."

Grace tilts her head, says, "Huh," and pulls a small card and a check from the envelope. "Maybe you know who did leave this, then?"

The card is simple; white with a fancy gold border. In the center is a note: *A moment of joy* in calligraphy. The check is more than enough to keep the shelter open another year. It is signed, but the ornate script is difficult to read. Avery turns it to the side, squints, and turns it to the other side. "I think that's an *S*."

Grace points to the last name. "That might be a *C*."

S.C.

Avery's attention is drawn back to the snow globe. *It's a cabin,* she realizes, *a cabin in the snow on Christmas morning.* She gives it a shake so the snow falls over the cabin, feeling a little woozy. *Could it be? No. That's insane.*

A moment of joy.

"Avery? Any ideas?"

She shakes her head to clear it, trying to think of something, anything, other than, *I've gone insane, and Santa Claus is real and also loaded, apparently.*

Grace says, mostly to herself while Avery has a momentary crisis of reality. "Just a random anonymous donation, I guess. I wonder how they got in. We need to beef up security big time. Unless people want to break in and leave fat checks, then who am I stop—"

"Donation!" Avery blurts. Grace stares at her open-mouthed and mid-sentence. "I, uh. The shop. The blankets? The shop that donated the blankets? What were they called? Sweetie? Sweets. *Sweet Chics.* I bet they did it."

Grace thinks, then nods. "That makes sense. Yes."

Her definitive conclusion makes Avery feel a million times better. Of course it was the shop. Of course it wasn't... that's impossible... She glances at the snow globe again before handing everything back to Grace. They stare at each other awkwardly, then look away from each other awkwardly. Now that the mystery is solved, and Avery isn't going to jail for dognapping, she can only think of the night before, when she told Grace in no uncertain terms that she liked her and wanted to be with her. And now here she is. And there Grace is.

From behind them, Tino bellows with laughter, and Grace clears her throat. "I'm just gonna..." She shuffles to the desk. Avery could join Tino and Deb and the other volunteers at the impromptu party. She planned to hang out with Rudy today, though. And maybe Grace would rather she left now.

"Avery? Would you mind coming with me?"

Grace hesitates at the doorway to the back, then leads Avery into the office, where she notes the adoption form and cash with a pleased quirk of her mouth. "Filled out the appropriate paperwork and everything." She's unusually shy and hesitant as she retrieves something from a desk drawer, tucking whatever it is behind her back and looking at her feet. "Um." Grace nibbles her bottom lip, then looks up at Avery from beneath her lashes. "I was planning on going to your place and making this big gesture, but you beat me to it." She holds out a red envelope and pulls her lip between her teeth.

Avery opens the envelope and immediately tears up. "Oh! Pepper!" It's a photo of Pepper, sitting serenely next to Santa Claus on the day of the adoption event. There's also a card with a golden retriever wearing reindeer ears, and inside Grace has written: *I'm sorry. Give me a second chance?*

"I was going to write 'do you like me back; check yes or no.'" Grace's cheeks darken with a blush. Her face turns more serious. "Avery, I like that you're mellow and laid-back and I shouldn't have gotten angry at you for being yourself. It was my insecurities that were the problem, not you. I talk this big game about being able to let go so easily when these dogs find their happiness somewhere else, and then I find someone I like so much and I was so afraid that you would disappear and just move on to the next person that I couldn't deal with it."

Heart racing, Avery forces a poker-face, and asks, monotone. "Do you have a pen I could borrow?" Grace stares at her. "Never mind, here's one." Avery snags a pen from the desk, hunches over, draws a little empty box, writes "yes" over it, and marks it with a check mark. "Here you go," she says, handing it back to Grace. "Official forms are very important."

Grace glances at it, then launches herself into Avery's arms and plants a hard, eager kiss on Avery's lips. Avery pulls her closer, tilting her head and parting her lips until they fit together just right. "Merry Christmas, Avery."

Avery lifts her hand to trace the curves of Grace's beaming, bright smile: the smile that changed everything one dreary hopeless night, bringing Avery a joyfulness she'd forgotten. A moment of hope, a moment of joy. A moment of grace.

THE END

About the Author: Lilah Suzanne has been writing actively since the sixth grade, when a literary magazine published her essay about an uncle who lost his life to AIDS. A freelance writer from North Carolina, she spends most of her time behind a computer screen, but on the rare occasion she ventures outside she enjoys museums, libraries, live concerts, and quiet walks in the woods. Lilah is the author of the Interlude Press books *Spice, Pivot and Slip,* and the Amazon bestselling Spotlight series: *Broken Records, Burning Tracks* and *Blended Notes.*

Shelved

Lynn Charles

900 History

HEAVY BLUE-GRAY CLOUDS AND A bitter wind propelled Karina Ness into the library. On days like this, when most people hunkered down with a blanket and cup of tea, Karina preferred to begin here. The paycheck didn't hurt either. Rows upon rows of handheld fantasy worlds, tales of ordinary and extraordinary lives, brightened the darkest of days and lightened the foulest of moods.

As she prepared the circulation desk for opening, soft snow began to fall—a sure sign of autumn's departure into winter. By the time she unlocked the door to let patrons in, the ground had a light covering of wet snow. Huge flakes dotted Mrs. McCallister's navy coat as she shuffled in the door. They balanced on the tips of little Emma Raman's coal black eye lashes as she slipped her books into the return slot one by one by one.

"I'm gonna build a snowman after lib'ary time, Miss Karina!" Emma said, as she scooped up her now-empty bag. "Or maybe a snow *dog*!"

Karina voted for the dog and suggested tortilla chip ears, much to Emma's delight. Mr. Foster arrived and took his seat in the computer room to begin his daily hunt for World War II photographs. Karina never could get him to share what he did with the photos once he found them, if he did anything at all. If it was a slow day, she would sit next to him and listen to the same two stories he was willing to share: the one about the pretty woman at the bar in Germany who would slip him a free pint on Saturdays, and the one about the prettier woman who waited for him at home.

As a child, her father had tormented her about her love of books, telling her she'd end up a lonely old maid librarian. "Your nose in a book and your head up your ass," he'd mutter in the midst of a rant about her uselessness. He reminded her more of Mr. Wormwood, the horrible father in *Matilda*, than any sensible father should.

He never understood that librarians were heroes. They listened and never judged. Librarians helped find answers to the questions that sometimes kept Karina up at night as she grew into an adult: Why does my father hate me? Am I really a lesbian? What are the literary differences between Emerson and Thoreau?

They helped her believe, in spite of her father's awfulness, there was nothing she couldn't do. With that belief, she studied English at State and now worked toward her master's in library science.

She would be another young girl's hero.

During school breaks, she worked here, at Piedmont County Library, serving the two cities in the largely industrial county, Linden and Harding. While frustrations existed with the old-school director and administrators, she delighted in doing for the town's more curious population what the librarians of her childhood had done for her.

On this snowy late November morning, she was halfway through shelving fiction when she scented a newly familiar cologne. She slotted the last of the James Patterson books between "How many?" and "Books Do You Write?" and peeked around the corner. It was the third time in as many days the man had come. He was a strikingly handsome Black man and carried a sporty, well-used backpack, heavy with a laptop and various supplies. When concentrating—not that she ever stared at him—he would slowly rub his short, coiled, salt and pepper hair. Today he wore a soft, rusty orange sweatshirt that absolutely did not bring out his—

"Excuse me? Miss?"

—deep brown eyes and ridiculously pleasant smile. None of these features would ever, in a million years, make her drop whatever might be in her hand. Like a book. A book that now rested on her newly aching foot.

"Oh! Are you okay?" The man was at her side with her dropped book in hand before she could so much as form a complete sentence.

He was not only strikingly handsome, but tall and broad and incredibly cozy looking on such a blustery day.

"I'm good," she managed and plucked the book from his hand. She glanced at the spine label—*PEA* for T.R. Pearson—and blindly shoved the book into a shelf. "Did *you* need any help?"

"I did. Do. It's my computer, so I'm not sure if you can—"

She followed him to his laptop and missed half of what he said. Men never caught her attention, especially men who were clearly old enough to be her father. Or not. She mulled over his potential age, and—he was still talking. He touched her arm.

"Miss? Do you know how to work around the templates?"

She sat next to him and looked at his laptop. Ludicrously handsome or not, he had a mess on his hands. His document had once been a résumé, but now looked as if words had been thrown at the computer screen to see which ones would stick.

"Oh. God," she said and offered a pained smile. "This is a mess."

"Yes. I noticed." He sounded perturbed; she hoped at technology and not the help. "I tried to paste in this job description from another file and—"

"Kerflooey."

"Ker—flooey. Yes." He smiled as Karina scooted closer to the screen. "I haven't had to prepare a résumé since college, and that was on a typewriter. I'm feeling a bit—"

"It's okay. These templates are evil. Have you thought about making one on your own? No one's looking for fancy fonts and headings anymore."

"They're not?"

"No. And I'd—" She pointed to his mouse. "May I?" Once in control of the file, she skimmed through and slipped everything into its proper spot. Templates were evil but manageable, if you were crazy enough to know how to outsmart them. "Can I suggest something else?" He nodded, not taking his eyes off the screen. "I'd get rid of the objective, and, if you've owned a business as long as this says—"

"Well, I'm not lying about it!"

"No, no. I mean—of course not—since you've owned a business this *long*…" She continued to scroll and point and surreptitiously take note of his name and any other bits of information she could gather. Wesley Lloyd: age forty-six; bachelor's degree in English from State; lived up on Garfield Road, probably in the new apartments. "Employers will want to know the details about your business and your day-to-day responsibilities. You can list earlier employers and the dates you worked for them, but shouldn't need any other details."

"Maybe I should *tweet* them my résumé." He smiled again and air-thumbed a fake text.

"That would be awesome. No more social anxiety. No more hideous résumés. 'I have experience. Hire me.'"

"My résumé is not hideous." He squinted and stared at the laptop screen. "Anymore. How'd you do that?"

"We have résumé building classes the third Thursday of every month if you want to—"

"No. Absolutely—no. I hate these damned machines. Fought them tooth and nail up at the store until I couldn't fight anymore." He tapped her hand to take the mouse and fix a typo. "Which might explain why we went belly up."

"Westland Sporting Goods over in Harding," she said, reading. "You always had bikes or skis out on the sidewalk?"

"That's me. Was me." Mr. Lloyd sighed and stared at his résumé with disgust. "Isn't me anymore."

"Look, the lack of a POS system didn't put you under. Big Box Whatsits up in Greendale is what put you under."

"That too. Either way, I'm too young to retire and too old to hire, and, as you see, I'm horrible at computers. This job hunt should go beautifully."

"You have tons of hirable experience. Certainly someone—"

"Thank you," Mr. Lloyd said as he looked at her name tag, "Karina. You've been a great help."

Karina smiled and pointed to the description of his qualifications. "Don't sell yourself short, Mr. Lloyd. Let me know if you need anything else."

"Wes," he said. "Mr. Lloyd was my father."

Snow had piled, wet and heavy, throughout the day. As Karina trudged down Chestnut Street, the wind whipped her eyes, but the trees lining the road met the storm head-on, bright and bountiful with snow. Mother Nature seemed to be bringing Christmas a little early this year, which was fine with Karina. She had always had to look outside her home for any holiday spirit, and once this storm ended, the scenery would be perfectly set for daydreaming. Or... wallowing in the loneliness the season could bring.

But Uncle Tony's barbershop sign shone ahead of her with the promise of a pot of hot water for cocoa and an empty booth so she could finish winter break homework to the din of the barbershop's constant soundtrack. The junky old space heater would be waiting for her in the corner. And the best promise of all, she would have an evening with her favorite man on the planet.

"Rina!" Tony sang as soon as the bell chimed behind her. "It's coming down, huh?"

"Down? It's freaking *sideways*, Uncle Tony." She shrugged off her coat, shook the snow from it, and kissed Tony's scruffy cheek on her way to hang it up. "Oh, and half of your "o" is out again."

"Maybe you could change the name to Tiny's," Wilson said. Karina never knew if Wilson was his first or last name, but she delighted in him either way. He was a tiny Black man, skinny and full of mischief and good humor. Tony had said Wilson reminded him of Sammy Davis, Jr., and, after Karina asked her mom who the hell *that* was, she couldn't argue. As a younger girl, she had asked him if he could tap dance like Sammy Davis. He stood and did a simple soft shoe; she had been forever smitten. "Might be cheaper than getting that damned thing fixed all the time."

Tony grunted, wiped the stray hair from Wilson's shoulders, and released his chair to floor level. "Maybe Santa will bring me a new sign."

"Santa's not coming if you don't decorate," Karina said, bending to find a wall outlet for her laptop. "When are you going to put up the tree?"

"It's not even December."

Karina tapped the bank calendar that hung next to his station. "It will be tomorrow."

"I dunno, Rina. I'm thinking maybe skipping Christmas decorating this year."

"What? Why?"

"You're old enough to not need it and it's not like my customers—"

"Hey now!" Wilson interrupted. "I like your little tree. It reminds me of my nini's. She had that silver thing with the—"

"Grandma's holiday discotheque," Tony said, clearly familiar with the tale. "Everything rotated: the silver tree, the neon lights she shone on it, the train going around underneath." Tony opened up his appointment book. "Two weeks? Yeah… my tree is not a disco ball *and* I'm not so fond of Christmas anyway. You're gonna have to get your ho-ho-ho spirit somewhere else this year."

"Uncle Tony," Karina scolded after Wilson left. "What's gotten into you today?"

"Nothing, Rina. I'm fine."

He swept the floor, turned his back to her, and swept harder. Usually, his personality matched that of a typical neighborhood barber— friendly, outgoing, and quick-witted. He sparked conversation with clients using his shirts from obscure sports teams around the country: Peoria Rivermen, El Camino Warriors, and Steel City Yellow Jackets.

Unlike his customers' often-conservative hair and short cuts, he wore his thick Italian hair in a mop of loose, black curls. Recently, his mop had gained a few grays that mixed in like strands of Christmas tinsel. Karina had always thought his perennial tan and pointed nose and chin made him handsome in an unordinary way. "Remnants of my mother's sharp personality," he'd always say about his nose.

It was Tony's second Christmas alone since his divorce from her aunt, but maybe loneliness had set in stronger, now that the pain and embarrassment had settled. Or maybe a good snowfall made him feel cold and solitary like Karina—and hopelessly so at that.

He propped the broom against a wall. "What're you studying today? Give me a lesson."

"I have a paper due over break for my Lit for Youth class. I have no idea what I'm talking about. But I'll be convincing the professor that I do."

"Maybe you should have gone to law school. You're a master at convincing."

Karina considered Tony, his posture, and the rarely seen scowl on his face. "Maybe you should put up your Christmas tree."

"Maybe you should mind your own business."

Karina closed her laptop at the sting of his tone. "Should I go home? You're a grouch today."

"No, Rina, wait. I'm sorry." He flopped into a barber chair. It squeaked when he landed; the vinyl moaned under his weight. "Tell you what. Aunt Jodi hated real trees. I haven't had one in years."

"Let's go get one then. You can have one here *and* in your apartment!"

"Here is fine." He stood and gently smacked her back with the towel that perpetually decorated his left shoulder. "Let me have one place where I can wallow in self-pity, huh?"

Over the years, he had listened to her wallow over school troubles and painful breakups, and he always took time with her when her dad's words stung harder than usual. After listening, he'd tell her to *Quitcherbitchin' and get busy doing something*. Coming from him, it snapped her out of her melancholy and got her on her feet again. "I *could* tell you to 'quitcherbitchin,'" she offered.

"And I could tell you to start working on your paper, Miss Librarian." He hovered and stared at her screen until she pulled up the Word document and typed an entire sentence. "We'll go to the tree farm tomorrow after work?"

Old Man Peters arrived for his weekly buzz cut, and the rhythm of the barbershop picked up again: white noise to Karina's studying, a steady comfort like Uncle Tony's ever-present—if occasionally grouchy—love.

* * *

THE FOLLOWING DAY, AFTER REMINDING Mr. Evanston that he had been banned from the library for two weeks because he kept asking women if he could touch their hair, Karina was able to escape the circulation desk and hide in the stacks to pull requested holds. Wes camped out in his usual seat surrounded by colored pens, a leather notebook, and, of course, his spiffy new laptop. When she arrived at the OR-RA row of Fiction, Wes flagged her over.

"Do you teach the computer classes?" Wes asked.

"No. I'm just—" She waved at her computer printout and half-full cart. "—*here*. A minion. Doing minion things."

"Minions are important." He smiled at her as if he had a secret. "A minion once told me: Don't sell yourself short."

"Mmm, smart minion."

He pointed to his résumé. "Here, I worked on it some more. What do you think? Would you hire me?"

She didn't need to look to know she'd hire him. He was friendly, polite, funny, and, based on the résumé, smart enough to run a business for close to twenty years. He had won the formatting battle and cleaned up some of his job descriptions and proven qualifications. It was fine, though dull and mechanical.

"What kind of job are you looking for?" she asked him.

"One that pays." He smiled and opened his notebook filled with plastic-sleeved printouts of job listings; he was more organized than most of the staff at the library. "I have a few options, but honestly, I'm pretty open. Management of some sort."

"So, this is a good base résumé, but you're going to want to tweak it for each job you apply for."

"What? The cover letter doesn't do that? One size no longer fits all?"

"Welcome to the twenty-first century."

"Is that what you had to do to get this job?"

"No. Minions don't have to provide résumés; we have to prove we can spell our names and recite the alphabet."

Wes patted the seat next to him, and she took the invitation. "Not your dream job, I take it?"

"It's a step. I was an annoying patron who wants to be an annoying librarian, so they gave me an opening."

"You're helpful, not annoying."

"Well, you're not the conservative circulation manager. Her, I annoy. Regularly. Because this is a library, not a Christian bookstore."

"See, now. You proved it. You're the kind of librarian I *liked*."

"You were a library kid too?"

"I read like a fiend. Still do, but the books at school didn't include many people that looked like me."

"Sadly, they still don't."

"No. And once I was a teenager, I couldn't find books that helped me understand why I thought boys were much cuter than girls." He smiled. "No offense."

"None taken. I mean, you're *wrong*; girls are much cuter than boys."

Wes smiled. "See? I needed librarians like you. Mom would take me up to the city library where they had more options. Once I could drive, I'd go and find the deepest stack and read everything I could."

"Because you couldn't take them home..."

"Nope. Especially with Dad." Wes sighed and closed his laptop. "You've been a great help. And don't you *dare* short change yourself or what you do here. Kids in these small towns need you."

"Thanks," Karina said as she stood. "Good luck."

"Oh, you're not getting rid of me that quickly. I'll be back tomorrow. I have to… *tweak*… as you say. I might need a helpful librarian."

That evening, Uncle Tony picked her up to find a Christmas tree for his shop. In Harding, they passed Westland Sporting Goods. Brown paper covered the windows; the sign remained unlit.

"Did you ever shop there? Westland?" she asked Tony.

"I think I got my bat there when I played softball a few years back. Is it closed?"

"Yeah, the owner comes to the library. Super nice guy. Lost the business and now he's scrounging for jobs, something he hasn't done for over twenty years."

"I wouldn't know where to start."

"I've been helping him with his résumé. It's weird seeing a whole life condensed onto one piece of paper."

Tony scoffed. "Antonio Trovato: barber. How 'bout one *line*?"

At the tree farm, Karina stood in awe. Yesterday's snow still clung to the trees' limbs. Utility lights dangled from cords draped between thin wood posts and splayed a glittery golden glow onto the rows of trees. It reminded Karina of a scene in *Polar Express*—a clear vision of the childlike magic of Christmas.

"What was your favorite book as a kid, Uncle Tony?" she asked as she fanned her hand along the branches to knock off the wet snow.

"*James and the Giant Peach*. Dad would do all the animal's voices. Half the fun was when Mom would come in all ticked off because I was putting off bedtime. He'd smile and nod and as soon as she closed the door, he'd go right back to it." He mimicked a cartoon-like voice, quoting the Old-Green-Grasshopper. "There are a whole lot of things in this world of yours that you haven't started wondering about yet." He stopped in his tracks and stared at a small tree—four feet tall, if an inch—and cocked his head. "How about this one? He's nice and round."

"Tiny but sturdy. Do you have a box to put him on?"

"Yeah, I think I have a crate in my gar—" He looked at Karina with sad eyes. "Maybe Aunt Jodi kept it… and the Christmas train we stored in it."

"Do you want me to ask her?"

"I dunno." He sighed and looked at the holiday scene: families with mitten-handed children tossing snowballs or finding patches of flat ground to make snow angels, couples cuddling against the cold as they chose the perfect addition to their holiday home. "Maybe this isn't a good idea, Rina. She's going to have all the ornaments too."

"For your *house*, but you have all the ornaments your customers have given you."

"They're all barbers with red and green scarves and creepy smiles."

"It's thematic. Let's get it." Karina spotted an orange-vested worker walking by. "Excuse me!" The person didn't immediately return, so Karina headed to the end of the row to find someone else. Before she got there, Orange Vest returned.

Karina stopped dead in her tracks.

The girl was stunning: tall and blonde with dark eyebrows and thick eyeliner. She walked with a swagger, and she gripped a bow saw in her hand like she knew how to use it. When Karina couldn't look her in the eye any longer, she scanned down to the name tag pinned to her vest. *Merry Christmas, Hailey.*

"You like this one?" Hailey said, grabbing a blanket from a nearby stack. Her voice vibrated with a deep end-of-a-cold rasp.

Karina stared. Tony nudged her until words blurted from her mouth. "Yes! Yes, um… we like this one. A lot. *So* much. It's—" Hailey grinned and tossed the blanket onto the ground, lifted the lower branches and began to saw the trunk in even, practiced strokes. The keys that hung from her belt loop jangled, the nylon of her puffer vest swished, and the long side of her bleached hair flipped in rhythm.

Karina didn't speak another word as Tony paid and helped Hailey lift the small tree into the back of his truck. She might have waved to the girl as they left; she might have giggled and missed the door handle getting into Tony's car. Tony said nothing until they got onto the main drag in Harding.

"You may not drop out of grad school to become a lumberjack," he said.

"I can do anything I want," Karina said, unable to hide the smirk on her face. "Besides, I don't want to become a lumberjack. I want to... date one. Apparently. Did you *see* the way she used that saw and how *strong*... and her eyes were the most... oh, god. Oh, *god.*"

"She was awfully cute. If I didn't know your barber, I'd say you went to the same shop."

"Did you hear her laugh?"

"I can't say as I noticed."

"Well, I noticed. And I think you and I need a new attitude this Christmas." She sighed, as fanciful holiday stories swooped and swirled in her mind.

"Oh no, you don't. Don't drag me into your little love story."

"Love is not little. It's huge. And it'd do you good to get out and stretch your social circle."

"I like my social circle, thank you. Clients by day, and me, my couch, and a stack of books by night. Merry Christmas. All the eggnog is mine."

"You are hopeless."

"And you love me."

"Against my better judgment."

800 Literature

"HAVE YOU STARTED GETTING READY for Christmas yet, Wes?" Karina had tried to pry a little Christmas spirit out of her parents over the weekend to no avail. But in spite of their best efforts, she hadn't lost the thrill from the tree farm. The smell of pine lingered, the snow on thick branches comforted, and the shine she caught in Uncle Tony's eyes when he admired the tree decorating the corner of his shop gave her hope that at least *he* was not lost to the joy of the season.

Given the look on Wes's face when he glanced up from his laptop, however—"I mean, do you celebrate?" she asked, backtracking. "I shouldn't assume."

"I do. Did. Used to. It's not a favorite holiday, I'm afraid," he said, as she sat next to him. "You're in a good mood today."

"I am." A blush warmed her cheeks.

"Out with it..."

"It's nothing." She couldn't lie for long; Christmas might have been *part* of her elevated spirits, but... "I met—no, I *saw* this girl. At the tree farm."

"Ah, so it's not Christmas spirit that has you, it's—" He dropped his voice low and deep. "—a *love* bomb."

"You're worse than my uncle."

"Maybe I'm smart like your uncle. Was she cute?"

"Yes, *and* she might have flirted with me," she said with a dreamy sigh. "In spite of my dad's Scrooge-y behavior this weekend, I'm still giddy."

"Is Dad a fun scrooge, or—"

"Or. He's a jerk three-sixty-five, so that's nothing new. Won't put the decrepit tree up before the twenty-fourth, tosses on thirty-year-old tinsel and his grandmother's scratch-and-dent ornaments, and calls it a day."

"Maybe they're important to him?"

"The only thing important to Dad is that he's in charge."

"So go back to the tree farm and get one for your room. Bonus: love bomb."

Karina laughed. "I doubt she remembers me." She moved to leave but stopped. "You don't spend the holiday alone, do you? I mean… at least I have Mom."

"I have dinner with a couple friends. Enjoy the quiet. Try to forget—" Wes reached for his mouse and focused on his laptop. "I found a few jobs to apply for. You wanna see if my résumé is specific enough for them?"

"Sure," she said. She touched his arm and offered a sad smile and an apology. "I didn't mean to upset you."

"You didn't. Every year gets easier."

"You lost someone."

"A long time ago. I probably wasn't much older than you are now. Ian and I bought Westland together."

"Oh, I'm sorry. And here I am whining about my ugly tree."

Wes looked at Karina with a warm compassion she had seen from only one man before: Uncle Tony. "I had a jerk for a dad too," he said. "It's hard loving someone who won't live up to your simple expectations."

"Thank you," she said, as she stared at his laptop. "So, what did you find?" He had named each résumé file with the prospective job: a management position at the gym up on Manchester, and a job at—"Wes. You do not want this job."

"I can't afford to be picky. Money's tight until I sell the Westland building."

"This isn't going to pay you enough to buy a stick of gum every third Tuesday." The job was for a clerk at a used bookstore on Sullivant. The place was a dump. It remained open because the owner's grandfather croaked and left her the building. The stock consisted of donated, yellowed, moldy-smelling books that had lived in various citizens' basements since the Nixon years. If not Roosevelt. *Teddy* Roosevelt.

"Okay," Wes conceded, "but the place is a mess. They need a manager. I can start—"

"Wes."

With one blink, his look morphed from that of a bumbling paternal father into an irritated professor. "Does the résumé look appropriate for the jobs or not?"

"I don't think the bookstore will need a résumé," she said. "Can they read?"

"Now you're being bratty." A grin defied his harsh tone. "I love bookstores. I've always wanted to be a writer, so maybe surrounding myself—"

"You have? Wes! You need to write, then. Don't work at some two-bit bookstore for a pittance." Karina caught her supervisor eyeing her across the room. She got up and shuffled the books on her cart while they continued to talk. "Have you started anything?"

"I have scraps and notebooks filled with ideas. That's why I bought this," he said, pointing to his laptop. "But, rent."

"But, fulfilling a *dream*!"

"Electricity."

"A *novel*, Wes. How long have you wanted to? Why not now?"

"Since I was a kid—since Dad read me *James and the Giant Peach*."

She stopped shuffling and blinked. "*James and the Giant*—"

"What? Don't you like Roald Dahl?"

"I *love* him—*Matilda* is one of my favorites," she said. "Someone else mentioned that book last week, is all." *It's kismet.*

Filled with images of tree farms and bow saw-wielding girls, Karina began to spin dreams of romantic Christmases: a trip to the farm to help Uncle Tony and Wes pick out *their* tree; snowball fights at Greendale Metro; kisses under the mistletoe she had snuck into Uncle Tony's apartment.

"—can see how you like that one." Wes looked at her, obviously waiting for her to respond. She hadn't the slightest notion what he'd been talking about. "*Matilda*," he helpfully offered. "You seem a lot like her: smart, curious, crappy dad…"

"At least my mom tries," she said. "And I don't have Matilda's courage to fight my crappy dad."

"What do you mean you don't—look at you." She'd have been uncomfortable if his gaze hadn't been so kind: over her hair, shaved close on one side and long to her chin on the other; the line of piercings that trailed down one ear; her funky, oversized glasses, and the corner of a tattoo—a shelf stuffed with books—that peeked from the open collar of her shirt. "You fight him by being yourself."

Karina touched the buzz cut side of her hair, a cut Uncle Tony had given her after four-too-many home hair coloring debacles. "You'll look cool *and* piss off your father," he'd said. "Trust me." And he was right: She looked cool, and dad was furious.

But right now, she wanted to hear more about James and how his giant peach affected Wes's dream to be a writer. "So, how does a book about an oversized stone fruit inspire a little boy to write?"

"It's full of wild imagery, you know? Mom and I read it every night for months, and when she'd turn out my light, I'd grab my flashlight and notebook and write new adventures with the grasshopper and the ladybug." Wes chuckled. "I missed a lot of sleep."

"I think Mr. Dahl would approve," she said.

"True, but now I need to send these résumés off, because car insurance is not free."

On her way out for the day, Karina grabbed the library's copy of *James and the Giant Peach* and gave it to Wes. He immediately flipped to a specific page, sat back in his chair, and began to read.

Forty-five minutes later Karina stood outside in the blistering cold because, in true Mr. Wormwood style, her dad hadn't bothered to pick her up. Her mother told her that walking five miles in negative wind chill—in the dark—wasn't asking too much. With no other option,

Karina buttoned up tighter and headed out. She wasn't out of the parking lot when an unfamiliar car pulled up.

"Do you need a ride?" The passenger window lowered, and Wes's breath ghosted in front of his face. Cool jazz played from the car stereo. A lifetime of, "Don't accept rides from strangers," and "It's against library policy," made her pause. "At least wait in the car so you can stay warm," he added at her hesitation.

"I'm not nearby," she conceded. Her fingers might never thaw.

"I'm not going anywhere but home. Hop on in."

Karina did, plopping her enormous bag filled with everything important—books, notebooks, a cell phone, tablet, and a bag full of colored pens—onto the floor. "Thank you. My dad is an asshole."

"We determined that earlier." He put the car in drive, cranked up the heat, and grinned. "Point the way!"

She chewed on her bottom lip as she gathered the courage to mention the daydreams that had kept her mind occupied that afternoon. "I've been thinking," she said. She kept her eyes on the road ahead in case her next sentence flopped like a basket of rotten tomatoes. "You might like my Uncle Tony."

Wes remained quiet; his finger, softly tapping to the music, never paused. "Huh. What's so special about Uncle Tony?"

Karina dared a glance Wes's way. He seemed cautiously interested. "Well, he's… I mean, he's—" She was *not* going to say Uncle Tony's interest in men was the main impetus. That was absurd and wrong, *but*— "He was married to my Aunt Jodi."

"Your *Aunt* Jodi." Wes pulled up to a traffic light. "If he was married to your *aunt*—what makes you think he'd be interested in me?"

Karina rolled her eyes. "There *are* such things as bisexuals, you know."

"I—I do know, yes. I'm sorry." He looked at her with a pained smile. "I'm so out of the dating game that I—yes." He continued to tap his steering wheel to the music. "You said 'was' married—is that why it's past tense?"

"Yeah. He didn't come to terms with it until later and… she wasn't keen on the idea."

"That's a shame," he said. "Thing is, I'm not too sure I'm keen on getting back *in* the dating game."

"But it's Christmas!"

"What does that have to do with—" Before taking off from the light, he shot a look at her. "Your love bomb and your Christmas spirit are still tangled."

She ignored him; of course they were tangled. That was the point. "But, Wes… walks in the snow and packages with pretty bows and eggnog under the tree."

"You know, some people *like* being alone at Christmas."

"Oh, come on. No one likes it; they put up with it. You said you were my age when—look, it was a *long* time ago, and maybe it's time—"

"How old do you think I am?"

"You're forty-six. Turn right up here."

"Huh. Someone did more than *fix* my résumé, I see." The smile he'd been visibly fighting this entire conversation finally broke free.

"Look, Uncle Tony is lonely, and you seem—"

"Lonely?"

"Well. Yes? And I think he'd make you laugh, and he loved *James and the Giant Peach* as a kid too…" She lingered and hoped that revelation would spark the ultimate flame. When he didn't flinch, she rushed on. "And he makes the most amazing *pasticiotti* that should never go unshared."

"*Pasticiotti?*"

"It's these custard-filled pastry… pie… things, and they take forever and a day, and he destroys his kitchen and my waistline. He shoves them off on his clients because—" She stopped rambling. Wes was laughing, and they'd driven right by her house. She directed him around the block.

"Does Uncle Tony know you're trying to hook him up with a failed businessman?"

"Who wants to write books," she said, trying to encourage him.

"But can't pay his rent?"

Karina sighed. "No. He's as stubborn as you. Green house on the right." Her dad's old, rusty Town Car sat in the drive. "Aaand, the asshole's home."

"Uncle Tony?"

"My *dad*. I wouldn't want you to meet an asshole. I like you. And I love him."

"I like you too," Wes said. Karina made no move to get out. "Why is this so important to you?"

"It's not," she lied, feeling the heat of him staring at her. "I thought it'd be nice. For both of you. You know, meet for coffee or, or a day at the gym."

"You need to stop reading all those romance books you shelve."

"Maybe you need to start reading more of them. In fact…" She dug through her bag and pulled out a book. "Here. It's out in my name, but I know you're good for it."

Wes flipped on the dome light. "*How They Met*. David Levithan." He gave her a look that felt like a dismissal to her bedroom without dinner.

"It's all first-meeting stories." She shoved the book closer to him.

"He writes for teens, right?"

"Yes, but I still like his books," she said, as he flipped to the table of contents. "Will you at least think about it?"

"About the book or your uncle?"

"Define 'it' however you want," she said, looking at her house with a lot less joy than she looked at Wes, or books.

"You okay? The house is dark."

"Mom works nights. Dad's probably in the basement. He tinkers around with his model railroad every minute he's not at work." When her dad wasn't doing that, he was giving her shit about something. Wes's car was warm. *Wes* was warm.

"Does he hurt you?" Wes asked.

"No. Not physically. He's just a miserable bastard."

Wes didn't stop staring; he tapped his finger on his steering wheel again. Karina still didn't move. "I might be crossing a line, and, if I am, ignore me. We'll pretend I never did," he said.

"Oh… kay."

"Give me your phone."

She did, and he typed as he spoke. "If you ever need anything, call, okay? I don't feel good about dumping you here and pulling out of this driveway."

"I'm fine, Wes. I am. But…" She lifted the phone and pocketed it. "Thank you. Will I see you at the library soon?"

"Yes. I can't pay for the Internet until my damned building sells."

She was certain now. He *had* to meet Uncle Tony. They would fall in love instantly, of course, and, after a perfect Christmas together, she'll visit their apartment and cook for them and happily watch whatever obscure sporting event they both loved. Maybe she'd convince Uncle Tony to get that darling schnauzer puppy he's always wanted. A new family; it would be perfect.

* * *

ON THURSDAY MORNING, KARINA KEPT one eye on the clock and one at the disaster of the DVD section she tried to straighten. *Edward Scissorhands* hid in the Ms next to *Moulin Rouge,* and *Scent of a Woman* sat upside down behind *Night at the Museum.* She had a perfect matchmaking plan; the mess the patrons had left wasn't doing a decent-enough job to distract her. She looked at the clock again: ten-twenty-five and no sign of Wes, but Tony stood at the holds shelf looking perplexed. She made herself busy.

"Did you put this in my name?" Tony asked before she felt him near.

"Possibly." She stared at the row of DVDs that was so out of order, someone had to have purposely shuffled them. Uncle Tony stood quietly with *How to Repair a Mechanical Heart* in his hand. "You know I did. You haven't used the library in ten years."

"It's been maybe *two*." He pointed to the title. "Mechanical heart… are you trying to tell me something?"

Karina stared at him; of course she was. "You've been a grouchy curmudgeon, lately… grumpy as Old Man Peters, and he's been alone for forty years."

"Since when have I been a curmudgeon? I'm friendly." He stood up straighter, and Karina had to stifle a laugh; he looked like a stubborn ten-year-old who's been told he didn't do his history homework right. "I'm friendly and personable and—"

"And *miserable* since Aunt Jodi kicked you out on your ass last year."

"Rina, it's Christmas. Everyone's into their own shit, myself included." He looked at the book again. "My heart is not mechanical or in need of repair."

"That's not what the book is about—not really." She growled as she tossed two misplaced copies of *Captain America* onto her cart. "It's about two guys who go on a road trip—one's out, one's not." Uncle Tony's look morphed from general impatience to cautious irritation. "Oh, come on. Give it a chance. I don't like seeing you so down. And Wes is—"

"Who's Wes?"

"The guy who owned Westland Sporting? I think you'd like each other."

"So you're giving me a book about two—what, teenagers?—who go on a road trip." Uncle Tony sighed and scanned the synopsis. "Huh. It does sound kind of good. I still don't get how this is supposed to un-curmudgeon me."

"Books help me remember anything can happen." She fixed the mis-ordering of six DVDs in two seconds; Tony peered to check her work. "And," she said, pushing him out of the way to move to another shelf, "most times, *anything* has to start with me."

"Fair enough." He flipped through the pages. "Speaking of *anything*, did you go to the tree farm again? Find out about Haaaiiillleyyy?"

"Stop it. I have absolutely no reason to go back there."

It had taken her father a grand total of forty-eight hours to crush Karina's high.

"She was doing her *job*; a smile means nothing," he'd said when he walked in on Karina telling her mom about Hailey the evening Wes took her home. This morning's parting words, said out of the blue as she poured milk in her cereal, were equally discouraging. "No one your age is going to want a simpleton library clerk. I'm telling you; you're headed nowhere."

She'd heard it all before. After a while, his words became the air she breathed. *A smile means nothing, simpleton, headed nowhere.* Her daydreams of romantic holidays were meant for everyone else, not her.

"You *just* said anything can happen." Tony shook the book in her face. "Come on... blonde hair, pretty eyes, stellar bow saw skills. That has to come in handy somehow."

"She barely noticed me."

"She... oh, my god, who has the mechanical heart? She noticed you. Besides, you have matching hair." He yanked a copy of *Slumdog Millionaire* out of the Ns and handed it to her. "Your patrons are pigs."

"They can also hear."

"Sorry. How can someone so hell-bent on hooking everyone else up be so oblivious to her own—" Tony stopped and dropped his emoting hands to his sides. "What'd your dad say this time?"

"Nothing worth repeating, and I am not hell-bent." Karina pushed her cart into the main aisle and glanced at the reading tables in Fiction, hoping to see Wes. No sign of him.

Tony stepped behind her and whispered in her ear, "One, your father is a dick, and two, you sneaky shit. You were hoping that guy would be here, and we'd meet." Karina grinned, big, fake, and desperate. "Oh, my god, you are worse than the people in those ridiculous Christmas movies Aunt Jodi loved to watch."

"I am not. I think you'd like him. Not my fault you're so stubborn."

Tony reached for his wallet and shook his head. "I'll take the book, but I'm not guaranteeing I'll read it." Karina kissed his cheek. "If you want to go to the farm, I'll take you. Buy a wreath for your front door or something. Besides, it's obvious you need some friends."

"I have friends—it's movie night with the girls. You wanna come?"

"No, thanks." He lifted the book. "I have a new book to read."

After the DVD section was in perfect alphabetical order, and after she'd almost given up on him, Wes arrived. He shoved a couple of business books into the return slot and grinned at Karina as if he had a secret. The last book out of his bag was *How We Met*; he wiggled it in her general direction and shoved it into the slot.

"Finished already?"

"I am."

"So?"

"So?" Wes grinned and winked.

"Oh, my god, you are being such a boob."

Wes leaned his elbows onto the desk and pointed toward the bin. "Here's something you don't know about me; I am quite often… a boob."

"Did you like the book, Boob?"

Wes grimaced. "Yes, I did. It was sweet and sometimes heartbreaking. I see why adults like Levithan's books. He understands—" Wes waved his hand in front of his face. "—fluttery early-on stuff."

"That's the best part, isn't it?"

"It is. Advice for your future—never go into business with your lover," Wes said. "It kills the fluttery early-on stuff, and you're left alone to run a business you were never sure you wanted."

"Ian?"

Wes nodded.

"Oh, I thought—" Karina leaned in and whispered. "I thought he *died.*"

"He did. Two months after we split. At Christmas."

"Wes. My god, I'm so sorry."

"It's okay." He shrugged. "He finally had the hernia surgery he'd been putting off; something went wrong. His dad called a week later to tell me. There weren't any services." Wes shrugged again. The lingering pain was evident if for no other reason than he wouldn't look Karina in the eye.

"No wonder the holidays are so hard."

"I manage. But," Wes said with a smile that was too bright and full. "I liked Levithan's writing. He gets us."

They looked at each other for long, understanding moments until Karina patted his hand and broke the quiet. "You just missed my Uncle Tony." Granted, it had been two hours; the meaning of "just" was irrelevant.

Wes stared her down, shook his head, and grinned. "I owe you a thank you, by the way."

"Yeah? What for?"

"I got a bite at the gym. I'm not sure what's up yet, but I interview tomorrow."

* * *

THAT SATURDAY AFTERNOON, KARINA STOOD near the reference section knee-deep in a project that, if she followed the directions properly, would become a life-size Christmas tree made of books. So far, it looked as if she had been trapped by a runaway literary stampede. Boxes of discarded books littered the floor. This had looked like a fun project on paper, but now she feared she bit off more than she could chew.

"See, this is why I stopped decorating for Christmas," Wes said as he stood near a stack of four stuffed boxes.

"It is not why you stopped. Do you see any over-sized books in the box by your shoulder?" He shuffled through and pulled out three coffee-table books. She put them in place and asked if he got the job at the gym.

"I'm going to start teaching some classes; see if it's a fit." He pulled the book she'd placed on hold for him from his bag. "*Sweeney Todd:*

The Demon Barber of Fleet Street," he said. "Please tell me your uncle is not a barber."

"What's wrong with barbers?"

"Well, nothing—" Wes frowned at the book. "I mean, the idea of reading a graphic novel for the first time in decades is appealing, but 'Demon Barber' isn't helping your cause."

"I have no other cause than to broaden your reading interests." She put more books on top of the ring surrounding her.

"You're going to need to step out of there if you don't want to become a permanent fixture." He offered his hand, and she stepped out and gathered more books. "Also, you are not putting books on hold for me to broaden my reading interests. You are trying to finagle me into dating your uncle by softening my cold, bitter heart with sweet books. This," he said, shaking the graphic novel, "does not speak to the appealing nature of your uncle."

"Okay, fair. But Johnny Depp is hot, and he was in the movie." She grimaced at her ridiculous argument and slid a half-empty box onto the floor with a thud so loud the lady using the copy machine cried out.

"Sweeney Todd *kills* people and grinds them into minced meat pie!"

"You know the story then?" Karina grinned, wide and silly. He frowned in return. "Not all barbers are psychopaths, Wes," Karina said as simply as if she had to explain snow fell from the sky, which it was doing again—while the sun shone.

"Date my uncle; he's not a psychopath," Wes said, mocking her. "You need to take some marketing classes."

"You need to start showing up earlier in the morning or closer to closing to make this easier."

"Is that when he's here?"

She feigned interest in her tree-building directions—stack books in a circle decreasing in circumference to the top; fill center with more books as you go; decorate with twinkle lights and a topper—and mumbled, "Maybe."

Uncle Tony arrived first thing Monday morning. Karina was still in the midst of her opening tasks when the smack of a book on the desk jolted her away from her concentration.

"I liked this one," Tony said. "There should always be kissing marathons for old lovers."

"You think?" Karina checked in *Two Boys Kissing* and tossed it on her cart. "I can't think of one ex I'd want to marathon *House Hunters* with, much less kiss for hours on end."

"Mmm, there were a few that got away I wouldn't mind."

"But see, now you're confident in who you are, you don't need those boys from your past." It was a cheap segue; she knew it. She wiggled her eyebrows in anticipation anyway. "I have an idea."

"I'm not sure I trust you."

She ignored him. "You quit yoga because you didn't like the instructor, Tracy, yeah?"

Tony squinted, clearly not ready to agree to much of anything.

"She's pregnant and quit," Karina continued. "They have a new instructor, and he's—well, he could be a lousy teacher, but he's cute." She stopped, caught herself blushing, and tried again. "Truth is, he's the kind of gorgeous that makes lesbian me drop books, okay? And he's sweet and your age and happens to be available." The last word came out like a song.

"And his name is Wes. You need to work on your subtlety." He found his name on the holds shelf. "*Dangerous Liaisons*? Karina Ness, I swear to *Pete*—"

She took the book and slid it to her coworker, Rhonda. "Check this back in for me; I miscalculated." She walked him to the door before he could say another word; this was no longer a time for jokes. "Tonight at seven. I'll come by after work, and we can go together."

"Don't you always go with friends?"

"We meet there. Lucy won't go anymore because Tracy quit, and girls are stupid anyway."

"You like girls."

"I like to date and kiss and—" she blushed and tripped over her tongue.

"Ha! I think you need to go find your lumberjane and ask *her*."

"Lumberja— I'm asking *you*, because I love you." She rubbed Tony's small paunchy belly, and he glared at her and stepped away. "You said you needed exercise."

"That was after Thanksgiving when I had eaten half a bird and an entire pie by myself."

"You did not." Karina stomped her foot. She was so frustrated, she wanted to stomp it again. "Look, if nothing else, I think you and Wes would be good friends."

"I have friends."

"Can you stop being such a—a—"

"Curmudgeon?"

She leaned closer and whispered. "Asshole is what I was thinking, but sure, we'll go with that."

Tony sighed and kissed Karina's forehead again. "Tonight at seven?"

Karina bounced on her toes. "Pick up a light dinner on the way. You're paying."

300 *Social Sciences*

KARINA AND TONY ARRIVED A few minutes before yoga class began. Since it was two weeks before Christmas, the class was half its normal size. The few who were there unrolled yoga mats, stretched out from long days on their feet or at desks, and chatted quietly.

"Karina!" Wes said. His smile brightened half the dimly lit room. "I didn't think you'd come!"

"I told you this was my normal class time."

Before she could introduce him, Wes offered his hand to Tony. "You must be Uncle Tony."

"Tony Trovato," he said as he shook Wes's hand. "You don't have to call me 'Uncle,'" he added with a wink.

He actually winked. Karina looked at him as if she'd never met him.

"So, Not-Uncle Tony, have you been kidnapped or are you genuinely interested in yoga?"

"I used to come regularly; it's been a few years."

"It's been a few years since I've taught, so we can fumble through this together."

"Right. I'm gonna…" Karina stepped back and unrolled her mat close enough to hear Wes and Uncle Tony talk. Uncle Tony freaking *winked.*

"I probably should apologize—" Uncle Tony said as soon as she stepped away.

"You don't need to; she's an adult." He caught Karina's eye. A slight parental threat lurked behind his kindness. "She's awfully fond of you."

"She's a good kid. About the only family I have left," Tony said. "And from what I hear, she's pretty fond of you too."

"Ah. Well," Wes said as he bent to collect a mat and yoga blocks, "let's see how we all feel about each other after an hour or so of fumbling, huh?" He handed Tony the supplies, shot Karina one more warning "glare," and sat cross-legged on his mat wordlessly directing the students to do the same.

Karina patted the empty spot next to her, sat up, and crossed her legs until Wes began. Instead of standard meditative chants, nature sounds, or ethereal floating chords as musical background, the room filled with soft, smooth jazz. His peaceful baritone voice blended into the music's groove as though he was part of the recording; its gentle rhythms kept everyone's bodies fluid and in sync with his instruction. She had always enjoyed yoga, but Wes' leadership was downright invigorating.

Uncle Tony remained quiet, focused. He followed Wes and kept up easily. After a refreshing hour, Wes led them through the final positions of the evening. They relaxed in *shavasana*—fully relaxed, flat on their backs—and Karina tried to focus on her breath as instructed. All she could think about was rewinding time to experience the class again.

"Extend your legs. Keep your shoulders away from your ears," Wes said, slowly walking around the students. "If there's space between your lower back and the floor, wedge those blocks under your thighs." He bent to help Mrs. Swanson in the back of the room. "Doesn't that help?" he asked her, and she giggled in response. *Dear god.* He continued to walk among the students as he talked. "You should be thoroughly comfortable; sink into the floor, focus on your breath." He stopped between Tony and Karina, and she couldn't help but smile up at him.

He lifted a scolding finger and squatted next to Tony. "Can I?" he said, as he reached out to touch Uncle Tony's shoulder.

"Yes, please. My back's tighter than a rubber band."

Wes lifted Tony's shoulder from the floor and settled it into the correct position. The groan Tony emitted was so serene, so *satisfied*, the rest of the class chuckled. Wes arranged Uncle Tony's other shoulder; he groaned again. Deep, full breaths noisily filled his lungs. Karina glanced at him; his peaceful grin would have been ridiculous if it wasn't so genuine.

Wes remained squatting next to Tony and said, still using a soft, meditative voice, "Can I recommend you pump up your customers higher in their chairs? Your traps are a mess."

"I'll do anything you say. *Anything.*" As far as Karina was concerned, Tony might as well have accepted a marriage proposal, or, at the least, a movie night proposal.

Wes verbally guided everyone to relax each part of their bodies as he moved about the room. By the time everyone had rolled to their sides and sat up, Karina had lost track of time. Tony's smile exhibited a peace she hadn't seen in years.

With a final, "*Namaste,*" students slowly moved to collect their belongings. Wes spoke with each person as they left, calling them by name. He was able to eke a tentative commitment from Tony to return next week. Karina promised to be there.

"I'll bring my girlfriends, too. They were afraid without Tracy—"

"I'm glad you both came," he said and moved on to the next student.

Once in the car, Karina stared at Tony.

"What?" He turned the heat on full blast.

"So?" she said, incredulous.

"So?" The blush that had colored his cheeks since Wes touched him was faint, but still visible.

Karina grinned at him. "Did you enjoy that?"

"I want to go back *tomorrow,*" he said. "I feel amazing." Karina tossed her workout bag onto the floor and rolled her eyes. "You're upset."

"Not upset," she said as she snapped her seat belt buckle. "Did you like *Wes*? I know you liked yoga. Your moans were pornographic."

"Well, *excuse* me." He reached for her hand and gently pinched her. "I liked Wes just fine."

"And?"

"And tomorrow is a new day. When is your Lit for Youth paper due? Are you off from the library?"

Defeated, Karina locked her door and stared out her window. "Friday and yes." He wasn't interested. That was that. The wink was friendly, the shoulder adjustment was professional, and Christmas would be as dull and miserable as always.

"Good," Tony said. "Come work at the shop. You need to show me how I should move my clients to fix my—what'd he say?"

"Traps—trapezius muscles. You're starting to look like an old woman with osteoporosis."

Tony didn't say anything the rest of the ride home. She tried to read his expression as streetlights illuminated his face in the moving car. The grin never left—not really—but she could have been seeing with blind hope. When he pulled into her drive, he kissed her cheek.

"Thanks for inviting me. I had a good time."

"Will you come next week?"

"One day at a time, Rina."

Three days later, Wes hadn't shown up at the library at all, and neither he nor Tony had returned either of the last books she'd given them. Until now, they'd flown through their books, and even if they'd feigned disinterest in her more ridiculous choices, they'd read everything. Now? Silence.

Karina finished her paper and emailed it to the professor. She should enjoy the rest of winter break, but she couldn't shake off her disappointment that yoga class was simply yoga class. The books were but a silly game. Wes was just a friendly guy at the library and Uncle Tony… well, he remained stubborn and alone.

It was preposterous to have expected sparks and instant chemistry and glitter bombs, but the irritation persisted. It didn't help that her dad honed in on her mood and danced on it every chance he got. "Told you that girl wouldn't amount to anything," had been that morning's parting words.

Wes came to the library that day; she greeted him with barely a nod. As she walked away to shelve a cartful of books, she heard Rhonda say, "Don't ask me. She's been quiet all week."

They stayed in separate corners. Karina caught Wes staring at her, but she would turn back to her work without so much as a blink. She had put one *final*—she'd promised herself—book on hold for him. He had it in his hand as he approached her in Nonfiction. "*A Christmas Carol*," he said simply. "Why do I have the feeling you've cast me as Scrooge?"

"Well, you're certainly not Tiny Tim," she said, staring at a bookbinding. *Modern Dating: A Field Guide*, 646.77 ATI.

"I'm feeling more like the Christmas goose—basted and carved into pieces. Why are you upset with me?"

"I'm upset with everyone," she said as she shoved the book into place so hard it pushed the book on the other side onto the floor. "Shit."

"I've got it." Wes went around the stack, retrieved the dropped book, and wiggled it through a small empty space into Karina's line of view. "Where do you want this?" He motioned to her cart.

"It's *numerical*, Wes. I'm sure you can put it back."

Wes dropped the book onto her cart anyway and retreated to his laptop. Karina swore again, finished unloading, and plopped herself in a chair across the table from him. "What's wrong with me?"

"Darling, I'm not sure I know." She glared at him—he *had* to know. "What?" As usual, his expression was friendly. Today, friendly didn't cut it.

"Forget it. I've been out of line; you're a patron. I'll leave you alone." She grabbed her empty cart and stalked to the circulation department.

"Karina, come on now." Her cart caught on a floor mat, wobbled, and began to topple. Wes was there, one hand on her arm, one on the cart. When she met his eyes, he said, "I know why you're upset, but I want you to explain it to me."

"I'm not sure I can."

"Come see me on your break?"

"I'm embarrassed," she said. "I'm sorry."

Wes smiled and tried again. "Don't be. Come talk to me."

An hour later, after catching more of his concerned looks, her pity party lost its fire. She joined him for her break.

"Is that your novel?" she asked him, diverting.

Wes turned his laptop away from her. "Not for anyone's eyes yet," he said. She looked over his shoulder and tried to read. "If you don't behave, I'm telling your supervisor you're goofing off."

"It's my break. I'm allowed to goof off."

He closed the lid and looked at her with the fatherly patience she only saw from Uncle Tony. "I liked your uncle," he said, cutting straight to the point, "but if these things happen at all, they take time. And at my age, they usually don't happen."

"Well, that's ridiculous. There's no reason to shut it all down because—"

"Why is this so important to you?"

She couldn't answer that question any better now than when he had asked her ten days before. "I *want*, okay? I want for Uncle Tony. I want love and Christmas stories and snowball fights and shared mulled wine." Wes nodded, smug, as if she'd given the right answer for the toughest question on the final exam. "What?"

"Are you sure you want those things for Uncle Tony... or for *yourself*?"

Karina scoffed. "Those *things* don't happen for girls like me."

"Says who?" Karina fell silent. Through quiet moments where she fought the urge to unleash a wall of tears, Wes's hand rested warm and comforting on her arm. She put her hand on his, unable to look at him. "Your father gets no say in who you are or who you find happiness with."

"I know." She hated that he understood; she loved that he understood. "But you and Uncle Tony—"

"You need to take care of yourself and let the old farts fumble around on their own."

At that, she looked at him. "No more books?"

"Are you kidding me? Meeting you and reading these books helped me make it through this month," Wes said. "Please, more books." A mischievous grin lit up his face. "Have you seen the cute girl from the tree farm again?"

"No. How would I?"

"I don't know, maybe she reads. Maybe it's Christmas, and she works at a tree farm, so there are a million good reason to go back." He poked her shoulder. "Maybe the fates are kind, and she'll be buying milk the next time you buy eggs."

"I hate eggs."

Wes leveled his gaze and pushed on. "If I remember correctly, you need a Christmas tree for your bedroom."

She squeezed her fingers around Wes's hand. *Your father gets no say in who you are or who you find happiness with.* He also had no say in how she decorated her own bedroom—Mom had made sure of that years ago.

"I think that might be a genius idea," she said.

"Good. Busy tonight?" Karina shook her head. "I'll pick you up at six-thirty."

WES ARRIVED BEFORE KARINA'S DAD'S post-dinner complaints began. Because Wes cared, because Hailey might be at the tree farm with her bow saw, flannel shirt, and dark eyeliner, nothing her dad said could have hit its target anyway.

The moment they stepped into the lot, Karina spotted Hailey's orange puffer vest and flannel shirt. She was working with another family, but when Wes and Karina passed her, Karina could have sworn—

Wes bumped her shoulder; they followed the signs to the smaller trees.

"Did she double take me?" Karina asked out of earshot.

"She *so* double-took you. Double-taked?" Wes cocked his head. "The girl looked at you at least three times."

Karina stopped in her tracks and stared at Wes. His eyes lit up the space more than the dangling utility lights. "You're as bad as me!"

"Maybe." Wes pointed three trees down. "Is that too tall?"

It was, but the third one they considered wasn't. It had plenty of branches for ornaments, was short enough to fit on her desk and pretty enough her mom's appreciation of it would drown out her dad's insults.

When a round, scruffy man approached to help, Wes was the first to say they were still thinking. Hailey arrived next, saw in hand and a crooked grin on her lips.

"Find one you like?" she asked.

Wes choked. Karina hit him in the arm and nodded. No words came out, which was a blessing. All she could think of saying was, "I like *you*. Will you come plant yourself in my bedroom?"

Hailey sawed and chatted and wrapped the tree in plastic netting. She dragged it to the register and insisted on ringing Karina out herself. The total was five dollars less than posted.

"I found an extra discount for you." Hailey leaned on the counter and rested her chin in her hand as Karina dug into her wallet for cash. "This is your second trip," Hailey said.

"I—yes." *She remembers me.* "It is. My uncle needed a tree and I decided I'd like one for my room." Cold and shaking with nerves, Karina's fingers couldn't separate and grasp her bills. She looked at Hailey, who promptly licked her lips. "You take plastic?"

"Anything you wanna give me."

Wes made a hasty escape toward the car. With one more look at Hailey, who now stared Karina straight in the eyes, Karina swallowed and gave Hailey her debit card. A blank piece of scrap paper and a pen accompanied her receipt.

"Can you put your phone number on that?" Hailey asked. "In case— uh, in case there's a problem with the card?"

Karina's heart skipped, her breath skipped. "And my name?"

"Yes," Hailey said, a flash of nerves now evident in her eyes. "Definitely your name."

"It's Karina," said as she took her time to make sure her handwriting was legible.

"Beautiful." As if choreographed, they stared at Karina's tree, out to the parking lot, and back to the tree. Hailey picked it up by the trunk. "I'll load this for you since your—"

"Friend. Wes is my friend, who is probably standing by his car laughing his ass off."

"*Unhelpful* friend." Hailey laughed and dragged the tree behind her. "Let's make him help."

Karina wasn't sure how the tree ended up in the back of Wes' car or how the rhythmic scratching of pine needles on his back seat's upholstery became the accompaniment to his Christmas jazz, but before she knew it, they sat in her driveway. She had been replaying the moments with Hailey until she was downright giddy.

"See?" Karina said, sassy and confident.

"See what?"

"It's not *that* hard to put yourself out there."

"I *took* you to that girl." Wes yanked the tree from the car and dragged it to her door while Karina followed and laughed. "Don't you dare take credit for your successful evening."

"Oh, come *on*. You have Uncle Tony's number from yoga. *Call him.*"

"Do you need help getting this inside?"

"No. Dad's home and he's—"

"A bigoted asshole. Got it." Wes kissed her cheek. "You'll call me or Tony if things get too bad?"

"I will." Before Wes got in his car, Karina made one more plea. "Call him!"

Karina's dad grunted at the tree and told her she couldn't have any of the family ornaments to decorate it. The family ornaments were ugly anyway; she'd won this round.

On yoga night, Wes and Tony chatted while students settled into their places. Karina stretched, but was more focused on trying to listen in. At one point, Tony threw his head back and laughed so uproariously everyone stopped what they were doing and stared. Tony's blush didn't disappear until class was so far into flow poses he had no choice but to focus and concentrate.

"I'm gonna—" Wes said, as he stood behind Tony's lazy-looking warrior two pose. He put his hands on Tony's hips. "Tuck your pelvis."

"And my shoulders are wrong," Tony said as he adjusted them himself.

"There you go, now keep them there into the next pose." Wes spoke to the class; his voice was like liquid silk. "Right arm down to your bent knee, left arm to the sky." He stayed behind Tony and moved with his own commands. "Look up at your hand... that's it."

When he moved to check on Mrs. Swanson's sciatica, he caught Karina's eye and sweetly scolded, "Look up at your *hand*, Ms. Ness."

Her desire for these two idiots to hook up might have been misplaced, but dammit, it was sincere and, besides, they were adorable—and bullheaded.

Five days before Christmas, Karina took one more book to Uncle Tony—her closing argument. She plopped *One Hundred Years of Solitude* on his workstation as he trimmed Wilson's sideburns. "This is what's going to happen to you if you don't *do* something. You like him."

"Him?" Mr. Wilson said. "Are you—"

"Going to cut off your ear if you don't look straight ahead." Tony caught Wilson's reflection in the mirror. "Which I'm not. Straight." He grinned, looked at the book Karina had given him and continued trimming. "Says who?" he asked Karina. "One hundred years is an awfully long time."

"Says me. I should know," she said. "I... have a *date*."

Tony turned off the trimmer. "So, now you're an expert?" He read the book's synopsis. "I've heard of this one," he said, still reading. "So, you're saying if I don't hook up with who you think I should, I'm going to be alone for a hundred years, dream up a town, and find nothing but bad fortune?"

"You already live in Linden," Wilson said. "How much more unlucky can you get?"

"It's the *title*, you boob. It's a *joke*." She yanked the book from Uncle Tony's hand and told Wilson to hold on for a moment. "Move over." She nudged Tony aside and pumped the chair up another inch or two.

"There. Old woman with osteo, Uncle Tony. You're going be so hunched you'll have to start cutting hair from the floor."

Tony grunted and revved up his trimmer. He stopped before it reached Wilson's neck. "Wait, you have a *date*?" He focused on his target and began to trim, wiggling his arms at the new work height. "This feels weird."

"You're weird, and I do. Hailey's taking me up to Greendale to see the zoo lights."

"Lumberjane?" Uncle Tony looked entirely too pleased. "Does your dad know?"

"No," Karina said, squaring her shoulders. "He doesn't have a right to my love life."

Tony smiled, the soft fatherly smile that had encouraged her since she was a child. "No. No, he does not. And now…" Tony brushed Wilson's neck. "Maybe you'll leave me alone about mine."

"You'd be sad and miserable if I left you alone." With a pointed tap on the book, Karina headed out, but not before hearing Wilson say, "You're too young to live your life alone, Tony. Maybe she's got a point."

*   *   *

"UNCLE TONY, I SWEAR TO *god*, is your maintenance guy ever going to fix those outside stairs?" Karina stomped the snow off her feet and unwrapped her scarf. The weather had been relentless, but Uncle Tony's invitation to help make this year's *pasticiotti* wasn't one to pass up. It was the weekend before what promised to be a beautiful white Christmas, and Uncle Tony's apartment smelled like chocolate pudding. "Have you bugged him about them again?" she asked, making her way into the kitchen. "Someone's going to get—"

She stopped in her tracks, smacked her hand to her mouth, and stifled a squeal.

Uncle Tony had been busy. A layer of flour covered the kitchen table; a stack of pustie tins waited to be filled. More importantly, leaning against the counter by the stove, completely engulfed in a filthy, leg-wrapped-around-a-thigh kiss were none other than Uncle Tony... and Mr. Wesley Lloyd.

Those conniving little shits.

She cleared her throat. Wes jerked upright. Tony's foot smacked the tile floor; his eyes were dark, his lips were swollen, and his hair was more askew than usual. Neither of them uttered a word or looked in her direction.

"You *did* know I was on the way," she said, skipping the part where she did *not* know this was going on. In light of the intensity of the kiss, "this" was not new.

"We—" Uncle Tony cleared his throat. Wes showed excessive concern with the consistency of the chocolate pudding and stirred as if his life depended on it. "We did. He, um... had some chocolate on his finger, and—"

"Stop. You're still my uncle. Ew." She butted her way between the two men to stir the vanilla custard and bumped Wes with her hip. He finally looked at her.

"Hi," he said with a grin so mischievous she'd have considered grounding him if she had the power to do so.

"Hi? That's all you have to say for yourself?" She took the custard off the burner and turned to Uncle Tony. "Hot pad?"

Uncle Tony took the pan. "It's your fault, you know."

"My *fault*?" She looked at Wes and sighed. "Come here, Boob." He bent to her, and she wiped a smudge of vanilla custard off his forehead. "I've never known this task to be so messy."

"Has she always had a way to make you feel like you've broken curfew or something?" Wes asked.

"Yes. You should have seen her butting in when I was dating her aunt."

"I was *six*. You were interrupting my time with her."

Tony looked at the pan in his hand as if he hadn't realized he was holding it. "Chocolate done?"

Wes and Uncle Tony reached into the same drawer for hot pads. Wes knew where the hot pads were in her uncle's apartment. She couldn't decide if she should scream or laugh. "Are you two going to tell me what in great *hell* is going on here, because, honestly, I feel like I've entered a low-grade movie set."

"Low-grade?" Tony said, incensed and comically dramatic. "I'll have you know—"

"Oh, stop it," she said. "You could have saved a whole bunch of grief and *told me!*"

Tony put the custard in the fridge, and they settled in his living room. "We thought about it," Tony said, taking Wes's hand, "but we wanted—" Tony looked at Wes as if he wanted him to explain.

"We wanted to make sure this was ours… not yours," Wes said, his eyes begging for understanding.

"I was pretty pushy."

"No kidding—" Tony started, but Wes interrupted.

"You were sweet." He kissed the half-assed scowl from Tony's brow. "It was probably fate anyway. We'd have met at the gym—"

"Or the grocery getting milk and eggs?" she teased, remembering Wes's mention of that fate for her. "So how long…"

"The night after yoga," Wes confessed. "I mean, I called him that night."

"That night? You'd already called him when we went shopping for my *tree?*"

"Yes." Wes shot a look to Uncle Tony so warm it could make flowers grow in three feet of snow. "It was the first book you gave me. All those stories about people meeting, but *then* having the courage to take the second step."

"So, it *is* my fault."

"Entirely." Uncle Tony said. "As soon as I heard the nerves in his voice—"

"And then, you gave me that book," Wes said, nudging Tony with his shoulder.

"How I got that past you at the library, Rina, I'll never know," Uncle Tony said. "You're *everywhere*."

"Wait, you put a book on hold for him? Is this the new way to flirt?"

"It's *your* fault," Wes and Tony said together. Karina stared. She didn't know either of these men—speaking in unison, sneaking around in a secret love affair.

"Fine. My fault. What book—or do I want to know?"

Tony pointed to the coffee table where William Burroughs' *Naked Lunch* sat.

"Were you trying to terrify him or seduce him?"

"That's what I asked," Wes said, laughing. "That damned book's had *hearings* for its obscenity."

"It was a *joke*! The title made me laugh and—"

"And I read it anyway," Wes confessed.

"And agreed to lunch…" Tony said, heat in his eyes. "In spite of the content."

"And then we got n—"

"*That's* more than enough, thank you," Karina said, shaking her head at these two idiots.

"So, like we said, this is your fault," Uncle Tony said one more time. "And we couldn't be more grateful."

A-Z Romance

KARINA WORE THE DEEP GREEN sweater her mother gave her that morning. Her first thought upon opening it was that it was Hailey's favorite color. She didn't recall sharing that detail with her mom, and certainly deep green suited the season, but she chose to believe it was her mother's extra Christmas gift—a way to quietly approve of the new romance.

At the drafty living room window, she hugged her arms close to herself. The aged pine tree in the front lawn weighed heavy with fresh snow, and the yard sparkled like glitter as the sun peeked from disappearing clouds. As calm as the scene was, nerves buzzed under Karina's skin. Hailey would arrive any minute. She had suggested that, instead of Karina running out to meet her as she had done time and again, today Hailey would come in and meet her parents.

"Maybe your dad will soften when he *sees*..." Hailey had suggested with great hope in her eyes.

Karina wasn't convinced, but the time for worry was over. Hailey had arrived and was walking to the door with a wreath in her hand. Before Hailey could knock, Karina opened the door and kissed her, needing to steal a measure of Hailey's confidence for herself. "Come in. I'm a wreck."

"But," Hailey said as she stepped in, "I bring you tidings of great joy!" She wiggled the simply decorated wreath, eyed a nail from a previous door hanging, and hooked it on. "Nothing to be worried about."

Karina kissed her again and called to the back of the house. "Mom! Dad! I'm leaving!"

And while the introductions weren't the warmest of the holiday season, her dad behaved like a civilized human being. He ran his finger over the deep red ribbon Hailey had added to the evergreen wreath and actually told her it was "very nice." He watched carefully as Hailey helped Karina with her coat, and, when they stepped outside, he called Hailey's name.

"Yes, Mr. Neff?"

"Um... drive careful." He looked pointedly at Karina. "The roads are slick today."

Hailey smiled, the smile that she'd offered Tony and, later, Wes—one she seemed to keep pocketed to assure the people in Karina's life that all would be well. She took Karina's hand. "I promise."

For a man who had planned to skip the holiday, Wes' apartment was decked out from foyer to living room to hallway, and, she imagined, to the kitchen and bathroom. A small, decorated tree filled the corner of his living room, and, as Wes took Karina's coat, she stepped in for a closer look. On Uncle Tony's tree, all the ornaments related to the barbershop; Wes' had a hanging Santa holding a baseball glove, a reindeer on a skateboard, and an ice fishing snowman.

"I could be insulted," Hailey said as they gathered, wine glasses in hand.

Wes followed Hailey's gaze to his very artificial tree and laughed. "It was a last minute thing. We did all this last night."

"You didn't have to, you know." Karina found a Santa yogi and laughed. "Dare you to show up to class like this."

"Only if I get to be an elf," Uncle Tony teased. "We knew how much you wanted a special holiday, and—"

"Uncle Tony." She kissed his cheek. "I have more than I ever wanted right here."

"Hey," Wes said, grabbing a book from the coffee table. "I've been meaning to ask you about this." He handed Karina a copy of *Blackbird*. "I can't find it in the library's catalog, and since we've talked about books that help the LGBT community, I thought this would be a good addition. It's funny. Talks about race and sexuality." A drawing of a Black man sprawled across his bed decorated the corner of the cover.

"Sure. I'll make sure to read it too." Seeing folded gift wrap and discarded bows near a few other books on the coffee table, she asked, "Did you guys exchange books for Christmas? How sweet!"

"Yeah," Tony said. "Since it's all still new, we figured—" He flipped the book to the title page. "Look what he wrote."

"Tony, the book that helped me see myself. Thank you for seeing me," she read. "You guys…"

Wes grabbed a copy of *Maurice* and handed it to Hailey. "He got me this one. I read it in college, but it's time for a re-read." Karina knew this classic. The Edwardian tale had brought many of her friends comfort when the world told them their lives were doomed for despair and misery. She read Uncle Tony's inscription to Wes: *Because I believe in happy endings.*

Before she could say anything, Uncle Tony waved the final book— or books—in front of her: two identical copies of *James and the Giant Peach* with a tag in Wes' handwriting: *To Wes and Tony. From The Old Green Grasshopper. Never stop wondering.*

"See?" Wes said. "Entirely your fault."

After dinner, they gathered again in the living room with *pasticiotti* and mugs of eggnog. Wes pulled two presents from under the tree.

"You got us presents? We didn't bring anything." Karina greedily grabbed the package with her name on it anyway.

"You already brought us everything." Wes said. "Hailey, why don't you open yours first?"

Hailey laughed as soon as she opened her package. "*The Evil Librarian.* Is this a warning?"

"The librarian is a dude, but… also a demon," Tony said. "I figured it might still apply to your—" He pointed at Karina. "Situation."

"Is that what I'm in?" Hailey asked. "A situation?"

"Oh, honey," Tony said, "you haven't been around long enough to totally *grasp*—"

"That's enough," Karina said as she opened her present. "I *chose* to keep you as my uncle because you're nice to me. Don't blow it." Her book was *Emma*, the Jane Austen classic. "I *know* this one. She doesn't want love but spends her time hooking everyone else up! How on-the-nose of you."

"Do you know how it ends?" Wes asked.

"Well, yeah. Love was right there all the time, but—" She took Hailey's hand and kissed her knuckles. "But not like this."

"Sappy..." Wes lifted a manila envelope from the mantle. He bit his lip, looked at it again as if it might change into something else, and finally handed it to Karina. "Thank you. For everything."

"I didn't—"

"I've known you five weeks, and you've changed my *life*. Now open it."

Karina pulled a small stack of printed pages from the envelope. "Untitled." She gasped and kept reading. "A Novel by Wesley Lloyd. Wes!" She read the first couple of sentences and flipped to the second page and the third. "Wes! You're doing it!"

"This is the first chapter. I have more, but they're still a mess."

She couldn't decide whether to focus on his proud smile or on his words sitting right in her hand—words he'd been avoiding writing for years and now had entrusted to her. To *her*.

"I want your honest feedback," he said. "You *know* good stories."

Karina leapt to her feet and threw her arms around his neck. "I'm so happy you've done this. I'll read it tonight. Call you tomorrow. Find you an agent—anything."

"You can find me an agent?"

"Of course not, but honest feedback, that I can do." She snuggled back into Hailey's side and skimmed, flipped to the front and skimmed again. As much as she wanted to spend the evening here, she also couldn't wait to curl up in bed with these twelve pages and read them again and again and again.

Hailey, Wes, and Tony chatted quietly. Karina finally put the chapter down to listen and to watch the way Wes looked at Tony when he spoke, how Uncle Tony leaned his body so their shoulders touched while they sat on the floor near the tree, how Hailey's hand on Karina's thigh was solid and secure, and how the slight movement of her thumb said, "I'm happy to be with you."

It was all right here, the way she'd always wanted: a snow-covered day, packages with pretty bows, and perfectly spiked eggnog. But mostly, she'd wanted people who loved, people who believed—family.

Conversation stalled, and Wes lifted his mug. "A toast. To telling good stories."

"To *living* them," Karina answered. "Merry Christmas."

FIN

About the Author: Lynn Charles' love of writing dates to her childhood, when thoughts, dreams, frustrations, and joys poured onto the pages of journals and diaries.

She lives in Central Ohio with her husband and adult children where a blind dog and his guardian cat rule the roost. When she's not writing, Lynn can be found planning a trip to New York or strolling its streets daydreaming about retirement. Her novel *Black Dust* (2016) was named a finalist for a Foreword Reviews INDIES Book of the Year award. Her other novels include *Beneath the Stars* (2017) and *Chef's Table* (2014).

interlude**press**™

 interludepress.com
 @InterludePress
 interludepress
 store.interludepress.com

interlude  press
you may also like...

Summer Love edited by Annie Harper
Published by Duet, the Young Adult imprint of Interlude Press

Summer Love is a collection of stories about young love—about finding the courage to be who you really are, follow your heart and live an authentic life. With stories about romantic, platonic and family love, *Summer Love* features gay, lesbian, bisexual, transgender, pansexual and queer/questioning characters, written by authors who represent a spectrum of experience, identity and backgrounds.

ISBN (print) 978-1-941530-36-8 | (eBook) 978-1-941530-44-3

Sweet by Alysia Constantine

Alone and lonely since the death of his partner, a West Village pastry chef gradually reclaims his life through an unconventional courtship with an unfulfilled accountant that involves magical food, online flirtation, and a dog named Andy. Sweet is also the story of how we tell love stories. The narrator is on to you, Reader, and wants to give you a love story that doesn't always fit the bill.

ISBN (print) 978-1-941530-61-0 | (eBook) 978-1-941530-62-7

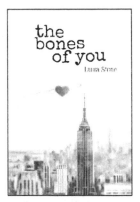

The Bones of You by Laura Stone

Oliver Andrews is wholly focused on the final stages of his education at Cambridge University when a well meaning friend upends his world with a simple email attachment: a video from a U.S. morning show. The moment he watches the video of his one-time love Seth Larsen, now a Broadway star, Oliver must begin making a series of choices that could lead him back to love—or break his heart.

ISBN (print) 978-1-941530-16-0 | (eBook) 978-1-941530-24-5

CPSIA information can be obtained
at www.ICGtesting.com
Printed in the USA
FFOW02n1922221117
43608977-42421FF

12/17